WITHOUT REPROACH

WITHOUT REPROACH

Janet Woods

This first world edition published 2008
in Great Britain and 2009 in the USA by
SEVERN HOUSE PUBLISHERS LTD of
9–15 High Street, Sutton, Surrey, England, SM1 1DF.

Copyright © 2008 by Janet Woods.

All rights reserved.
The moral right of the author has been asserted.

British Library Cataloguing in Publication Data

Woods, Janet, 1939-
  Without reproach
  1. Police - England - Dorset - Fiction 2. Romantic suspense
  novels
  I. Title
  823.9'2[F]

ISBN-13: 978-0-7278-6704-9   (cased)

Except where actual historical events and characters are being
described for the storyline of this novel, all situations in this
publication are fictitious and any resemblance to living persons
is purely coincidental.

All Severn House titles are printed on acid-free paper.

Typeset by Palimpsest Book Production Ltd.,
Grangemouth, Stirlingshire, Scotland.
Printed and bound in Great Britain by
MPG Books Ltd., Bodmin, Cornwall.

One

'Thank you for coming, Charlie would have appreciated it,' Lauren said as the three last couples left in a tightly knit bunch.

She closed the door with a sigh of relief. Charlie was buried. All that remained was to sort out the estate.

The police still didn't know the identity of the woman who'd died with him, and Lauren had never seen the car before. But it was strange that a woman had gone out without a handbag or identity of any sort.

'He was supposed to be arriving home from the US,' she'd told the two policemen who'd come to tell her of the accident. 'I dropped him off at Heathrow a month ago, like I usually do.'

The officers had exchanged a significant glance. She'd imagined it wouldn't take them long to ferret out what she knew and they suspected – that Charlie had never heard of the word, fidelity.

Betty was in the lounge stacking cups and saucers on a tray. Lauren's mother-in-law looked tired. 'It was hot today and my ankles are swollen. My head aches too. I think we're in for a thunderstorm later.'

'More than likely. Sit down and rest, Betty. I'll clear up.'

Betty sagged untidily into a white leather armchair. 'A lot of people came to the funeral. He was popular, was my Charlie. I can't believe he's dead. I wonder who that woman in the car with him was, and what he was doing in Essex.'

'He probably came home late, bought that car and gave her a lift.'

'But Essex is hardly on his way home, it's in the opposite direction. And why would he buy an old car when he had a BMW in the garage? The police said the identity on the car had been scratched off, and it had false plates. Somebody will report her missing before too long, I suppose. If not, they might be able to identify her through dental records.'

Lauren doubted if she was her husband's girlfriend. The woman had been about Charlie's age, and he liked them much younger. At twenty-five, and after four years of marriage to Charlie, Lauren had already passed her use-by date. Only the ring on her finger had reminded him that she was still alive and he was still married to her – on those occasions she wished it hadn't.

She gazed at the photograph on the table. It had been taken on her last birthday. As one does on such occasions they were all smiling happily for the camera. Charlie looked younger than his forty-two years. He was handsome and well preserved, despite a slight thickening at the waist.

Sitting on the other side of him was Monica Spencer, the office receptionist, her plump red breast pressed familiarly against his shoulder. She couldn't be more than seventeen and she wondered if Charlie had been screwing her.

After the first two years their marriage had become a farce. More and more often of late, Lauren had been considering divorce.

She carried the crockery through to the stainless steel and glass kitchen and stacked it in the dishwasher. God, she hated this house! Her husband had bought a perfectly comfortable dwelling with the money she'd brought into the marriage, gutted it, then filled the spaces he'd made with ultramodern junk. There was nothing homely about it, and it was hard work to keep it shiny, even with a cleaning lady to help. Once the estate was settled she intended to sell it and buy something smaller.

'What will we do now Charlie's gone?' Betty called out, almost reading her mind. 'You won't put me in a home, will you?'

'Don't be silly,' she said, returning to the lounge because she hated shouting back and forth. 'We'll see what the solicitor has to say tomorrow. There's the business to be sorted out with Brian Allingham yet. What would you like for dinner tonight, Betty?'

'Nothing much. A salad would be nice, and some of that apple pie in the freezer with some custard. I think I'll go upstairs and rest.'

The phone rang as Lauren drifted back to the kitchen. When she picked up the receiver a young, hesitant voice said, 'I'm sorry to bother you. I found a card in the drawer and wondered . . . is Mr Parker there?'

Probably a schoolgirl wanting to know about video distribution for a project. She didn't want to tell a child that he was dead. 'I'm afraid not. I'm Lauren Parker, can I help you?'

'No, it doesn't matter. There's the doorbell . . . I expect it's my mum. I'd better let her in.' The phone went dead.

Betty was halfway up the stairs. Her calves were knotted with veins and her voice sounded breathless.

'Are you all right, Betty?'

'I'm fine. Just a bit out of breath.' She thumped a fist against her chest. 'You've got to expect it at my age. At sixty-eight I'm no chicken.'

'And neither are you old. You should lose weight and get some exercise.'

'I can't be bothered. Who was that on the phone?'

'It sounded like a child. It wasn't important.'

'As long as it wasn't that man who said Charlie owed him money. I must say, you don't seem very upset about Charlie.'

Lauren wouldn't have wished him dead. 'Of course I'm upset, just a bit numb. The doctor gave me something to carry me over the past few days. There was so much to do, and to organize.'

'A pity you wouldn't give him any children. Charlie was upset about that. I'd have liked a grandchild.'

Charlie had lied to his mother, but he hadn't lied to her. 'I'm too old to want the mess of babies and toddlers in the house,' he'd said when the honeymoon had worn off and she'd brought the subject up. 'You've got class, and the know-how to arrange my social life. You look good on my arm, babe. I don't want your figure spoiled by having kids and going all domestic on me.'

Charlie had his life all mapped out, and everybody had to slot into it his way.

So she'd stopped wanting a child in case she got one like Charlie, who'd turned out to be a shallow, selfish, and possessive man, full of false flash. But for all his expensive suits, his cars and his charisma, and despite living life to the hilt – nothing could take the barrow boy out of Charlie Parker.

Malice narrowed Betty's muddy eyes. 'I notice that your mother didn't come to the funeral.'

Lauren's mother had made it quite clear that she'd disapproved of Charlie, and had been furious. 'How could you marry a man like that, nearly twice your age and so totally beneath you?'

'Oh, stop making such a fuss,' she'd said. 'Having a baron in the ancestral cupboard doesn't make us anything special.'

'A pity you hadn't been a boy to carry on the name.'

'Even a boy would have inherited a debt along with the title, and would have had to sell Grantham.'

'At least he'd have understood that one simply doesn't marry that far beneath them.'

Now, Lauren would be the first to admit that her mother had been right, but not to her mother. Portia Bishop had not attended her wedding, and they'd hardly communicated since. The last time her mother had written it was to tell her she'd married an Italian businessman, who just happened to be a count. Her name was now Portia, Countess Demasi.

'I sent her a card telling her when the funeral was taking place. I imagine she's in Venice for the summer with her husband and didn't receive it. They travel a lot. Brian Allingham didn't come either.'

'Thank God. I never cottoned on to him, or his tarty wife,' Betty grunted. 'Venice is damp and mouldy. Your mother isn't getting any younger. She'll come back with rheumatism, you mark my words.' With that final dig, Betty continued on up the stairs.

Lauren slept well, considering. Showered and dressed she went downstairs to make her first cup of tea. She'd take a tray up to Betty, for Mr Gregson the solicitor was due at ten and her mother-in-law would want to be there.

Gregson was preceded at nine by a policeman in plain clothes, who offered his card and introduced himself as Detective Sergeant Ransom.

Showing him into the sitting room and trying to resemble a grieving widow, she asked him, 'How can I help you, Detective Sergeant Ransom?'

'We've discovered the identity of the woman in the car with . . . *your husband.*'

He was nicely spoken, and had amazing eyes the colour of pewter. In fact, he was an extremely attractive man. 'Oh, really? I was hoping you would.'

He stared hard at her. 'Were you?'

'Well, of course. She might have a husband or children waiting for her to return.'

'She had both husband and child.'

'Oh, I'm so sorry.' Puzzled, she gazed at him. 'You were going to tell me; who is she?'

'Jean Parker.'

She shook her head slightly. 'I didn't know Charlie had an extended family. Betty never said.'

'Betty?'

'His mother. She lives with us . . . me, but she's still in bed.'

He appeared slightly taken aback. 'Would you wake her please, Mrs Parker.'

'She's awake, but I doubt if she's dressed yet. Look, is something wrong? If it is I'd be obliged if you'd break it to her gently.'

Betty duly came down, grumbling at being asked to hurry. Lauren made the introductions.

'Oh hell!' the detective said. 'I didn't expect this complication, and nobody told me there was a mother.'

'Men usually have mothers, that's how they get here,' she said helpfully.

A dark eyebrow rose and his expression indicated that he thought he might be dealing with a lunatic. He cleared his throat. 'Is that so? Hmmm . . . interesting. Look, there *is* no way to break this to you gently. The deceased woman in the car was the wife of Charles Parker. The car was supplied by a friend of hers . . . a scrap dealer.'

The first thing Lauren did was give a nervous huff of laughter, but there wasn't even a glimmer of amusement in the detective's wintry eyes, which were watchful in the extreme. She exchanged a glance with Betty, who looked mystified. 'You've made a mistake. I'm Mrs Parker. Charlie and I were married for four years. I have a marriage certificate that says so.'

'So had the woman who was killed with him.'

'It must be a forgery.'

'No, Mrs Parker. It's not. She's been his wife for seven years. There's a daughter. She's sixteen.'

'There you are then,' and Betty folded her arms on her bosom. 'It can't be Charlie's daughter if they've only been married for seven years, can it?'

Lauren exchanged a glance with the detective, who raised

an eyebrow. She said, 'Betty, it's quite possible Charlie fathered a child sixteen years ago. You're his mother, surely you must have had some suspicions about this marriage.'

Betty looked belligerent. 'Not a soddin' thing. It's a mistake.'

The detective shrugged. 'I'm afraid it's not.'

Lauren said, 'Are you telling me I wasn't legally married?'

He nodded. 'If he was married to you as well as the woman he was with when he died, then Charles Parker was a bigamist.'

It wasn't the time for levity, but Lauren had a job hanging on to her laughter. 'How wonderfully Charliesque this is. So for four years I dropped him off at Heathrow airport, supposedly on business, and this other woman . . . Jean Parker picked him up. Then she must have dropped him off a month later, and I picked him up. It's so farcical it's a wonder we didn't run into each other.'

'Jean?' Betty said suddenly. 'Her maiden name isn't Higgins, is it?'

The detective nodded.

Betty went red in the face. 'That conniving little slag . . . she lived down the road. Always after the men, she was, and got her claws into my Charlie when she was sixteen. He wanted to marry her but I threatened to break his stupid neck if he did. Her mother was on the game, and Jean had learned a few tricks from the old tart. They moved abroad somewhere, and good riddance. Jean must have come back with this kid in tow and told Charlie it was his.' Lauren was the recipient of a scornful look. 'My Charlie always wanted a kid. Well, I don't want anything to do with the daughter, and that's that.'

'No, *that* is certainly not *that*, Betty. We can't pick our parents, so it's not the girl's fault.'

The detective gazed upon her with sudden approval and she allowed herself to smile warmly at him. He blinked.

'Bad blood,' Betty muttered and burst into tears. 'This is too much. I'm going back to bed.' She slammed the door behind her when she left.

'I'm sorry to be the bearer of bad news,' the detective said awkwardly.

'You're just doing your job. Thank you for being so kind. It's a mess, but I'll sort it out with the help of the solicitor. What's the girl's name?'

'Katie.'

'How is she taking the death of her parents?'

'As you'd expect. She's not a bad kid as teenagers go these days, and the welfare is looking after her. She thinks you're her aunt and is hoping that you'll offer her a home.'

Lauren drew in a deep breath, considering it. She felt sorry for the girl. Not only had she lost both her parents, she was also being rejected by her grandmother.

Not if Lauren could prevent it though. She knew what it was like to have nobody to turn to. If her own mother had been part of her life, and if her father hadn't died just as Charlie came on the scene, she doubted if she'd have made the mistake of thinking herself in love with him. Besides which, her curiosity was raised.

Betty had said she'd like a grandchild, and here was one ready-made and toilet-trained. 'I'm not adverse to the idea, and I'm sure Betty will come round eventually. But the girl must be made aware of the truth before we even meet – and it must be her choice.'

'Obviously, and the welfare officer will take care of that. But once Mrs Parker gets over her shock of learning about Mr Parker she might see things a little differently about Miss Parker . . . Mrs Parker.' His rueful grin was attractive. 'Four Parkers can get a little confusing.'

She chuckled. 'Yes, I suppose it must. You may call me Lauren if you prefer. As things stand it might be better if I revert to my maiden name.'

'Which is?'

'Lauren Bishop. Do you have a first name, detective?'

He looked slightly abashed. 'It's Theodore.'

'Would you mind if I called you Theo, Theodore? Detective Sergeant Ransom is rather intimidating – but then, in your profession I imagine it's supposed to be.'

He smiled at that, but his grey eyes still had a watchful, hawklike look to them. 'Just Theo will do. You don't seem surprised by what's happened, Lauren.'

'It's the sort of thing Charlie would do, that's all. He was a wheeler and dealer. But he had charisma, and a certain boyish charm about him. Though it could get annoying, I could never stay mad with him for long, either, even when he lied and I knew it. I never thought he'd do anything really bad though.'

'He had a juvenile record as long as your arm, mostly petty

stuff. Shoplifting, selling stolen goods et cetera. And he did time for possession.'

'Possession of what?' she said cautiously.

'*Drugs* . . . with the amount in his possession he could have been done for dealing, but it was a long time ago, he was young, and the magistrate was lenient and gave him the benefit of the doubt and a light sentence to go with it.'

'Drugs?' She was horrified. 'He never said.'

'It's not something a man would tell his . . . *wife*. If I may say so, you don't seem very upset by his death.'

Theodore Ransom was long-legged and lean. Her glance took in his taut body. He looked fit, and would be more at home sprawled in the depths of an overstuffed armchair with his legs stretched out.

But then, hardly anyone but Charlie had suited the pristine starkness of this furnishing style. She remembered a photograph of him, his silver hair abundant, and wearing an impeccable grey suit. His flamboyant red tie had matched the glass tulip in the crystal vase on the glass table next to him and his arm had been a stretch along the white leather of the couch, his cufflinks and ring displaying rubies. Dapper was the word attached to Charlie.

The last time she'd seen him he hadn't been so dapper. His face had been livid, bruised and swollen, his hair matted with blood. She banished the image with a shudder. The woman with him she had not been able to identify.

'You don't have to tread on eggshells, Theo. For various reasons our *marriage* was over two years after it began. I was thinking of divorcing him. All the same, I wouldn't have wished for his death. It was hard when I identified him. The doctor gave me some pills. They helped. They stopped me thinking about . . .' She shuddered. 'The doctor said it was instant. I'm glad he didn't suffer.'

His expression softened. 'You don't seem the type of woman who'd get involved with a man like Charlie.'

'I wasn't long out of school when we met at a nightclub. My mother had gone abroad, and I'd just lost my father. Charlie was very kind to me over the next few months. He made me laugh. He retained the ability to do so right up to the end . . . and even now, after he's gone. *Bigamy!* It's ludicrous. This sort of thing only happens to other people.'

'Did you know that Charlie Parker peddled porn?' Theo asked softly.

Her smile faded and she stared at him. So that was the layer of scum that had settled on the bottom of Charlie's pond. Matters no longer seemed so funny, she thought, as she gazed into the detective's astute eyes. 'You're very good at questioning, Theo.'

He inclined his head in acknowledgement. No false modesty about this man, he accepted praise where it was due. 'He and his partner filmed it in a warehouse they rented. His wife . . . the woman in the car with him, was in it up to her ears.'

'Do you suspect me of being involved?'

'It's the nature of my job to be suspicious. *Are* you involved?'

'Certainly not. Did Jean Parker know about me, d'you think?'

'There's no way of knowing that. It's possible, though the girl, Katie, thinks she has an aunt.'

'So you indicated.' Lauren remembered the phone call. 'I think it might have been his daughter who rang me yesterday . . . just after Charlie's funeral. She said someone was at the door and it might be her mother, then she rang off.'

'It was probably us at the door, informing her that her parents were deceased. Apparently Jean Parker was driving him to the airport when the accident occurred. The girl didn't think to report her missing because her mother often went off for a day or two afterwards without telling her.'

'How dreadful for the poor girl. And I thought Charlie might have been held up in the US when he actually couldn't have been waiting for me. I was notified that same evening.'

'Brian Allingham has emptied the company accounts and fled, by the way.'

Almost an aside, as if it didn't signify. *Layer upon layer, Charlie and his associate were being exposed for what they were.* This man was an expert. 'I wondered why he wasn't at the funeral.'

'We think he's gone abroad. I believe he has a villa in Spain.'

She paled and her hand went to her mouth. 'Oh, my God! Did you say he'd emptied the company accounts?'

He nodded, then said, 'We've already searched the business premises, now we'll have to search this place, I'm afraid. I'll obtain a warrant and we'll be as unintrusive as possible under the circumstances.'

A trifle stiffly, she told him, 'You're welcome to search it now if you wish.'

'Uniformed officers will help conduct the search, and a warrant will cover any legalities. If you have a computer it will be taken away and examined.'

'Of course. Charlie has . . . *had* a laptop, which he always took with him, and there's a desktop in his office. His office is across the hall if you want to look at it.'

'We'll wait for the warrant to come.' He drew in a breath. 'There's worse to come, Lauren.'

After a moment to collect herself she said, 'How much worse can this get? You'd better give me it now. I'd rather know it all.'

'The nature of some of the material was child pornography.'

She stared at him, uncomprehending for a moment. Then as his words sank in nausea began to roil in her stomach. 'Excuse me,' she gulped. Pressing a hand to her mouth she headed for the small cloakroom off the utility room. She returned a few minutes later, minus her breakfast and with tears welling in her eyes. 'I'm sorry. I don't usually give in to moments of weakness. I was trained not to as a child, you see,' she said ruefully.

His voice was sympathetic. 'It was a lot to take in.'

'I suppose you get hardened to this sort of thing in your job.'

'To some extent, but it's hard to keep control of the emotions when kids are concerned.'

The doorbell rang.

Her glance went to the clock. It had no numbers, just hands and a tick. She'd never been able to tell the time accurately by it. 'That will be Mr Gregson, my solicitor. Considering what you've just told me I'd like you to stay, Theo. I'll show Mr Gregson in, introduce you, then make us some coffee. I could do with some, myself. Perhaps you'd explain to Mr Gregson what's been going on.' She gave him a faint smile. 'You'll allow me to move out of your sight without arresting me, I take it?'

He gave her a glimmer of a smile, then nodded. 'I think I can allow you a little leeway.'

'That's encouraging. While you talk to Mr Gregson I'll tell Betty what you've told me.'

'Is that wise?'

'She'll have to know sooner or later. I imagine this will make the news networks, so I'd rather she learned it from me.'

Betty had been proud of what Charlie had made of himself, but she would have composed herself by now, and be wondering if her son had been up to anything else. If nothing else, Betty was a realist. 'Don't worry, Betty is tough when she needs to be.'

Before she went upstairs Lauren opened Charlie's safe. She removed the twenty-five thousand in cash that was in there. Then, feeling guilty, she put it back in again.

'Damn it, it's Charlie's money, now it's mine. I'll need it and it's now or never,' she muttered. Taking it out again she stuffed it under her jumper, then wiped her fingerprints from the tumbler. Charlie hadn't had a clue that she'd known the combination, but if nothing else, he was predictable and his birth date had been the most obvious choice.

Once upstairs she stuffed the money inside several pairs of boots and shoes, then went to see Betty. Apart from a few exclamations of distress Betty took the news as though she'd been expecting it. 'I never dreamed my Charlie was such a bloody rogue,' she said, rocking back and forth. 'I'm so ashamed I can hardly think straight. What will people think of us? What are we going to do, Lauren?'

Lauren put an arm around her, and this time Betty left it there. She seemed to have aged ten years in ten minutes. 'Charlie was a grown man and you've done nothing to be ashamed of.'

'Other people won't see it that way.'

'I know. The only suggestion I can make is to listen to what the solicitor has to say, then I'll ring a friend of my mother who deals in real estate. Perhaps he's got a place in the country on his books that we can move into at short notice, until this blows over.'

'I'll hate living in the country.'

'It will only be for a short while. We'll take Charlie's daughter with us if she'll come.'

Betty's mouth flattened into a thin line.

Sharply, Lauren told her, 'What's happened is not Katie's fault. She's the biggest victim in this. Not only has she been orphaned, but how do you think she'll feel when this gets out? She's young, she won't be able to cope and will need our support.'

Betty shrugged. 'Just don't expect me to like her, especially if she looks like Jean Higgins, the common little whelp.'

Gazing round at her mother-in-law's room, pink walls and

purple satin bedspread, a feather boa decorating the mirror, Lauren found it hard not to shudder. 'I'll sell this house when things are settled. I've never liked it.'

'Neither have I,' Betty said in a moment of candour, 'But are you sure it's still yours to sell?' And her caustic tone warned Lauren that Betty was well on the road to recovery.

Lauren hadn't thought that far ahead, but she now had the feeling that everything was about to go horribly wrong. 'My money bought it, but there's only one way to find out, isn't there? We'd better go down and see the solicitor.'

She got what she was now expecting. Exactly nothing! Charlie hadn't left a will, and there were too many debts to clear. Besides, he had a daughter.

It turned out that Katie looked surprisingly like Charlie, with wide brown eyes and dark hair. She was a bit on the plump side, and her face wore a sulky expression, though it was strained.

Her glance took in her surroundings as she sneered, 'This is a bit posh isn't it? Better than what me and my mum lived in. Being someone's bit on the side must pay off.'

Lauren bit on her lip. 'You've been told the circumstances, Katie, so let's get one thing straight to start with. Recognize that you're not the only person who's been affected by your father's unfortunate death. You've been given a choice of making a home with me and your grandmother in the country, or you can stay here and allow the welfare department to take care of you.'

The welfare officer concerned, a harassed looking woman in her fifties, said, 'She'll go into a shared house, then on the housing list for single accommodation. She'll be eligible for a pension until she finds work.'

'My name is Katie Parker, not she.' The girl gave the woman a speculative sideways look before offering Lauren a challenging one. 'Why can't we just live here?'

'Your father borrowed money left, right and centre and was up to his ears in debt, so everything belongs to the bank. I won't be able to pay the mortgage owing so the house will be repossessed. Your home, my home and the contents. All I'll have is my car, which is several years old, my clothing and some savings from a legacy.'

She felt a twinge of guilt as she remembered the cash, which was now stuffed inside a body suit she wore, for safe keeping. Over it was a loose blouse.

'We're leaving within the next hour so make your mind up quickly, Katie, because I'll have to make room in the car if you're coming with us.'

'I don't think we should take the little trollop,' Betty said from her seat in the corner.

'Who's the old hag making all the noise?' Katie said provocatively.

'You watch your lip, young lady.'

'I will when you watch yours. How d'you get off calling me names. You don't even know me.'

'I'm your grandmother.'

'Well, tough luck for both of us, Grannie. I'm coming with you, so you'll have to put up with me. I haven't got much luggage.' Katie threw her bag to the floor. It was stuffed to the seams and the head of a small teddy bear stuck out through the open end of the zipper, as if it needed to breathe. For some reason the sight of it touched Lauren's heart as the girl said offhandedly, 'It's got to be better than living in a boarding house, I suppose.'

Lauren smiled at the girl, mainly because she'd managed to render Betty speechless. Nevertheless, she said, 'That was rude, Katie. I'd prefer it if you apologized to your grandmother.'

Katie tossed her a grin. 'Sorry, Gran.'

'I should think so, too,' Betty muttered, her feathers obviously ruffled.

The welfare officer sighed with relief as she handed Lauren a card. 'I'll be going then. Ring me if you need any help.'

'Katie's not a child, she's a young woman who can, no doubt, act sensibly.'

'Course I can.'

Lauren looked around her. Her life here had crumbled away. Now she'd have to make a new one for herself . . . for them all. 'Ah well,' she said. 'It's no good hanging around here. We might as well go too.'

Theo Ransom uncoiled to his feet. 'I'll see you into the car.'

She wouldn't be sorry to leave here, she thought, as the front door closed behind them with a definite click.

'Safe journey. Don't forget to do your seat belts up, Mrs Parker. Miss Parker.'

While her passengers were settling themselves into the car

Lauren said to Theo, 'Thank you for your help. I don't know what I would have done without you.'

'You're a nice lady, Mrs Parker.' His eyes wandered to her body and a faint frown touched his forehead before his grey eyes looked into hers.

It is my money; I'm not stealing it, Lauren thought and made her eyes round and innocent. When she sucked in her padded stomach her padded breasts swelled. He grinned as he took a quick glance. Damn! He was a breast man, when hers were on the smallish side. But at the moment they were worth at least five thousand pounds apiece. She felt extremely fat, and intended to take the body suit off at the first roadhouse they came to.

Straight-faced now, he said, 'I forgot to pat you down, Mrs Parker.'

'*Miss Bishop,* and I thought we'd decided on Lauren,' she said with a desperate smile. Wracked by guilt she found herself squirming under his amused gaze. Then she found her courage and looked him straight in the eye. 'Some other time, perhaps.'

He chuckled, and standing with his back to the car, said, 'I might take you up on that. Do you know the combination number to the safe?'

'Charlie never gave it to me,' she said, and so quickly that his eyes narrowed. Squeezed by guilt she couldn't look at him. He'd searched her room himself while she'd stood in the hall outside the door. She was surprised he hadn't thought to look in her shoes. He *had* looked there. *He knew!* She was wearing this body suit for nothing and he knew exactly what she was hiding under it.

'As for the safe, Charlie was predictable. Try his birth date, fourteen eleven sixty-six.'

'In what order?'

She rallied. 'Try them all? Why is it that I've formed the impression that you're keeping something from me.'

His smile was deliberately enigmatic when he took her hands in his. 'I get the same feeling about you. If you have any idea what that something could be, contact me. Live dangerously. Contact me, anyway, just for the hell of it. By the way, if I find any cash in the safe I'll give you a receipt for it.'

He knew about the safe money, she was certain now. He was going to allow her to get away with it, he'd just stated his price. 'You have too high an opinion of yourself. I certainly will not contact you. You're too unsettling. What d'you do for pleasure, Theo, pull the wings off flies?'

'I'll contact you, then.'

'If you feel you must.'

When she attempted to withdraw her hands he released them slowly so their fingers grazed across each other's palms. It was such an erotic action that she thought her palms must be smoking when he said quietly, 'Oh, I do feel I must.'

She smiled. Sliding into the driver's seat she knew she was grateful for the unexpected gesture of his. The only other money she possessed was a savings account in her maiden name, which contained a useful legacy from her grandmother – something Charlie hadn't known about. Theo had checked the deposit date, then told her to keep it. 'Your grandmother isn't responsible for Charlie's debts.'

She looked back at him in the driving mirror. He was standing in the drive, watching them go, and there was something lonely looking about him. Just before she turned into the street she waved out of the window. He smiled and waved in return.

'The copper fancies you,' Katie said.

'I shouldn't think so.' The rush hour was over, and for that Lauren was grateful as she drove the loaded car off into the evening light. 'Dorset, here we come,' she said.

'Where's that?' Katie asked.

Betty sniffed. 'Where d'you think it is, Bangladesh? Don't they teach you anything in school these days?'

'Oh, put a sock in it, Grannie. You're just like the teacher I had. If you keep making sarcastic remarks when I ask a question how d'you expect me to learn anything?'

Katie was right, and Lauren decided to put a stop to it before it really started. 'We've got at least a three-hour journey in front of us and I'll have to concentrate on my driving. I'm not going to put up with the pair of you bickering all the way. You're not children. If you can't be polite to each other don't talk at all. Katie, there's a map book in the side of the door. You can look up Dorset in that . . . in fact, it would be helpful to me if you could work out the route as we go, so we don't get ourselves lost.'

When the car fell into a tension-filled silence she switched on the radio. After a while Betty began to gently snore.

'She sounds like she's sawing wood, doesn't she? My dad used to snore like that.'

Lauren chuckled. 'Yes, I know.'

'I'm sorry for what I said earlier about you being his bit on the side. Did you love him, my dad? I mean, you're a lot younger than him.'

'I'm twenty-five.' She slanted the girl a glance. It was natural that she should be curious. Lauren decided to be truthful with her. 'I did love him at first. I've been thinking of getting a divorce recently though.'

'I liked him at first, too, then when I got to know him, I didn't. He always gave in to my mum over me. She didn't like him making a fuss of me. She was jealous and used to accuse me of encouraging him. She beat the hell out of me when Dad was away. She kept asking me if he did things to me, like her father did to her. As if he would. He wasn't like that, whatever the papers say.'

Knowing what she did about Charlie now, Lauren could understand why her mother had wondered. 'I'm sorry you didn't like your parents. I didn't get on with my mother very well either, but she didn't beat me. That must have been horrid.'

'You're all right, you know,' Katie said. 'My dad did love me. He wrote it in my autograph book. But he wasn't allowed to show it because he just couldn't stand her nagging.'

It sounded as though Katie had convinced herself.

After a while came the rustle of pages being turned, then she began to sing softly to the music. Lauren joined in.

Two

'This is it?'

Head out of the car, Katie spelled out the lettering on the mouldy looking gate. '*Blackbird's Nest*. Yep, this *is* it. What a dump!'

The two-storey brick and slate cottage seemed to lean sadly into a darkening sky.

Lauren's heart sank as she looked up at it. 'Daniel had said it was all he had. Everything else was let for the summer. I hope he remembered to get the electricity switched on.' At least the rent was cheap, she thought.

'Are we there yet?' Betty said, looking fuddled as she jerked out of her latest nap.

'Yes, we are.'

'And about time, too.'

'The key should be under the doormat. I'll open the door. Let's get unpacked.' Thank goodness they'd eaten at a road-house, and she'd thought to stop and buy supplies at a supermarket on the way, using her ill-gotten gains. 'We'll take the groceries into the kitchen first. Unpack the candles and matches in case we need them, please, Katie.'

They didn't. A solitary light flickered on, then made up its mind to afford them a dusty shine. She had a quick look around the place. It needed a good clean, and thank goodness she'd thought to buy light bulbs. She twisted one into a greasy cord and socket hanging from the stained kitchen ceiling, then looked at the cook top in the resulting flood of light. Her nose wrinkled as an army of cockroaches scattered. The place needed more than a clean, it needed a good scrubbing from head to toe – and that was before anything else.

'Ugh, I'll chase that bugger out in the morning,' Betty said when a spider scuttled into its nest in a corner. 'I'll make us a cup of tea, shall I? That stuff at the roadhouse was gnat's piddle. It reminded me of the war and just after, when everything was rationed. We used the tea-leaves over and over again until there was no colour left in it. Then we mixed it with bran and peelings to feed to the chickens.' She angled Katie a look. 'You lot are spoiled rotten these days. You don't know what it's like to go hungry, what with the welfare system, and all.'

Betty would have only been a couple of years younger than Katie's age when World War Two ended, Lauren thought.

Katie snapped back, 'If you want to go back to the delights of the old days, you can always hand your pension back in and see how you manage.'

'I earned that pension, Missy. I worked in my father's fish shop from the age of twelve, filleting the fish and laying it out on the slabs, my fingers frozen to the marrow in the winter. He got himself blown up by a bomb when he should have been in a shelter. "I'm going out to watch the show," he said to my mum and me. Didn't watch it for long, did he? There was nothing left of him to bury.'

Lauren knew better than to interrupt Betty's tirade, since it would relieve her tension. Katie's shrug seemed to egg Betty on.

'Then it was working on my husband's barrow when I married. My Sidney was a lazy bastard, though . . . by God, the men in my life have been utter fools.' When Betty savagely turned on the tap, Lauren knew she was thinking of Charlie. The pipes juddered and banged, then after a while rusty water came trickling out of the tap. Betty suddenly burst into tears. 'What will become of us?'

'We'll manage,' Lauren said with more conviction than she felt. 'You're tired, we all are. Everything will seem better in the morning, when we're rested.' She made a cursory inspection of the place. 'It could be worse. I'll make a bed in that little sitting room off the living room. I think the sofa lets down. It will save you going up those steep stairs, and besides, there are only two bedrooms. And the bathroom is downstairs, what there is of it.'

The room tacked on the side of the house contained a dirty old tub and a pedestal with no seat and a rusty tank and chain. She'd be surprised if it flushed. That *did* surprise her later, though, and with a good flow of rusty water.

Betty loudly blew her nose. 'Don't think I'm sleeping on the sofa like a lodger for ever. Tomorrow, I'll buy myself a proper bed.'

Lauren grinned as she wondered, from where? But she didn't say anything.

Katie suddenly whooped with triumph. 'Look, the water is clearing, Gran,' and she held the electric kettle under the flow. 'You sit down. I'll make the tea, and there's a packet of chocolate digestive biscuits to go with it.'

'Thank you, dear. They're my favourites. Is there a television?'

There was a valve radio which took a little while to warm up and crackled.

'I expected war music to come out of it,' Katie said, and her wide grin suddenly reminded Lauren of Charlie, so she felt a little pang of remorse.

'Vera Lynn, the forces' sweetheart. Now *she* was a real singer, and a proper lady with it. You wouldn't catch her shaking her naked bits at the audience like some of today's hussies who call themselves singers.' Betty began to hum in opposition to the crackling radio.

Lauren added a new kettle to her shopping list, when the one belonging to the cottage took twenty minutes to boil the water. It was furred up. She could rent a television for the six months' duration of the lease, and a new radio was inexpensive. New mattresses for the beds too, she thought. The ones on them were stained and dirty. But they would have to do for tonight. She just hoped there were no bed bugs in them.

They went to bed almost as soon as they'd put the sheets on them. Lauren threw her window open wide, allowing the warm night air to flood into her room. The darkness and quiet seemed absolute after the city. There came the soft hoot of an owl. She smiled, for it reminded her of her childhood.

Katie lay awake long into the night. The mattress was lumpy, the darkness around her musty smelling and the quietness smothering. She imagined death must feel like this, only colder.

Thoughts swirled through her brain – thoughts she wasn't entirely uncomfortable with now she'd been orphaned, for life seemed very precious to her now she knew how quickly it could be snuffed out.

Hard to think she'd considered topping herself, but hadn't been able to decide which method to use that wasn't painful. If she hung herself she might change her mind at the very last minute, then it would be too late. The same with drowning. Cutting her wrists would be messy, and she hadn't been able to find the courage to make that first cut into the vein pulsing at her wrist. Throwing herself from a tall building was out, since she was scared of heights. Like other methods it would be too late if she changed her mind halfway down, and anyway, she might land on someone who was walking innocently underneath, and she didn't want to kill anyone else. It occurred to her that perhaps she wasn't quite ready to die just yet, else she wouldn't keep talking herself out of it.

Reaching out for the torch Lauren had given her she clicked it on. A thin beam of light cut through the darkness and shone on to the curtain rail. Two pairs of red eyes gleamed. 'Mice!' She laughed when they gave a squeak and fled, and tried to catch them with the beam. They disappeared behind the grubby curtain.

The wallpaper was hanging off in strips. What a shack! It was a wonder the place hadn't been condemned. How had she ended up here, living with strangers? Wasn't it enough that she hadn't been wanted or loved before?

But then she considered the alternative, surviving on the welfare in a cramped women's shelter, where it wasn't safe to go out during the day, let alone at night. She shuddered. At least she'd have someone to turn to here. Her father's tart didn't seem too bad. Lauren was pretty and she spoke nice . . . softly and sort of posh.

Her grandmother was something else altogether. She had the East End in her voice, stronger than her father. When Katie had wondered what her grandparents had been like she'd imagined a softly spoken woman who'd given her hugs, and who'd baked cakes. In reality, Granny Parker was as hard as nails with a smart mouth – a woman who didn't want her around, either.

Tears of pity came to her eyes. Adults were good at telling you what to do, but not so good at putting it into practice. At least she'd known where she stood, before. Now they had to hide away from the press, and all because her stupid parents had turned out to be perverts. She wished she'd told them about Brian Allingham. It would have served them right.

Switching off the torch she pulled the covers over her head and began to cry.

After a few moments there was a light tap on the door and Lauren said, 'Are you all right, Katie?'

'I was just thinking about things in private,' she sniffed, annoyed at being jerked out of her self-pity.

'It's hard not to think, isn't it? It's the quiet, I expect. It doesn't allow for distractions. I dare say we'll get used to it.'

'I saw some mice on the curtain rail.'

'Perhaps we should rename the cottage Mouse's Nest, then.'

Katie giggled and drew her teddy bear against her face. It had been a birthday present from her father when he'd come back into their lives. Not that his presence had changed much. Her mother had always yelled at her.

'I'll give you something to cry for if you don't shut up.'

And although her father had given her his attention at first, and had treated her OK, it hadn't taken him long to regard her as a nuisance. Yet, she'd give anything to have them back and to be asleep in her own bed.

'Goodnight, dear. Sleep tight. Things will seem better in the morning. And if they don't, there's always the morning after that one to try out.'

It was nice to have someone who cared if you felt sad. Katie warmed towards the woman. 'Goodnight . . . Lauren.'

Betty had risen early, before the others were awake. She'd cleaned the bathroom as best she could, but the electric water heater didn't work.

She went through to the kitchen to make herself a cup of tea. While she was waiting for the kettle to boil she scrubbed out the mouldy interior of the small fridge then switched it on and unpacked the groceries they'd bought. The mice hadn't been able to get at the margarine, but they'd discovered the biscuits.

'You greedy bastards, those are my favourites,' she muttered. Fetching a pen and notebook she started a list, muttering to herself, 'Bed. Plastic containers, buckets. Mop. Dusters.' Her glance went to the spider web. 'Insect Spray. Mousetraps.' She crossed mousetraps off and said 'cat' before writing it down. Charlie had never allowed her to have a cat. He'd said they left hairs over everything. But now he was gone she could do as she liked.

The milk was long life. Eggs and bacon went into the fridge. Fruit, bread.

The cupboards revealed packets of this, bottles of that, all old, nibbled and dribbled on. The packets and shelves were sprinkled with mice droppings. 'You lot are going on a diet,' she said and scooped the lot into a tin bath. She carried it outside and tipped it into the dustbin. When she got back inside she began a second list

'Flour, sugar, tomato ketchup.' As the list grew longer she wondered if she had enough money. She should have. Charlie had been generous with his cash over the years, and she'd saved most of it for a rainy day.

The sudden exertion had made her short of breath. Her son hadn't allowed her to do anything, and she was out of condition. Perhaps Lauren was right and she should diet and exercise. She made her tea and took it through to her allocated room, opening the French windows on to a sunlit conservatory full of pots of dead foliage. It would be pretty once she got some plants growing. Geraniums were easy to grow and made a cheerful display, even though the smell was a bit off.

There was a utility room tacked on to the conservatory. A door to the garden was choked by honeysuckle and weeds. It would need cutting back before it could be opened. An old-fashioned mangle stood next to a modern stainless steel sink and draining board. Lauren would probably prefer a washing machine. So would she.

She started a new list. Washing machine. Potting mix and plants. Opening her sewing basket she lifted off the top layer and began to take rolls of money out of the partially darned pair of socks she'd hidden it in. The plod who'd looked into her sewing basket hadn't given the socks a second glance. The money was of mixed denomination, each roll secured with an elastic band. She hadn't realized that Charlie had given her so much over the years.

Now she knew how he'd earned it, it somehow seemed tainted, and the sooner she got rid of it the better she'd like it. After all, she still had her cheque account to fall back on. Her pension money had been paid into that.

Then there was the key he'd given her to look after, just before he died.

'It belongs to a storage facility,' he'd said when she asked. 'It's nothing to do with the business. It's private. I keep . . . *stuff* there, as insurance for my old age. One day we'll buy a villa overlooking the Mediterranean sea and live the good life. But don't tell anyone. Not even Lauren, and especially not Brian, though I think he's got wind of it. Act dumb if anyone asks about it. Don't go there and don't lose it unless something happens to me. You're the only person I can trust.'

Betty now wondered if she should tell the copper about the key. She picked it up and turned it over. All it had was a number on it, but she knew which storage place Charlie would have used. She put the key back in her sewing box and decided to forget about it for the time being. She didn't see why the banks should get everything and would wait for the dust to settle before making a decision.

She was still trying to figure out what her purchases would cost when she heard the girl come running down the stairs.

The bathroom door slammed open, then the sound of heaving came to her ears. After a while it stopped and the toilet flushed. Betty went out and stood at the bottom of the stairs until Katie came back. The girl's face was pale, her eyes watery from her efforts.

Betty's eyes went to the podgy stomach under the thin nightie. Katie still had some puppy fat so it was hard to tell. Nevertheless, she sneered, 'Got yourself a bun in the oven, have you? I don't know what the duchess will say when she finds out. Most likely she'll throw you out.'

'You think you know everything, don't you?' Katie threw at her. 'It was the food we had in the roadhouse. There was something wrong with it and it gave me an upset stomach. I'm all right now.'

Betty laughed. 'I had the same as you and it didn't upset me. I'm not such a fool to believe it's the gripe.' Going back into her room Betty started another list. 'Wool, patterns, knitting needles. Crochet hook.'

Lauren woke to the beautiful song of a thrush in the delicate white and purple clematis curling up over her window sill. For a moment she wondered where she was, then she remembered. Her gaze wandered around the room with its peeling paper and flaking paint. Something was different, and it took a few moments to realize there was no sense of urgency in her.

There was a delicious smell of bacon frying. Pulling on her dressing gown she went down the narrow wooden staircase that led straight into the living room.

Katie had found a tablecloth from somewhere and was setting out the cutlery. Betty was singing to herself in the kitchen, which was a nice size for a cottage. Giving Katie a smile she said to Betty, 'Can I do anything to help?'

'There's only room in the kitchen for one cook. Tell you what you can do. When you're dressed you could take me into that big town we came through yesterday, if you would. I've got a shopping list as long as your arm.'

'That's Poole,' Katie said, importantly airing her newly discovered geographical knowledge.

Lauren smiled at her. 'Yes, it is. How observant you are. I want to shop too. I need some paint, as well as utensils. I thought

I might strip the wallpaper off and paint the walls cream for now. It will make the place look brighter.'

'The owner should pay for that. We'd better compare lists. We don't want to double up.'

'I don't mind paying for it. I want us to be clean, and paint won't cost much.'

'You'd better ring the agent and tell him the water heater doesn't work. The owner will have to pay for the repairs to that.'

'Daniel did say to tell him if there was anything that needed repairing. He said he'll send somebody round to cut the lawn, too. And he'll be round to check the inventory tomorrow.'

'The fridge works. I've cleaned that, and thrown away the rubbish in the cupboards. I've also cleaned the bathroom as best as I can.'

'Thanks, Betty. You should have left it for me to do.'

'I'm quite capable of helping out, besides, there's plenty more to do.' Deftly turning over an egg she slid it on to a plate with two slices of bacon and some tinned tomato and handed it to her. 'Here, get that inside you. I think we've got a busy day ahead.'

'What about you and Katie?'

'I've eaten, and she only wanted toast.' Betty seemed about to say something more, then she shrugged. 'I'll bring you some tea in.'

Lauren glanced at the clock on the mantelpiece and panicked. 'I never sleep this late. It's gone eleven o'clock!'

Katie grinned. 'It's only half past eight, the clock's stopped.'

Lauren rang Daniel about the hot water.

'I know about it, Lauren. The electrician should come today. It's probably a fuse. I'm sorry the place is in such a mess.'

'I'll clean it up. I hope you don't mind if I strip the wallpaper off and paint the walls.'

'Go ahead. There's a maintenance fund so give me the accounts and I'll charge the owner. He won't replace any of the contents though.'

'The furniture will do once it's cleaned up, except I'll be buying us new mattresses. What shall I do with the old ones?'

'Put them outside with the dustbins, along with anything else that's past it. I'll bribe the dustmen to take the rubbish away and remove it from the inventory. I'll be along this evening with the lease, if that's all right with you. About seven?'

'Fine. I'll be in.'

Katie elected not to go shopping with them. 'I'll wait here in case they come to fix the water heater. Leave the washing up. I'll do that and I'll wash the kitchen cupboards and the larder shelves, so it's clean to pack the stuff into.'

'Is there anything you need at the shops? Do you have a shopping list, Katie?'

'I haven't got any money.'

'I have money that used to belong to your father. We'll have to eke it out a bit, but you're entitled to have some of it. What colour paint would you like for your bedroom?'

Katie's eyes gleamed. 'I've always wanted yellow walls, a nice golden colour, like a sunset. And if you can afford it I'd like some art things, so I've got something to keep me occupied.'

Lauren wrote it down. 'Anything else?'

Katie shook her head. 'I can't think now, though I'll probably come up with a thousand things after you've gone.'

'That's always the way. If you've got a mobile you can call me.' She wrote her number down and handed it to Katie. 'I'll get the landline switched on while I'm out, ex-directory.'

Betty impatiently hooted the horn.

'How can you stand the old bat?' Katie said. 'She's so bossy.'

'Betty's not so bad when you get to know her. She's hurting at the moment, trying to come to grips with Charlie's deception. She was very proud of her son.'

'I could have told her he was no good . . . if I'd known about her, that is.' Her eyes were troubled for a moment, then she stated vehemently. 'My father was a cheat, a liar and a *pervert*. I hate him. He's ruined my life!'

A youthful exaggeration stemming from youthful passion. Katie probably hated him for dying and leaving her alone. She'd felt the same anger when her own father had died. 'You have most of your life ahead of you. What you make of it will have nothing to do with Charlie and everything to do with yourself. Try not to let what he did ruin it.'

When Katie's face screwed up, Lauren wondered if the girl was going to break down again, but Betty put her finger on the horn and kept it there for half a minute. She grinned when

Katie aimed forked fingers towards the open door. 'I'd better go before she flattens the battery. Will you be all right on your own, Katie?'

Lauren sensed uncertainty under the girl's toughness when she said, 'Oh, don't worry about me. I was often left on my own. In the end I was so used to it I resented the parents coming home. That last time . . . when mum didn't come home, I felt . . .' She shrugged. 'I don't know, guilty for thinking that way and betrayed by them both, I guess.'

'You're bound to. We all feel betrayed by Charlie.'

'But they were my parents. They should have cared more, and so should I.'

'I expect you all did, deep down.' She reminded Katie, 'You did say that your father wrote that he loved you in your autograph book. Sometimes it's hard to express what we really feel out loud, especially when people don't come up to our expectations. Don't torture yourself over what you can't change, Katie. Things have a way of working themselves out eventually.' Gently she kissed the girl's cheek. 'Don't forget to ring me if you think of anything else.'

'I will.' Tears were glistening in the girl's eyes as Lauren closed the door behind herself.

Three

After the two older women had gone Katie boiled the kettle and filled up the kitchen sink. She found a ragged hand towel to use as a cleaning cloth, and an old bottle of detergent under the sink was still effective as a cleaner.

Afterwards she washed the dust from the crockery and cutlery and replaced it in the dresser, displaying the prettier stuff and hanging the cups along a row of hooks. It looked nice like that.

A middle-aged man came to fix the electric heater. 'Here for the summer, are you?' he said.

She nodded.

'I've checked her out and there's no leaks. She's not a trouble-some water heater. They don't like standing idle though, and

I dare say the switch was in the on position when the electricity was switched on and she blew a fuse. I'll show you how to replace the fuse if she goes again.'

A few moments later Katie found herself standing in front of a fuse box in the utility room, with its bewildering array of switches and fuses. 'This here is the mains switch. It disables everything, so make sure you turn it off here first. These things are your fuses. See, they are labelled. Loosen these screws at either end and put in a new wire, like this, then screw them down again. Not too hard though because it might break the wire.' Deftly he showed her how then placed the repaired fuse in her hand. 'Push it back in . . . that's right, straight in. Now turn on the mains switch . . . now the water heater switch. Good, give her twenty minutes and you'll have some hot water. I doubt if she'll go again.'

'That's a relief. Would you like a cup of tea?'

'I reckon not, Missy. I'm off up to the big house. They've opened it up to the public at weekends and they intend to sell cream teas in the conservatory. They need some more electrical sockets, and right quick.'

Katie smiled when he said, 'You're a quick learner. I reckon I'll have to take you on as an apprentice when you leave school. I'll leave some fuse wire in the box in case she plays up again, but you can always light the fire if you get stuck for hot water; it's got a back boiler. But it would warm the place up too much in summer for most folk, I dare say.'

What was a back boiler? she wondered, after he'd gone.

It didn't take long for the hot water to appear from the tap. She found a china potty decorated with roses in the utility room. Filling it with warm, soapy water she cleaned the dust from her bedroom furniture, then from Lauren's. As an afterthought she went downstairs and cleaned the old hag's room.

There was a pale-blue vacuum cleaner in the cupboard with the grand name of Constellation. It was round and resembled a space ship. Removing the dust-filled bag she inserted a new one then took the cleaner upstairs, plugged it into a socket and flicked the switch. It began to roar.

'You work,' she said with some surprise, and grinned because the cleaner had no wheels, but seemed to float on air. She remembered her father's collection of Star Trek movies and hummed the signature tune, then said in a deep voice, 'You're about to go where no man has gone before . . . or woman come to that,' she added, and sent the nozzle to probe the corners of the ceiling. After she'd sucked down all the cobwebs and their contents she fitted the brush on the end and applied it to the grit on the floor. Floors done, she backed down the wooden stairs, singing to herself.

She'd just finished the cleaning when her mobile rang. 'Take me to your leader, bristle head,' she said in a robot-like voice, and turned the cleaner off. As the motor faded to a whine she grabbed the phone up and said in her normal voice, 'Katie Parker.'

The silence at the other end was unnerving. Voice trembling a little, she whispered, 'Who is this?'

The silence deepened, then there came a low chuckle followed by a hollow voice. 'I know what you're doing. I can see you. Remember what I said about keeping your mouth shut.'

It had been several weeks since she'd heard from him. Turning the phone off, Katie closed the door and locked it, then shut all the windows and pulled the curtains across. Going upstairs she hid under her bed and hugged her teddy bear against her trembling body.

'She hasn't been idle while we were out,' Betty said, inspecting the clean shelves and cook top with approval. She opened the oven door and tut-tutted. 'She missed that, and although she's done my room she's ignored the corners. She doesn't like me very much.'

With the amount of nagging Betty had been doing Lauren didn't bother to wonder why. 'Give the girl a chance. She's not the cleaning lady.'

'She left the cleaner in the middle of the floor. I nearly tripped over it. And why has she got the windows shut and the curtains closed on a lovely day like this?'

'Perhaps she's gone out.'

Betty bawled, 'Katie!'

Her words were greeted by a sob, then the door to the right of the stairs creaked open and Katie's tear-stained face came around the door. 'Thank God it's you.'

'Oh, my Lord,' Betty said at the sight of her. 'You look scared out of your wits. Who else were you expecting?'

'Him.'

dressed from head-to-toe in pink sparkly stuff or in your bunkers."

"I am your girl. I think somehow I always knew even when I tried to talk myself out of it." Full of love, contentment flowed through her veins. "My answer is yes, Christian. I'll marry you."

He kissed her on the lips. "Merry Christmas, LeLe."

She stared at the snow falling and clinging to his hair. So handsome. So strong. And hers.

"Merry Christmas, Christian." She placed her palm on his chest and felt the beating of his heart. "Maybe there is a little Christmas magic in Hood Hamlet, after all."

* * * * *

Mills & Boon® Large Print
April 2012

0312 Rom LP

'Him. What d'you mean by him?'

Katie's face was closing up. 'Nobody. I fell asleep and dreamed someone was watching me through the window, that's all.'

'So you walked in your sleep and closed all the curtains, just in case. Pull the other leg, it's got bells on. You've been up to something, girl, and I'm going to get to the bottom of it.'

'Oh, all right. I'll tell you, if only for a bit of peace and quiet.' Katie came down the stairs, flicking her hair back over her shoulder and looking more confident now she had company. 'Somebody rang me. He said he was watching me. It's happened before and I know he didn't follow me here. I got a bit spooked, that's all.'

'Oh, is that all. You should get yourself a new telephone number.'

'I've tried that.'

'Well, buy a whistle and the next time he rings you give it a good old blow and knock his eardrum for six.'

'Have you reported it to the police?' Lauren asked her.

'What for? They wouldn't do anything. It was just a crank call. School kids, I expect. They dial numbers at random and if a woman answers they try and frighten them.' She changed the subject. 'By the way, the heater's been repaired. The man showed me how to mend a fuse in case it goes again.'

'I could have showed you that. Dearie me, kids of today know bugger all.'

'If you know so much why didn't you fix the water heater to begin with?'

'Because we rent the place and that's what electricians are for. Anyway, it's not my job, is it?' Betty heaved a sigh. 'I'm worn out. You can help Lauren empty the car. Fish the new kettle out first and I'll make us a cup of tea. And there's a present for you in the basket.'

Katie stared at the wicker basket in astonishment. 'A present! For me?'

'That's what I said, didn't I? If I can't give my own grand-daughter a present, who can I give one to. They didn't cost nothing, so don't think it's anything special.'

When a mewing noise came from the basket Katie rushed to open it and cried out in delight. 'It's a kitten, no . . . *two kittens!*' Picking up the tabby one Katie cuddled it against her chest. 'Which one's mine?'

When Charlie's smile nearly split the girl's face in half, it wrenched at Lauren's heart. She realized that she'd still appreciated Charlie's personality, even though she'd no longer loved or respected him. That's what had held her back from divorce.

Betty grinned at Katie, more than a match for the girl. 'The tabby one seems to like you, which doesn't say much for his taste. I prefer the ginger one, myself. He reminds me of your grandfather, sort of sly looking. Same colour hair too, what he had of it.'

'I like mine best. I'm going to call him Tiger.'

'Tiger it is then. Reckon I'll call mine Ginger. They were advertising for homes for them in the vet's window. They've been fixed, and are nearly out of kittenhood. That's why I took them both, to make it easier for them to settle down and be company for one another. Besides, the vet would've had to put them down if nobody took them. Another month and they'll be chasing those old mice out of here. Tabby's are good mousers. See that dark M marking between his ears? That's a dead giveaway, that is. M for mouser.'

Katie giggled. 'Thank you, Gran. My dad would never let me have a cat, or a dog. He said—'

'Yeh, I know what he said, luv.' Betty finished for her, '"They leave too much hair on the furniture." I don't know where Charlie got his tidy nature from, that I don't. Certainly not from his parents.' She fell silent, then turned and walked into her room, closing the door behind her.

Katie's smile faded. 'Was it something I said?'

'You mustn't blame yourself, Katie. We all need time to ourselves now and again. Betty was thinking of your father, I expect. She'll be out in a minute to make the tea, and I bought a packet of doughnuts.'

'My gran's tough, isn't she? When they told me about her I was excited. I expected her to be different.'

'Betty has lived a tough life. Your father tried to give her the life he thought she deserved, which was the one he wanted for himself. She couldn't change, and she never really fitted in. Her toughness is mostly front.'

Lauren gazed around her. 'You've done a good job with the cleaning. It was kind of you. But don't wear yourself out. We have plenty of time.'

Katie flushed with pride.

'The new mattresses are being delivered this afternoon. After lunch perhaps you'd help me bring the old ones down. I've bought new bedding for us, too. And a washing machine.'

'I'll help you move that old mangle out. It will weigh as much as an elephant, I expect. It will make things easier if we cut back that creeper too. I'll see if there's some shears in the shed.'

'We'll also have to move the sofa out from Betty's room to make room for her bed. I thought we might push it out into the conservatory. It's not very big, but if we can't shift it, it'll have to wait until Daniel comes with the lease, this evening.'

'What's he like, this Daniel?'

'I can't really remember. I've only met him a few times when I was a child. He was a friend of my mother. Oh, I've bought a small television, as well. Perhaps you'd help me carry the box in. It's got hand grips so we should be able to manage it between us.'

The kettle began to whistle loudly as they went to the car. When they returned, carrying the boxed television between them, Betty was in the kitchen busying herself with the cups and saucers and grumbling, 'A body can't have a minute's peace.'

Betty had forgotten that she wasn't the only one who might like a minute's peace, Lauren thought.

A little while later, seated and drinking their tea, Betty picked up the newspaper she'd bought and spread it on the table. Immediately she gasped. 'Oh, my gawd!'

Lauren gazed at her in alarm, then at the newspaper.

'Shit!' Katie said.

There on the front page was a photograph of Charlie with a woman Lauren had met only after she'd died. Katie's mother, Charlie's legal wife. A smaller photograph of herself was published next to it, her hair shoulder length and curling into her chin.

Bigamist! the headline screamed. *The house that businessman Charles Parker used to share with the second of his wives stands empty today. It's believed that Lauren Parker has gone into hiding after the man she married five years ago died in a car accident with his legal wife, Jean Parker, aged 40. The deceased couple's daughter is being cared for by the welfare department. Meanwhile, the police are investigating Mr Parker's affairs. It's believed that his business partner, Mr Brian Allingham, has fled abroad . . .*

'It's not a bad photo of you,' Betty said.

'Easily recognizable,' Lauren said. 'It won't take too long for someone to recognize me, if they haven't already.'

'I could cut your hair really short,' Katie chipped in. 'I've been working in a hairdressing salon every Saturday for the past year, and my boss taught me how to cut hair. She was going to take me on as an apprentice in the new year. I used to cut my mum's hair, and I've brought my hairdressing scissors with me. We could change the colour, too.'

Lauren looked at the photo of the dead woman. Her haircut was a smooth bob.

'Yours would look better layered, it would encourage the curl,' Katie said, as though she'd read her mind. 'And if you buy some hair colouring the next time you go shopping I could colour it for you. Highlights would be nice because it looks more natural and it would blend in with your own hair colour.'

'I didn't realize that you were so talented. There's no reason why you shouldn't take up that apprenticeship once this thing blows over, is there? Though I'm not sure that I want to go back to London to live, myself.'

'No, I suppose not,' Katie said vaguely.

'Let's do it, then. I'll trust that you know what you're doing.'

Katie grinned. 'If you wash your hair I'll cut it while it's still wet.'

An hour later Lauren gazed at herself in the mirror while Katie worriedly waited for her reaction. The dark, feathered cap made Lauren's face look elfin, her eyes large and her mouth generous. 'I love it like this, Katie. It feels as though I'm looking at someone else. I don't think it needs colouring.'

Katie relaxed with an audible hiss of breath and said with enough embarrassment to alert Lauren to the fact that she was unused to compliments, 'You'll get used to it.'

Betty smiled. 'Even Charlie wouldn't recognize you.'

There was a sudden silence and they all gazed at each other. Mention of Charlie's name had reminded them all why they were here.

The phone rang so suddenly and loudly that they all jumped. Lauren could have sworn that Katie went pale. It was an old telephone with a dial front and a clamouring ring.

'Shall I get it?' Betty said.

'I'm nearest.' Gingerly, Lauren picked up the receiver.

'Lauren Bishop?' a man said.

Cautiously, 'Yes.'

'It's British telecom. I'm just testing that the line works.'

'That was quick. I only just ordered the service this morning.'

'Despite reports to the contrary we can be quick sometimes.'

'As you've just proved. Thank you. It's working perfectly.'

'Who was that?' Betty and Katie said together.

'The linesman to say the telephone is on.'

'As it has just demonstrated.' Betty picked it up, turned it over and fiddled with a little wheel. 'There, that should turn the sound down.'

'The number is ex-directory.' Fishing in her bag Lauren came out with the contract, copied the number on to a piece of paper and placed it under the phone. 'Please don't give it out to just anyone, in case the wrong people get hold of it. And tell them not to pass it on. Also don't give anyone our address unless you ask me first, otherwise we'll have the press swarming all over us.'

By the time Daniel arrived the furniture was more or less in place. He was younger than she expected, about forty-five, elegant in his country style and with an easy confident manner.

'Lauren, how lovely to see you again,' he said, and he kissed each cheek before holding her at arm's length. His blue eyes were appreciative. 'Look at you, absolutely exquisite.' He gazed around the place. 'Not what you're used to, but you've worked wonders already.'

'Not by myself.' She indicated the two other women and introduced them.

'Parker,' he said. 'Now . . . where have I heard that name lately?'

'It's a common name,' Betty said defensively.

'Yes, of course it is . . . I meant no offence.' But Betty's manner had alerted Daniel and awareness had come into his eyes.

They signed the lease and Lauren handed over the rent money. Daniel raised an elegant eyebrow. 'Cash?'

'If you'd prefer a cheque I could manage it.'

He handed her a receipted rent book. 'Most people use plastic these days. Cash is becoming obsolete.'

'Christ, I hope not,' Betty said.

'Just joking of course, Mrs Parker.' He smiled at Katie. 'Do you ride, Katie?'

Katie shook her head.

'A pity. Lauren could have taken you out. She still can if she wants to teach you, not at the weekend though. It's always busy with the riding school pupils then. Walk me to the car, would you, Lauren . . . have you heard from your mother lately?'

'She's married an Italian. I haven't met him yet.'

When he leaned against the sleek green bonnet of his Morgan with one leg casually crossed over the other, she smiled. 'Same car, Daniel. I remember having a ride in it when I was a kid.'

'I imagine that was with my father. It's a classic, handmade for him. I'd never part with it. Tell me about you, Lauren. I knew you'd married someone your mother didn't approve of but I never dreamed your life would have turned out to be such a mess. The older woman is . . .?'

'Charlie Parker's mother. The girl is his daughter from his legal marriage.'

'And you?'

'Someone who was fool enough to be taken in by Charlie. I was married to him – or thought I was – for four years. I had no idea that his activities were illegal . . . and neither did the other two. It's all blown up in our faces. We've lost everything, and we're in hiding until it blows over.'

'I see. I wouldn't have thought that the girl and her grand-mother were your responsibility.'

'Betty and I were unaware of the girl's existence, and poor Katie didn't know she had a grandmother. They both needed someone.'

'And that someone was you.' He smiled. 'You always were tender-hearted. Your mother would have walked away from this, you know.'

'I'm not my mother.'

'If you don't mind me saying so . . . you've turned out to be a much nicer person, Lauren. It goes without saying that I'll respect your privacy.'

Her face warmed at the compliment. 'Thank you, Daniel. I was hoping I could rely on you.'

'Come and have dinner with me on Thursday, so we can catch up properly.'

'You'd better ask Lucy first.'

'We're no longer married.'

'Oh . . . I'm sorry.'

'Yes, so am I. She left me shortly after you left. I still miss her. Seven for half past, OK?'

She nodded.

He fitted a flat, checked hat on to his head. 'There's only a few people left in the village who would remember you. John Dunne, who used to work at the manor when you were a kid. As for the newer people, they wouldn't recognize you from that photograph in the paper. The Misses Anstruther still live at Barnaby Lodge. Both have failing eyesight, so wouldn't have read the articles in the paper.'

'I'm surprised the twins are still alive. They must be in their nineties.'

'Ninety last birthday. The local paper did an article on them. I see you've reverted to your maiden name. A good idea. People are curious about newcomers to the district, and word has got around that the cottage has attracted a permanent let, despite the ghost.'

'Ghost?'

'It's supposed to be Harry Simpson . . . a lot of nonsense, of course. I guarantee there's no resident ghost. Besides, he died in a nursing home.' He leaped over the door into the driver's seat. 'Now, if there's nothing else I can do for you . . .'

'Actually, there is, Daniel. I need a job, so if you hear of anything I'd be grateful if you'd put a word in for me.'

He thought for a moment, then nodded. 'How would you feel about working at your old home.'

'Grantham Manor?'

'It's open to the public. Who better than the Honourable Lauren Bishop to guide people round while the owner plays lady of the manor. And if the girl wants a job they're looking for someone in the tea room for the summer holidays. Do you have a phone number?'

'We're ex-directory.' She gave him the number, then their mobile numbers. He wrote them down in his notebook.

'What are the current owners of Grantham like?'

'The Bamfords?' He shrugged, then grinned. 'They equate

brass to class and pronounce aich as haich. They paid too much for the place, but they're making a go of it, all the same.'

She smiled. Daniel had always had a mine of good summing-up phrases, she recalled. 'My father would turn over in his grave.'

'Ah, yes, but the hardships of genteel poverty was a natural way of life to him. If he were still with us he'd be living at the manor, and he wouldn't have noticed it falling down around his ears.'

Lauren tried not to think of her gentle father, who'd faded away gradually and without complaint, and had died in his sleep when her mother had been in London. She'd adored him.

'Damn,' her mother had said when she'd come back. 'I didn't think he was that far gone. If I'd known I'd have bought myself a new black coat for the funeral.'

'I missed my father for a long time after he died. He was the sweetest, and most impractical man I've ever known, and he loved Grantham. He wrote wonderful poetry and stories, and illustrated them himself.'

Daniel said gently, 'Your mother always said you were like him, a dreamer. None of that with the Bamfords. They have a knack for making money. Greg manufactures computer games and electronic gadgets. Samantha runs the manor as a business, and has let it out at a phenomenal fee to film companies on a couple of occasions. I'll talk to her, try and persuade her that employing you would be an asset, and she should pay you accordingly. I'll let you know if anything comes of it on Thursday.'

'Any children?'

'Two teenagers. Anthony and Phillipa, otherwise known as Tony and Pippa. They're a couple of brats, currently being educated and gentrified at public boarding schools. They'll grow up as to the manor born. There's no like-father-like-son senti-ment in that household. Both of them want their children to have the opportunities they missed out on. Greg's a nice sort of bloke . . . clever, and down to earth. I think you'll like him.'

'And Samantha?'

'I'll allow you to discover that for yourself, but she has her moments.' His smile had an edge of something in it that Lauren couldn't quite figure out. 'I'll see you Thursday, then. Can you remember how to get to my place?'

'Of course.'

'Right you are then. I'll be off. If you need anything else, do let me know.'

'Thank you, Daniel. I will.'

She watched him go, then went back inside and told Katie about the job in the tea rooms.

Katie seemed less than enthusiastic.

'Well, it was only for the holidays, and you don't have to decide now. I've given him your mobile number to pass on to Mrs Bamford. Did you get your art things from the boot of the car?'

'I thought you'd forgotten to buy them.'

'No, I just forgot to bring them in. I hope I've brought the right stuff. I've never been much of an artist, and was guided by the assistant. She seemed to know what she was talking about.'

'Wait,' she called out as Katie headed through the door. 'You've forgotten the keys to the car.'

Snatching them up Katie headed outside.

Lauren went into the kitchen, wondering what to cook for dinner. Betty was in there. 'I'll take over the meals if you like. I used to like cooking and it will make me feel useful. I want to pull my weight while we're here.'

'What will I do?'

'Nothing. Sit in the evening sunshine and start reading that book you bought for yourself this morning.'

'I'll feel guilty doing nothing.'

'You've done enough for one day. We haven't got to do everything at once, have we? It can wait.'

Yes, Lauren thought. It most certainly could wait. 'I might ring that detective and let him know our number.'

Betty grinned. 'I think he already has yours.'

'It's not what you think.'

'How do you know what I'm thinking?'

'Well, it's written all over your face to start with. This is strictly police business.'

'If you say so, Duchess. You shouldn't be too eager giving information to the cops, you know. They take advantage. Better you wait for him to ring you.'

'All right. I will.' If just to prove to Betty that it wasn't personal with her.

It was two days later when Theo rang, by which time Lauren knew from her reaction to his voice that it was definitely personal.

'How did you get my number?' she asked him. 'It's ex-directory.'

He chuckled. 'I'm a detective. Besides, if someone wants a number badly enough it can usually be obtained.'

'Has anything important happened?'

'Such as?'

'Such as . . . *anything*. Charlie having a twin brother perhaps. I thought that might be why you rang.'

His voice was like smoke when he enquired, '*Has* Charlie got a twin brother?'

'Theo Ransom, you were not meant to take that literally. You are quite the most aggravating man I've ever met. No, he hasn't got a twin . . . at least, not as far as I know.' She groaned. 'Wouldn't it be just devastating to discover that he did have one, and I was married to him.'

Theo's chuckle was equally devastating.

'Tell me, why did you call?'

'To enquire whether you'd settled in OK.' His reply was a little disappointing.

'That was kind of you. Yes . . . we have settled in.'

'I'll be down that way next week. Would you object if I dropped in on you?'

She kept it light. 'I wouldn't object at all. Come for lunch. Ring me first.'

'I will. I'm looking forward to seeing you again, Lauren.'

'I'm not sure if the sentiment is entirely reciprocated,' she said softly. 'You're a very confronting sort of man.'

'Am I?' His chuckle came again, laid-back and sort of warm and crumbly, 'I'm fond of home-made chocolate cake.'

'Home-made chocolate cake?' She gave a bit of a nervous giggle. 'It so happens that I'm an expert at baking chocolate cake.'

'When people laugh like that it usually means they're lying.'

'Laugh like what?'

'Sort of breathless.'

'I'll try and be more hearty next time I laugh. If you think you take my breath away you're daydreaming. I'm not lying . . . you'll see.' She hung up to his laughter.

Turning, it was to find Betty grinning at her. 'Now *that's* what I was thinking,' Betty said.

Lauren spread her hands and grinned at her. 'You don't have a recipe for chocolate cake, do you? It can't be too hard to make.'

Four

Exploring her surroundings two days later, sketchbook in hand, Katie came across a notice on a cottage gate. 'Bicycle for sale. Ten pounds.' The machine was black and solid, had a basket on the front, a bag on the back and a guard around the chain to prevent grease getting on to a woman's skirt. Not that she was wearing one, but an old pair of hipster jeans that were a bit tight, and a loose tee shirt. The bicycle ticked like a clock when she gave it a trial and rode it around in a wobbly circle.

'It's got new brake pads and inner tubes, and the dynamo works,' the old man at the gate said.

Katie was discovering that questions to Lauren always brought an honest answer, even if it was only of the – I don't know, but we can look it up in that set of encyclopedia on the bookshelf at the top of the stairs – variety. And Lauren would always sit with her on the stairs and help her find what she was looking for.

Now, Katie asked the old man, 'What's a dynamo? What does it do?'

'It's that bottle-shaped thing there. You push it against the wheel like that, then as you ride that little bit at the top turns against the wheel. It creates enough electricity to work the lights. I've put a new globe in.'

'How clever.' The bike was very cheap, but her former friends would have laughed if they'd seen her riding it. It didn't seem to matter here. Katie counted the money in her purse. 'Would you accept five pounds and forty pence for now? I can drop the extra off the next time I come this way. Or I could do some housework for you instead . . . or do a sketch of you or the cottage, if you feel you can't trust me.'

'Why should I feel that?'

'I dunno. Where I come from nobody trusts anybody else, and no wonder. They were all a pack of thieves.'

'And where was that?'

She remembered she wasn't supposed to talk about where they'd come from. 'We were on the outskirts of London, really, I suppose. I'm not very good at places.'

'Lundun, is it . . . that accounts for it then. Only bin there once and my wallet got stole. It were during the war when I was a young sprat like you. Lifted straight out of my waist-coat pocket by a dip with greased fingers, it was. I didn't feel a thing. Not like today, the thieving buggers would knock you over the head just for fun first.' His face became doubtful. 'Perhaps I shouldn't trust you after all, then, not with you being a Lunduner, and all.'

Katie saw the bicycle slipping away from her. 'Oh . . . you most certainly can. We're not all thieves.'

He grinned. 'That be all right then, Missy. I'll take your word for it. A sketch of me it is, then? What's an artist like you doing in these parts?'

'Oh, I'm not a real artist.' She took her sketch book and pencil from her rucksack and sketched the old man leaning on the gate, chatting as they went. He had an interesting face, leathery textured except for a smooth, ruddy pad over each cheekbone held there by a nest of deep wrinkles. 'We've moved into Blackbird's Nest.'

'Have you run into Harry Simpson yet? He used to own Blackbird's Nest before it got too much for him. They put him into an old folks' home. Hated it, he did. I've heard he turns up at the cottage now and again. He always liked to wander, did Harry.'

'I can't say I've met him yet.'

'You needn't be scared of old Harry. He wouldn't hurt a fly. What's your name then, girl?'

'Katie.'

'How d'you do, Katie. I'm John Dunne.'

She took the hand he offered. 'Pleased to meet you, Mr Dunne.'

'Blackbird cottage . . .? You must be one of the Bishops, then. I heard they'd moved back into the district. I worked for Lord Bishop up at Grantham Hall. A gentle soul, he was. Not very practical, though. His wife robbed him blind. Not that anyone saw her much. She married him, stayed long enough to drop her daughter then cleared off and left the pair of them to it. She came back now and again though, sometimes with a man in tow, sometimes without. It didn't take her long to find a man to squire her around, I can tell you. There was one after the other. I felt sorry for his lordship, I did, having to put up with her carrying on.'

Katie found the tale fascinating, and it was romantic to discover that she and Lauren had similar backgrounds – though in reverse.

'In the last year of his life we didn't see Lady Bishop again until it was time to bury her husband. Then she tried to do her own daughter out of her inheritance . . . what there was of it. A trust fund her grandma had settled on her at birth, I recall. Portia Bishop couldn't wait to get rid of Grantham. Not that there was much money left after taxes and debts were settled.'

Katie knew exactly how that felt.

'Lauren was more like her dad than her mother, except she had more backbone when her dander was up. There was no turn the other cheek from her. Mother and daughter had a right old dust up, shortly after they lowered the old man into the grave. It set the gossips' tongues wagging for months.'

And kept the old man's tongue wagging for years afterwards, Katie thought.

'You're not the Honourable Lauren's daughter by any chance, are you? No . . . she wouldn't be old enough to have a daughter your age. How old did you say you was?'

'I'm seventeen next month, and I'm a sort of cousin,' Katie mumbled. She handed him the sketch, anxious to change the subject. 'What do you think? I'm not very good yet, but I'm still learning.'

'Yup! I reckon that's the same face I saw when I looked in the mirror this morning, right enough. By God, look at them wrinkles. Seems like only yesterday that I was a youngster like you with hardly a whisker on my chin. Better sign your name in the corner, dearie. You never know when these things are going to become old masters. I reckon I can find a frame for it too, and I'll hang it over the mantelpiece. John Dunne, lord of his own manor, however humble, that's me.'

'It's a nice cottage and you have a lovely garden.' She wrote her signature in small slanting letters that fitted into the pencil lines, so if anyone wanted to find it they'd have to look hard.

John Dunne was cackling with the laughter generated by his own joke as he turned to walk away with his sketch.

With no money left to buy lunch with, even if she did find a cafe, Katie boarded her new transport and turned towards home to show off her purchase, ringing the bell at every curve in the road. The saddle was wide and comfortable as she whizzed down the hill, ticking away and gathering enough momentum to scale the next rise without too much effort on her part.

The newly discovered knowledge was buzzing in her brain. Lauren was the daughter of a lord. An honourable, the old man had said. A blue blood.

'No shit!' she said.

Loosening the earth around a weed, Lauren forked it out of the ground. The day was warm, the breeze languid drifts of fragrance from the south-west.

The lawn had been mowed that morning and the edges tidied, but the flowerbeds were dotted with poppies, harebells and the daisy-like mayweed, while the hedge supported purple thistles, toadflax and long waving fronds of goldenrod.

With a fork she gently eased the earth from the roots of the long clumps of dried grass threaded in the rose bushes, enjoying the sun on her back and the perspiration trickling down beneath her breasts. She sat back on her heels while she untangled the grass from the thorns.

The rose blooms were fat and heavy, but they hung down from twigs so skeletal that they'd be unable to support them upright. The bushes badly needed pruning, but this wasn't the right time of year. The pruning would have to wait until they were dormant – if she was still here in winter.

At the moment she couldn't imagine being anywhere else, and the house in London, with its impersonal interior and its closely shaved garden seemed ages away.

Attracted by the song of a thrush she gazed at the Rowan tree in the hedge, where its mate fed on the bright berries. How sweetly it sang. But the kittens were looking at it too, and their innocent kitten eyes were narrowed and cruel and their purrs deep with an instinctive bloodlust. She tickled them with a long piece of grass, bringing back their playfulness.

Lauren had just finished weeding the patch when Betty came out carrying a tray of tea, some slices of egg and bacon tart and a salad. She placed it on a rickety wicker table and took one of the seats, waving a wasp away. 'Come and get your lunch.'

'Is it that time already? You should have called me. I would have carried it out.'

'I'm not that old, and neither am I entirely helpless.'

Lauren smiled at her. 'I didn't say you were. It's a beautiful day, Betty. Stop being such a grouch.' Washing her hands under the garden tap she waved them around in the air to dry. 'That looks lovely. Did you make it?'

'No, the chef I hired, did.'

Lauren gave a light laugh. 'Oh . . . have we got a chef, then? I hadn't noticed.'

'There's no use being sarcastic with you, is there?'

'None whatsoever. You need to learn to accept a compliment gracefully.' Lauren kissed her on the forehead and seated herself opposite.

Betty blustered, 'Look at those hands of yours, Lauren Parker. Have you forgotten you're going out to dinner with that man tonight.'

'Actually, I had forgotten. And it's Lauren Bishop now.'

'Ah, yes . . . it was wrong of my Charlie to do what he did. I don't blame you for casting his name aside.'

'It does no good agonizing over it, Betty. In the end, all that was really damaged was my pride.'

'There . . . I knew you didn't care that he'd died.'

'I didn't say that. Can we drop this conversation, please?'

'Making you uncomfortable, is it?'

'As a matter of fact, it is. I did love your son at the beginning, otherwise I wouldn't have married him.'

'Charlie told me you didn't love him any more. He was going to pay you more attention.'

She drew in a deep breath. Betty had gone too far, and perhaps it was time she put her straight. 'Did he tell you why I no longer cared about him?'

Betty stared at her. 'It's obvious, isn't it?'

'What's obvious is that you're spoiling for a fight. You see only what you want to see. Perhaps it's time we cleared the air over this, since I'd prefer not to be blamed for your son's dishonesty. When I married Charlie he took advantage of my gullibility to cheat me out of my money. Our relationship had been a farce for a couple of years. It was me who wanted children, but Charlie refused to father a child right from the beginning. Now I'm pleased we didn't have any, especially knowing how poor Katie was treated by him.'

'Poor Katie? Knowing that slag who was his real wife I'm still not convinced Katie's his daughter.'

'You only have to take your blinkers off and look at her.'

'It would take more than that.'

'Then have a DNA test. By the way, Charlie also had several affairs, and with girls young enough to be his daughter. His latest was Monica at the office, I think. They were seen out together.'

'That slut.'

'Considering what's come to light, let's face it . . . it was Charlie who was the slut, along with other labels that could be hung on him. Petty thief, handler of stolen goods . . . possession of drugs, to name a few. Nobody told me about his record before he *married* me. Not even you.'

'He was just a kid.'

'Stop making excuses for him. Was he just a kid when he went through with that sham marriage to me? He knew exactly what he was doing. Charlie had all the charm in the world but he was weak, and rotten to the core. He cheated on all of us and he didn't give a damn for anybody's feelings but his own. No, Betty, you're wrong. I do care that he died. I care very much. I wish he'd lived so he could face up to his deceit and pay the penalty for it.'

'You'll be accusing Charlie of fathering Katie's baby, next.'

'Katie's baby?' Lauren stared at her in shock. 'Katie is expecting a baby?'

'Now who's blind,' Betty mocked. 'Haven't you noticed her being sick in the mornings.'

There came a gasp from behind her.

Losing her appetite Lauren rose to her feet and gazed at the ashen-faced girl, who was standing there holding a bicycle. 'Oh, my God, I hadn't realized, I'm so sorry,' she whispered.

But Katie was looking past her to where Betty sat, her face red with anger and affront, and embarrassment at being caught out.

'How could you even suggest such a wicked thing you inter-fering old witch. I hate you!'

Dropping the cycle Katie pushed past them and ran indoors.

'I didn't mean it,' Betty whispered.

'Shut up, you've done enough damage for one day,' Lauren said savagely and followed Katie inside and up the stairs.

A storm of weeping reached her ears.

'Katie,' she said against the door. 'Can I come in?'

A long, shuddering sob reached her ears and a forlorn voice informed her, 'It's not locked.'

The girl's face was tragic. Lauren held out her arms and Katie came into them like a lost puppy. 'Don't worry, I'll look after you.'

'I was going to tell you, but I wasn't certain, and I was too ashamed to go to a doctor,' the girl sobbed.

'There's nothing to be ashamed of these days. You'll have a beautiful baby to look after.'

'I don't want a baby, especially not this one.'

'How can you say such a thing, Katie?'

'It's easy,' she said bitterly. 'It was forced on me and I don't know who fathered it.'

'Don't know—'

'I went to a party at Brian Allingham's house about five months ago. Someone drugged me, put something in my cola so I was barely conscious. Brian said I was drunk and he'd take me home. He took me out to a car where two boys waited, then drove us to a building . . . a warehouse, I think. There, they pulled my clothes off and they raped me. I'd never had *sex* before and it hurt. When they'd finished with me Brian paid them, and when they'd gone he did it to me too, then he took me home.'

'Oh, my God, Katie. You must report him to the police.'

'There's worse,' she said quietly.

Lauren couldn't think of anything that could be worse than what the girl had already gone through. 'You'd better tell me everything.'

'Brian Allingham videotaped it. He said he'd show the tape to my dad if I told on him, and besides, he wouldn't believe me because it looked as though I was a little slag enjoying myself. He said he was going to call the film "The Rape of the Virgin", and if he'd known I was an innocent he'd have done it to me first.'

'Have you told anyone besides me?'

She shook her head.

'We must tell your grandmother what happened. She feels bad about what she said, and you need her on your side. You can't go through this alone.'

'I'm not telling her. She hates me.'

'No, she doesn't. She's hurting too, and needed to lash out, but it was aimed at me. If she'd known you were there she wouldn't have said it. Would you allow me to tell her?'

Katie nodded, then she began to sob again. Lauren held her tight and rocked her back and forth. After a while the girl fell asleep on her shoulder. Gently laying her on the bed Lauren pulled a cover over her, kissed her tear-stained cheek and whispered, 'That's right, you sleep. It will do you good.'

Betty was waiting for her at the bottom of the stairs. 'Is she all right?'

'She's asleep for now. There's something I need to say to you.'

'Are you going to tell me to leave?'

'No, but I'm going to ask you not to place me in the position of having to take sides again. We'll talk in the garden. Is the tea still hot?'

'I put the cosy on the teapot.'

'Then brace yourself for a further shock.'

Five

Daniel lived in the oddly named Crookhaven House, a solid, two-storey ham-stone farmhouse. It was topped with a chunky, barely weathered thatch with a row of windows set under what seemed to be bristling eyebrows. The farmhouse was set at the end of a short avenue of yew trees. Lauren couldn't remember it being so large, then as she got closer she noticed that a two-storey extension had been skilfully added at one side.

Behind the house was the stable block with meadows for schooling both horses and riders. A copper beech and a couple of oaks provided shade for the animals in summer. Beyond the meadow a bridle path led through a copse skirting Grantham estate – across a road it became a public right of way that meandered through the grounds, then downhill to a sandy cove that had been part of the estate until the ancient right of way had been rediscovered by the rambling clubs. It was twenty minutes by horseback, and triple that if one walked.

The house looked well cared for and prosperous as she drove through the yews. She'd been sorry to hear that Daniel's marriage to Lucy had failed. They'd seemed like an ideal couple, for Lucy had been as mad about horses as Daniel had been. Lauren smiled to herself. When she'd been fifteen she'd had a schoolgirl crush on Daniel. But then, so had every girl who met him. Daniel had regarded their adolescent looks and sighs with complete indifference, and had broken all their hearts in the process.

Preceded by two honey-coloured Labradors who sniffed her tyres and threw a couple of welcoming barks her way, Daniel emerged from the front door in jeans and navy crew-necked sweater, a smile widening on his face. 'You made it then?'

'I'm sorry I'm a little late, I couldn't decide what to wear. I hope you don't mind jeans. I thought we'd known each other long enough, by association if nothing else, not to have to stand on ceremony.'

Opening the car door Lauren eased herself out legs first.

Daniel laughed when he saw her jeans, which she'd topped with a pale blue embroidered blouse. 'I see you didn't.' He gently kissed each cheek. 'Welcome to Crookhaven House.'

'It looks good, Daniel.'

'I usually tart it up a bit in spring. It was re-thatched a couple of years ago. I managed to get a grant for that; and it's just lost its newness. Otherwise a tub or two of whitewash works wonders. Come in, I'll get you a drink. Gin was your poison, I recall.'

'Gin? I was only seventeen the last time we met and didn't drink. You must be mistaking me for my mother. I'll have a glass of white wine if I may.'

'I have a Chardonnay resting in the kitchen.' His eyes met hers for a moment and he smiled as he said softly, 'Actually, you're nothing like Portia, you know. How is she?'

'I really have no idea. She practically disowned me when I

married, and that was quite some time ago. She felt the marriage was unsuitable. With hindsight, I know she was right, but I'm not about to tell her that.'

He busied himself pouring her a glass of wine and a whisky for himself. 'I don't imagine that made much difference to your life. Portia was never much of a mother to you, or a wife to your father. Everyone we knew felt sorry for you.'

A stab of annoyance punctured her. 'Why?'

'Because they were such an ill-matched pair. Your father drifted around in a world of his own. Your mother . . .?' He shrugged and looked awkward. 'Sorry, Lauren. I'm out of line.'

She felt disorientated by this sudden attack on her parentage. 'I adored my father, and he never harmed anyone.'

'Everyone liked him . . . except for Portia. But he wasn't much good for anything, was he? He sat in that big house with it falling down around his ears, lived off Portia's money and read books while you waited on him hand and foot and worshipped him.'

She gazed round the kitchen with its ancient beams, its copper pots and its Aga cooker, and began to dislike him. He'd inherited a going concern from his father, who'd been part of the Olympic team and whose name had brought credibility to the riding stable he'd started. Lucy had been well off, so Daniel had obviously got to keep his business in the settlement, and with more beside. 'Why was it that Lucy left you? I can't remember.'

Daniel laughed. '*That* touch of nastiness you did inherit from Portia. You can't remember because I didn't say. You may recall that I had an affair . . . Lucy found out about it, but it was a long time after it was over.'

She remembered a snatch of something, but the exactness of it eluded her and was gone. Yet she was curious. 'May I ask, with whom?'

There was something odd about the look he gave her and he said quite gently, 'I'd prefer not to disclose that. It's really none of your business, Lauren.'

She set her glass down on the bench and lied, because she was hurting like hell. 'And neither is my life any of your business, Daniel. To be quite honest I don't give a damn about what you, or anyone else thought of me or my parents. Equally, I don't give a damn why Lucy left you, or whose money supported whom.

It's like the pot calling the kettle black, isn't it? Now . . . we can either change the subject and go on from here, or I can get back into my car and leave. Which would you prefer?'

Embarrassment flushed the skin of his face. 'My profound apologies for raising your hackles. I went too far. Don't go, Lauren, I've cooked us a wonderful meal and I don't want us to be on bad terms.'

Because he'd been big enough to apologize the tension dissipated and she met him halfway. *'You've* cooked it?'

'Believe it or not I enjoy cooking. We'll eat in the kitchen if you don't mind. It's my favourite room.'

Lauren could cook, but she certainly didn't have the flair for it that Daniel seemed to possess. A delicate asparagus soup was followed by succulent chicken and roast potatoes with a variety of vegetables. Then there was a dream of a pudding which consisted of strawberries and ice-cream on a bed of chocolate sponge, with rum trickled over it. The confection was dribbled with raspberry sauce and topped off with cream.

After an initial awkwardness they relaxed. 'That was the most wonderful meal I've ever eaten, Daniel. You should open a restaurant.'

A smile lit up his face. 'I considered it once, then my father died and I carried on with this place. It was the right thing to do. Restaurants are risky, and I'm lazy by nature. Finding the right position to attract the clientele, hiring the staff, the health aspect and the hours of work needed put me off. Because I enjoy cooking it doesn't follow that I'd make a success of running a restaurant. I do enjoy what I do here, it's something I was brought up to do, even though I wasn't in my father's class when it came to riding. I entertain a lot which satisfies my urge to cook.'

'You won lots of prizes for your horsemanship, as I recall.'

'Oh, I was competent. I didn't have the competitiveness that Dad had, and sometimes I think I won a prize because I was his son, rather than for my skills. You had a good seat on a horse, I recall.'

'Most little girls are keen on riding horses. I never had a craving to own one though. I always thought them to be rather smelly creatures.'

'They do tend to fart rather a lot.'

They both laughed, then Daniel said, 'For all that, horses

are beautiful, sensitive and intelligent creatures with a lot of strength and grace. But they're not the only iron I have in the fire.'

'Oh . . . what else do you do?'

Standing, he held out his hand to her. 'Come and see.'

He led her to the extension and she saw that it formed an L shape to the house.

'It's a workshop?' she said in surprise.

'Yes, it is. I've added a guest area over the top with an en-suite and a food preparation area, so the front of the place doesn't look tampered with. You can't afford to fall foul of the heritage people, or the council, come to that. I let the flat out on a weekly basis to singles or couples who want riding holi-days. Down here I restore old furniture. Sometimes I buy old pieces, do them up and resell them. See that dresser over there with the bracket base, that's my latest find. It's made of oak and has about ten different coats of paint over it. I think it dates back to the middle of the eighteenth century. I'm dying to start work and uncover the bare wood.'

'Then what will you do with it; sell it to an antique shop?'

'Advertise it for sale. I don't believe in giving money away to a middleman.'

'Yet you dabble in real estate.'

'Only rental properties, and that's on a commission basis. I've only got a few properties to manage. It's mostly a question of doing the inventories and making sure the properties are kept clean.'

'Blackbird's Nest?' she reminded him.

He shrugged. 'I didn't realize it was so bad. As it had no tenants coming and going I overlooked it. I do all right in the summer, people will pay anything for a cottage near the sea, but winter is a dead loss. I can probably find you something better come winter if you're still here. Blackbird's Nest is too isolated for most people.'

Alarm filled Lauren at the thought of having to move again. 'I like Blackbird's Nest now it's beginning to get straightened out. I'm happy there and the rent's fairly cheap.'

'Yes, well. The person who owns it might decide to put it up for sale. He asked me to get him a valuation a couple of months ago.'

'But I have a lease.'

'Yes, of course you have. I shouldn't worry. These things rarely move that fast, anyway. Come along, make yourself comfortable in the sitting room and I'll make us some coffee.'

The sitting room was furnished with restored oddments. There were two winged chairs covered in dark-blue brocade, and a sofa with cornflowers decorating the loose cover. The cool severity of a grey stone floor was relieved by the addition of a rug splashed with yellow, orange and blue swirls. An enlarged photograph of Daniel's father, his horse looking over his shoulder and his Olympic medal held up for display hung on the wall.

'Did you sound Mrs Bamford out about employment at Grantham?' she said when he set the tray of coffee on a low table made from six coloured lead light windows hinged together and lit from inside. A slab of grey marble served as a top. It was a simply made, but beautiful piece of furniture.

He saw her looking at it. 'I made that out of some old windows I bought from a demolition site.'

'It's spectacular, and imaginative.'

'I did ask Samantha and she's thinking it over. She's already got someone for the tea room – a niece who's coming to stay with her for the school holidays.'

Just as well considering Katie's likely condition, Lauren thought. If the girl was pregnant, the baby would be due round about February when the lease was due to run out.

'Come in with me, Lauren, I'm scared,' Katie implored her.

'Don't be silly, there's no need to be scared. It's only an internal examination,' the nurse said.

Katie was pale and covered in perspiration, and Lauren felt sorry for her. 'I'm sure you have nothing to worry about, but I'll stay with you if the doctor doesn't mind.'

'Are you a relative?' the nurse asked with a sniff.

Lauren was just about to shake her head when Katie said, 'Miss Bishop is my cousin, and I live with her. If she isn't allowed in then I won't go in either.'

The nurse sighed. 'All right, but its only a small cubicle, mind. You'll have to stand near her head, Miss Bishop.'

Although she held Katie's hand the girl was still upset, and she burst into tears when the doctor tried to examine her. 'It hurts.'

'That's because you're too tense. Relax,' he said.

But Katie couldn't relax. She gave a terrified scream when he touched her again. 'I don't want this baby, take it away.'

The nurse began to look annoyed and the doctor drew the sheet over Katie. He took Lauren aside. 'I can't examine her while she's like this, but even if I was inclined to refer her to a clinic she's too far along for an intervention. The scan shows that the baby is normal, and the mother is healthy. Is there any reason why the girl is so frightened.'

When Lauren nodded his eyes sharpened. 'I thought so.'

'You must understand that I can't break her trust over this.'

'Even though it might have an impact on her health and that of her baby?' He glanced at his watch. 'Look, it's time for my tea break and Miss Parker is last on my list for today. See if you can persuade her. Long term, the amount of tension she's suffering from can cause a lot of damage.'

'I'll try.'

Lauren succeeded with, 'Although you don't want to think about this, Katie, the fact is that the baby is not going to go away. If you don't want to talk about it yourself, perhaps you'd allow me to tell the doctor on your behalf. It would be best if you stayed with me, then you'll know what I told him.'

Lauren held Katie's hand and she gave a sob every now and again while Lauren related to the doctor the basics of what he needed to know.

Anger gathered in his eyes and he said gruffly, 'You should have reported the assault to the police, you know.'

'I'm too ashamed,' Katie whispered. 'I just want to get rid of the baby.'

'It can't be done, I'm afraid. It's too dangerous at this stage.'

'Then when it's born I don't want to see it. It can be adopted by someone, can't it?'

'No doubt a good home can be found for the child if that's what you want. But try not to blame the infant for the circumstances of its existence. We have to make sure that both you and the baby are healthy. I'll need to examine you, Katie, especially now. As it's obvious that protection wasn't used during the assault, I'll also ask the nurse to take some blood, just to make sure that you're free of any sexually transmitted diseases.' His voice lost its professional detachment when tears began to trickle down Katie's cheeks. 'I'll be as quick as I can, my dear, I promise.'

Katie bore the indignity with several sharp intakes of breath, between the encouraging words from herself and the doctor. Afterwards, he said, 'I'd like to refer you to a psychologist, who should be able to help you come to terms with what's happened. Her name is Eve and she specializes in helping victims of sexual assault. She doesn't have an office, but she'll visit you at home.'

'I've got Lauren to help me,' Katie said and held on to her hand possessively.

'But I'm not a professional, Katie dear. I'm just a . . . *relative* who cares about you. It would be better if you saw someone who knew what they were doing.'

'Promise you'll stay with me?'

'That wouldn't be fair to Eve . . . the counsellor. How could she do her job properly if I was there? I'll stay within reach until you feel comfortable with her. You could talk to her in your bedroom, in private. I'll be downstairs, or in the garden. Then, if you think you need me you could call me. But I'm sure you're grown up enough to handle it by yourself.'

Reluctantly, Katie agreed.

After they left the doctor's office they went to the shopping centre, both of them wearing sunglasses and hats that shaded their eyes in case they were recognized, for the story of Charlie Parker had taken on a life of its own. He was fast becoming a sort of folk hero, Charlie the cheerful cockney with a heart of gold that no woman could resist. There was a picture of Monica leaning on the desk, her cleavage the main focus. A close up of Charlie's face, positioned so he was looking straight at it.

MONICA COULDN'T RESIST HIM!

'*Charlie Parker made advances to me in the ladies loo on the day I started work for him,' aspiring model and actress, Monica Spencer gushes. 'He called me his fluffy kitten.'*

Lauren sighed. 'How very romantic of him.'

Surprisingly, Katie leaped to her father's defence. 'Show-off bitch! She looks more like a cow than a kitten with those big udders, and the fluff is all inside her head.'

Lauren laughed. 'Don't be too hard on her, she's only a few months older than you are. At least it takes the heat off us. I've bought you a present from the charity shop. It's a patchwork quilt with a big golden sunflower on it. We'll wash it when we get home. I'm going to start painting your room tomorrow, and I thought it would go nicely with that golden-yellow paint.'

'Can I help with the painting?'

'Of course. I'll do the ceiling first.'

'You know . . . you shouldn't have spent money on me.'

Lauren slid her a glance. 'Why not?'

'Because you can't afford it.'

'It didn't cost much, and it was Charlie's money. I stole it from his safe.'

Her brown eyes rounded like saucers and she breathed, *'You didn't!'*

'I did, but don't tell anyone. Besides, I enjoyed buying you a gift.' She wished there had been more money in the safe. Then Lauren remembered the astuteness of Theo's grey eyes and was pleased she hadn't been in the position of being tempted to take more. He was no fool.

They stopped off at the plant nursery on the way home and, on advice, bought a variety of pot plants for the conservatory. Betty had cleaned the brasses while they were out. Those around the fireplace had taken on a gleaming new lease of life. She'd washed the lace curtains, too, and they drifted lazily on the line in a faint breeze, like dancers warming up before a performance.

They found Betty asleep on her bed. Lauren gently shut the door on her snores, wishing that she'd take things a bit easier.

In the kitchen Katie began to unpack their groceries. 'What shall I do with this frozen cake?' she called out.

'Put it in the freezer for now.'

The phone rang, giving a discreet buzz now Betty had muted its clamour.

'It's Theo,' a deep voice said.

She laughed, delighted to hear from him. 'How odd, I was thinking about you just a few minutes ago.'

'That's encouraging. What exactly were you thinking?'

'I suspect it's not what you'd hope I was thinking.'

'And what might that be?'

'Tell me what you think I was thinking you were thinking and I'll tell you if you're close . . . I think.'

Now it was his turn to laugh. 'You're much too complicated.

What I didn't tell you is that I'm an expert at spotting a lie, and you were wishing you hadn't lied to me.'

Her heart gave a bit of a wobble. 'Lied about what?'

'About being an expert at making chocolate cakes. I'm an expert at eating them, and I'll be there tomorrow to sample the one you're about to make for me.'

'I'll guarantee it will be the best cake you've ever tasted. By the way, Theo, I'd intended to paint Katie's bedroom tomorrow.'

'And . . .?'

'You're exactly the right height to reach the ceiling if you get here early enough. It won't take Katie and myself long to do the walls.'

A heartfelt groan reached her ears. 'It's supposed to be my day off.'

'Well, don't think you're going to laze about eating chocolate cake.'

He laughed. 'How are things, have you settled in?'

'More or less.'

'But it's not what you're used to.'

'No, it's not . . . but in its own way, it's better.'

'In what way?'

'I can't explain.'

'Try.'

'I grew up not far from here and I feel . . . let me see . . . safe isn't exactly the right word I'm looking for. It's more of a, I fit into the landscape so can't be noticed, type of feeling, I suppose.' She gazed towards the kitchen and lowered her voice. 'I think I enjoy not being married to Charlie most of all.'

'I enjoy you not being married to Charlie, too.'

Things were getting too personal too quickly between them, but she enjoyed the danger of it. It had been a long time since an attractive man had paid her attention. 'How will you get here, Theo? Do you need me to meet you at the station?'

'I have transport. I'm looking forward to seeing you again.'

'Are you? Why?'

There was a short silence followed by a quiet chuckle. 'Do you need to ask, or are you just fishing for a compliment?'

'It was neither, but I shouldn't have asked. Now I have asked, I do need to say this. I'm still coming to terms with the consequences of Charlie's death and the circumstances of my freedom.

I like you, but it's far too soon for me to even contemplate becoming involved with anybody else . . . I think.'

'Watch those thinks, they have a habit of getting away from you.'

'Everything happened so fast that I feel a bit mixed up.'

'I'm well aware of that, Lauren, and I won't put any pressure on you, I promise. But does it hurt to let you know I find you attractive?'

It made her a little uncomfortable in a self-aware sort of way. It wasn't that she disliked it, but that she didn't actually want to contemplate the possibility of physical attraction between them – something told her that a sexual relationship with Theo would be intensely intimate.

'No it doesn't. Thank you, Theo. I'm just scared. I'll see you tomorrow.' She replaced the receiver in its rest, went through to the kitchen and removed the cake from the freezer. 'We're having a visitor tomorrow. We might as well just leave it in the fridge.'

'The policeman . . . yes, I heard. He's a bit scary.'

'Scary?'

'He looks you straight in the eyes when he talks. You have the feeling that he misses nothing. And he's fit. Have you seen the way he moves.'

'Describe it.'

'So fast and quiet that you don't hear his feet touch the ground.'

Lauren grinned. 'I hadn't noticed, but it sounds interesting, so I'll make a point of doing so when I see him.'

'Will you tell him about . . . me?'

The question hardly deserved a moment's thought. 'Of course not.'

'It wasn't a question, Lauren, it was a request. I was thinking that perhaps he might find the video Brian made. I'd hate to think of anyone seeing it, or putting it on the Internet. If it hasn't already been copied, then he might be able to find it and destroy it.'

Lauren was glad the girl was thinking straight. 'Do you want to ask him?'

Her voice rose a fraction. 'I couldn't talk about it to a man . . . I just couldn't . . . not yet.'

'Try not to get upset, Katie. It's bad for the baby.'

'Would you ask him for me? In private. I don't want my Gran sticking her oar in.'

Lauren gave her a quick hug. 'If that's what you want. What if Theo wants to ask you questions?'

'About what?'

'Katie, please stop being so obtuse.'

'I don't know what that means.'

'It means that you're acting dumb. Theo's a police officer. He's not going to look for that video and just hand it over to you. If the young men that took part in the assault on you can be identified then he'll want to prosecute them. That means he'll need you to sign a witness statement and appear in court.'

Katie paled. 'Forget it.'

'So you don't want me to ask him?'

'Yes . . . but nothing else. If he says no then he says no.'

The door to Betty's room swung open. 'Oh, you're back. I've just had a little rest. What did the doctor say?'

'Everything's all right, but he wants me to see a counsellor.'

'There was no such thing as counselling in my day. We just got over things and got on with it. The kids were looked after properly at home, and disciplined, too. They did what they were told, else they got a good smack for their trouble.'

The sting in Katie's tail flicked. 'How do you account for my father turning out so badly then?'

Betty's knuckles whitened. 'It was your mother who led my boy Charlie astray.'

'Yeah, sure it was. How can you suggest that your precious *boy,* who was in his thirties when he married, didn't have a mind of his own. He wasn't a fool, he was an out and out liar and a cheat, amongst other things.' She gave an exasperated sigh. 'Oh, it's no good arguing with you, since you thought the sun shone out of his—' She threw Lauren an apologetic look. 'Sorry, Lauren . . . I'll go and get the curtains off the line. It will give me time to cool off.'

'The saucy little cow,' Betty grumbled after Katie left.

'She has a point. You can be so insensitive at times, Betty. The girl's had a hard day, and it serves you right.'

Betty shrugged. 'I suppose I deserved it?'

'Yes, you did.' She kissed her on the cheek. 'Go and tell her you're sorry.'

'I've never said sorry to anyone in my life.'

'Then it's about time you did. Katie's a nice girl when you get to know her.'

'Anyone would think you were her kin instead of me. She worships you and hates me.'

'That's because I'm nearer her age, and I pay attention to her. You should try to meet her halfway. It's hard for her to imagine you as her grandmother, when you criticize her or grumble every time she opens her mouth.'

'I don't mean it.'

'I know that, Betty, but Katie doesn't. She's experienced nothing but negativity from adults for most of her life. She's an intelligent girl, so if your intention is to alienate her completely, just keep going the way you are.'

As Betty walked away, Lauren called after her, 'Detective Sergeant Ransom is paying us a visit tomorrow.'

'Paying *you* a visit, you mean.'

'He's going to help with the painting.'

'You'll want me to show you how to make a chocolate cake, then.'

A grin came to Lauren's face. 'I bought one of those fancy frozen cakes while we were out. Theo's a man, he won't be able to tell the difference.'

'A fiver says that he does.'

Lauren laughed. 'You're on.'

Six

Theo had made good time. An hour and a half had passed since he'd eaten a substantial breakfast at a roadhouse. His tyres had wound up the road since then. He smiled, for he'd timed it nicely, missing the morning rush hour by a fraction. The road had narrowed to one lane some time ago, and, according to his map the turn off should be just about . . .?

Coffrey Lane was well signposted. 'Yes,' he said and took the next right turn. Coming to a halt on top of a rise he looked about him. The countryside was overwhelmingly gold with ripening wheat. Down a long sweeping slope through fields dotted with wild flowers sheep slowly grazed their way through a verdant carpet of grass. In the misty distance the sea sparkled like a length of blue sequinned silk.

A song thrush darted out of a hedge next to him and flew into the air with a cry of alarm.

'Can you direct me to Blackbird's Nest?' he called after it.

The thrush didn't answer. Theo's glance was caught by a fraction of stone and grey slate roof visible through an over-grown hedge and the branched splendour of a copper beech tree. It was just a little way down the hill. 'So that's where you're hiding?' he whispered.

It was still early, just gone eight as he coasted his Ducati to a halt outside the cottage. The curtains were still drawn and there was a faint hum of insects in the still air. Taking off his crash helmet Theo thumbed Lauren's mobile number into his phone.

'Hi, Lauren,' he said. 'Did I wake you?'

'No . . . I've been up for hours, painting.'

Just at that moment the door to the cottage opened and Lauren followed two kittens outside. She looked cute in a short cotton nightdress with a pin-tucked bodice, her hair still spiky from the pillow. She'd had it cut. His glance went to her legs, long and slim with neat knees, as she walked barefoot into the wet grass like a miniature goddess.

'Liar,' he said and he smiled when she grinned, and wiggled her toes in the dew beneath her feet.

The sun chose that moment to appear between the trees to backlight her. Theo's mouth dried as her small waist and the flare of hips and thighs were shadowed against the light fabric. Lauren Bishop *was* a miniature goddess.

'Ah, I'd forgotten you could spot a liar a mile away, Sherlock. Where are you?'

'Not all that far away . . . outside your gate if you want me to be exact.'

She spun his way, her smile broadening in a manner that caused Theo all sorts of damage. A breathless giggle raised the hairs on his neck. 'Goodness, you have me at a disadvantage,' she said into her phone.

'A good place to be. At least I know how you look when you get up in the morning.' Adorable was the word that came to his mind. 'I'm sorry it's so early, I wanted to miss the rush hour.'

'Very wise. You look slightly sinister in black leather,' she said.

'I am slightly sinister.' He held up a plastic bag. 'But I do have more suitable clothes to change into. Can I come in?'

She backed away towards the cottage door still talking into the receiver, her wide smile making him feel welcome. 'I'd better get dressed first. Come into the garden and be entertained by Tiger and Ginger. They're brothers. I'll bring us some tea and we can drink that while the other two get up. They're awake.'

If he was the primitive caveman he felt like being, he could easily rush her, throw her over his shoulder and carry her off to his cave to have for breakfast. What a breakfast!

The kittens were practising stalking a blackbird, but the grass was too short to slink through and the prey too wise and too vigilant to be caught. After a while the cats became bored by their lack of success and engaged in a wrestling match with each other instead, before tiring, and stretching their stripes out in a patch of sunshine.

Theo picked up some tiny pieces of gravel and amused himself by lobbing them into the furry bellies presented to him. Tiger stretched and turned over on his side. Ginger lifted his head, opened one eye and gave him a warning look.

A few minutes later Lauren joined him, dressed in blue jeans and a cropped white shirt that displayed her navel when she lifted her arms.

His gaze raked hungrily over her. 'I like your new hairstyle. It suits you.'

'Thank you. Katie cut it after that photo of me appeared in the paper. She's very talented. I don't know how they . . . the papers . . . got hold of it.'

'I think the office girl might have given it to them. It's been cropped from that one of the three of you I saw on your table. No doubt she has a copy.'

He *did* have sharp eyes. 'Monica Spencer? Oh yes . . . of course. I'd almost forgotten about her. I suppose she must be out of a job.' For a moment her eyes were filled with vulnerability, and he felt desperately sorry for her.

She ran a finger over the smoky face shield of his helmet and wryly attempted a joke as her eyes went over his sleek gleaming red Ducati. 'Spaceship or motor bike, Theo?'

'Spaceship,' he said, for he had the feeling he was exploring new territory and was heading into the unknown. He reached out, and there was a precious moment of empathy between them as his hand gently squeezed hers.

Her eyes melted blue into his as she slid it away.

Her bottom lip seemed to have been created in a deliciously natural pout, and he was attacked by an urge to lean forward and capture it in a kiss. He didn't know why he was here. It had been drilled into him years ago that getting involved with a victim of crime had its pitfalls. They could become too dependent, cause problems.

Yes, he did know why he was here! He hadn't stopped thinking about Lauren Bishop since they'd met. She was like an itch he couldn't scratch. He needed to get to know this woman. She was elusive . . . clean, with not even a demerit point on her driving licence, which was still in her single name. How could a woman like her get caught up in the sordid schemes of someone like Charlie Parker? She wasn't stupid.

'How do you like it?' she whispered.

The cats came and jumped on her lap. They vied with each other for her attention as her fingers automatically caressed their chins and set them purring with ecstasy.

Abandoned, hot, spicy and extremely satisfying, like a good meal. He'd be purring if she stroked him too, he thought, and smiled at the thought of whipping this provocative morsel of a woman off to bed. He cleared his throat. 'Medium strong. Milk in first and two sugars.'

All alertness, the cats flew off her lap at the sound of a spoon tapping on a saucer and streaked towards the cottage door. She poured the tea into matching mugs, smiling at him as she handed it over. 'Have you eaten?'

'I had breakfast at a roadhouse.'

'Can you eat another? Betty is making pancakes.'

It had been years since he'd eaten pancakes and he couldn't resist the thought. 'With golden syrup?'

She smiled. 'You have a sweet tooth, Theo.'

'Yes, I do . . . but your smile satisfies it.'

The smile faded and silence gathered between them, so he thought he might have offended her. He ventured, 'Tell me what you're thinking.'

*   *   *

What was she thinking to even contemplate becoming involved with this policeman who was investigating the life of her late husband?

No, she hadn't really been married to Charlie. He'd been her former partner, even if it was on a shared basis – his bit on the side, as Katie had put it. But that hadn't been an accurate term either, since the past two years the relationship had been almost platonic, the marital duty perfunctory, as if Charlie felt he should service her. And she felt she should accept that attention because she had a ring on her finger. What did one call a bigamously married wife in legal terms? A fool!

Surreptitiously she moved her hands to her lap, slid off the wedding ring and pushed it into her pocket. Lauren couldn't imagine why she hadn't thought of removing it before. She had long held the old-fashioned belief that love, marriage and fidelity went together, even while she knew Charlie was cheating on her. The gesture gave her a euphoric sense of freedom, like an escaping slave might have had. Charlie would have laughed at that, would have enjoyed the thought that a small circle of platinum could have effectively shackled her to him. But that was Charlie.

This was Theo. What was she thinking, he'd asked her? Lord, it would make a tomato blush. She gazed into those long-lashed eyes of his and modified her thoughts, though she imagined that Theo was a man who would appreciate honesty.

She swooped in a breath and said in one rush, 'I'm thinking that your eyes miss nothing, that you're probably good at getting your own way and that it wouldn't be a good idea for us to become involved, but we probably will before too long if we keep seeing each other. I think I should run like hell in the opposite direction.'

'And will you?'

'I think that would be a wasted effort, Detective Sergeant Ransom. Do you have any wives, ex-wives or children I should take into consideration? I'm carrying enough baggage at present.'

'None that I know of.'

'Then I'm thinking you should break the ice and do what you've been thinking of doing.'

'I like this habit of thinking out loud. It makes thinking very clear.' Giving a chuckle he took her face between his hands, leaned forward and kissed her.

His mouth was warm, his kiss brief, but long enough for her to enjoy the tentative intimacy of its newness – so they wouldn't go through the day with expectations of anything more than friendship. It was not a sensual kiss, but just a little taste – the salting of butter on the toast, the sugary syrup on the pancake, the melting glisten of caramel on the crème brûlée that left no doubt that there was something infinitely more satisfying beneath the garnish.

Betty's raucous screech from the kitchen drew them apart. Their eyes met and they grinned, guiltily, as if they were schoolchildren caught in the act of kissing behind the bicycle shed.

'I thought I heard a parrot?' he said, his eyes gleaming with laughter, so she giggled.

'I think the pancakes must be nearly ready, Theo. I'll show you where you can change. Follow me, and mind your head on the beam just inside the door. Bring your cup and I'll take the tray.'

'I like a man with an appetite,' Betty said a few minutes later. 'Would you like some more, Theo?'

'Not unless you want me to burst. The last time I ate so many pancakes was when I was fourteen and staying with my grandmother for the holidays. She's gone now.'

'Didn't your mother make them?'

'Mostly I was brought up on boarding school food.' He gave a rueful smile. 'Mother didn't cook, not even when I was home for the holidays. We had a housekeeper of sorts. Several in fact, they kept leaving.'

Lauren could sympathize with that. 'Where did you grow up, Theo?'

'Oxford, mostly. My father, Elgar James Ransom is a mathematician. My mother is an academic and a women's rights activist. She kept her own name. You may have heard of her, Sarah Fanshaw. I was born to them later in life. Neither of them knew what to do with me. I didn't come up to their expectations academically. My grandmother had me during the school holidays until I was about eleven. After that I fended by myself along with the current housekeeper if they were away, or on tour.'

'Did you find it intimidating to have such academically brilliant parents?'

'Bloody feminists trying to make us take our bras off and

burn them,' Betty interjected. 'They should stay at home and look after their own kids – and if they don't want to do that then they shouldn't have them in the first place.'

'That's if they're given the choice in the first place – which was one of the options women were fighting for, and why there is now a birth control pill,' Lauren pointed out to her.

'A pity more women don't take advantage of it then.'

Katie giggled when Betty stomped off towards the kitchen with some of the dirty dishes, muttering under her breath. 'Don't get her going, else we won't hear the last of it all day,' she said with a breathless laugh.

'Mind your tongue, Miss Clever Britches,' Betty said, coming back in. 'You can help me wash up, then you can bring me that quilt of yours. It's ripped along one seam, where the machine didn't pick up the material, and needs a few stitches. You're lucky it didn't fall apart in the wash.'

'It's pretty, isn't it? Lauren bought it for me from the charity shop.'

'Did she indeed? You've got an eye for a bargain, I'll give you that, Lauren. It's hardly had any wear. Let's hope nobody has died under it.'

Katie shuddered and said worriedly, 'Do you think someone might have?'

Betty gazed sharply at her granddaughter, then laughed and patted the girl's hand. 'Don't you worry about that, my love. I was only joking. It's a factory second, anyone with only half an eye can see that. You can help me this morning, there won't be room for three of you in those tiddly bedrooms.'

A blatant attempt to make sure that Theo and herself spent time together alone, Lauren thought. Well, OK.

They spent the time being industrial, without a shred of anything personal to suggest an attraction between them – unless she counted the time when he gently moved a strand of her hair with his forefinger, and gazed into her eyes with a strangely intimate smile on his lips. The warmth had curled into her stomach and she'd become meltingly aware of herself and sensitized to every nuance of his movements.

While Betty and her granddaughter were doing the chores, Lauren fetched the paint, the trays and the rollers. It didn't take Theo long to paint the sloping ceiling. He offered to paint her bedroom ceiling as well, then painted his way down the stairs.

By lunchtime Katie's room was ready for occupancy, the lace curtains hanging at the window. Thrilled with the result she threw her arms around Lauren and hugged her tight. 'It's so pretty, Lauren . . . thank you. And you, DS Ransom.'

Betty had made a salad for lunch. 'That's enough work for one day. It's lovely out, why don't you two find a beach and have a nice swim.'

'I have my shorts,' Theo said.

'And I know of a nice beach. We can take the car some of the way, then it's a bit of a hike over the hill. Coming, Katie?'

The girl's eyes began to shine, then her hand made a tentative move towards her stomach and her smile faded. She seemed conscious of her lumpy figure. 'I haven't got a bathing suit and I can't swim very well. I'll stay here and keep Gran company.'

'I'm going to do a bit of gardening, then I'll probably have a snooze before I start on dinner. I don't need any company but my own for that.'

'Why don't you wear those baggy shorts of yours with a loose shirt over the top. You could swim in those,' Lauren suggested.

Katie nodded and went upstairs to change.

Allowing Theo the use of the bathroom, Lauren went to her own room and gazed critically at her two bathing suits. The blue bikini was a little on the skimpy side, and she didn't want to give Theo any ideas, at least, not before she was ready. She donned the black one-piece and pulled on a turquoise tabard of floating material that covered her from neck to ankles. Filling a foam drinks cooler with a flask of tea, water, apples, and a bottle of cola for Katie, she fished out some towels from the linen cupboard at the bottom of the stairs.

Betty came out of her room. 'The cop has gone out into the garden with Katie. While we're alone I just wanted to say something to you, Lauren.'

'Goodness, Betty, you look so serious. What is it?'

'I'm sorry what my Charlie did to you. I liked you right from the beginning, and I wish . . . well, I wish the other one hadn't happened. If it hadn't been for her he'd have come home safe and sound.'

'If it hadn't been for her then Katie wouldn't be here.' She gave Betty a hug. 'We can't change things so we have to learn to live with them as best we can.'

'That girl . . . Katie.'

'Your granddaughter, you mean.'

'Oh, I'm not daft. I know what you're trying to do.'

'I'm not trying to do anything. I like Katie. She's been given a rough deal and she needs a friend. It would have been better if that friend had been you.'

'I'm too old and set in my ways. Besides, the pair of you leave me out of things.'

'If I didn't know you better, it sounds as though you're jealous. I'm trying to make Katie feel part of the family. We don't leave you out, you push her aside. She wanted to stay home with you this afternoon, but you rebuffed her. It's possible she wanted to talk about her father, since it's something you have in common.'

'I wanted some time to myself.'

'I'm aware of that. The cottage is small, and we all need time away from each other. We also need to be aware that none of us can afford to alienate the other, because it would make living together unbearable. Together we can manage, but on our own life would be very difficult. I'm keeping my guest waiting. Was that what you wanted to talk to me about?'

Betty avoided her eyes. 'No. I intend to make out a will. I want you to have everything I've got to make up for what Charlie did to you. I have jewellery – stuff that Charlie gave me, and . . . a little cash . . . and some life insurance, you know.'

'No, I can't accept it. Leave it to Katie, she's your kin. She has nothing, and will have a child to support before too long . . . if she decides to keep it.'

Betty only just stopped herself from blurting out about the key and the storage facility Charlie had given her. She'd wanted Lauren to have that. After all, Charlie had spent all the money she'd brought to the marriage.

'You think she'll keep the little bastard?'

'I wouldn't be at all surprised if she kept your great-grandchild. The infant will be her flesh and blood, after all, and she needs someone to love and to love her in return. We all do.'

'You know, Lauren, for all your fancy ways you can be a real bitch when you want to.'

The shock of Charlie's death and the aftermath had begun to wear off and Lauren's initial numbness and disbelief had begun to turn into awareness and anger. That anger needed to be expressed. She didn't mince words, though she kept her voice low.

'And you're being all sorts of the same, Betty. For most of her life Katie has been neglected, or abused, and mostly by her family. I won't allow you to add to the damage that has already been done to her, or start in on an innocent child. Your *boy* Charlie was a cheat and a liar . . . a criminal who spoiled everything he touched. He was cheap trash and I really don't want anything of his to remember him by.'

'Then why are you making so much fuss of Charlie's daughter?' she sneered.

'Because she's a young woman, who through no fault of her own finds herself in trouble. And because I had an association with Charlie, so I do feel guilty on his behalf over her plight, and the need to be responsible for her welfare.'

'In the same way you feel responsible for mine, I suppose,' Betty whined. 'I'm sorry to be such a burden, I'm sure.'

Lauren gave her a disdainful look. 'Stop being such a pain in the . . . *behind*. This isn't about you, and you're not sorry, at all. Enjoy your quiet afternoon, Betty.'

Betty said, 'Don't you use that stuck-up tone with me, Duchess. If you mean arse, say it.'

Lauren glared at her, 'A pain in the arse, then. Are you satisfied?'

'*Awse*?' Betty laughed. 'I thought awses had four legs and a tail and neighed.'

'Oh, do be quiet, you wretch!' Lauren couldn't stifle her giggle as she pulled the door shut behind her.

'Shall I drive?' Theo said when she reached the gate, and held out his hand for the car keys.

She placed the handle of the cooler in it, and grinned. 'I don't see why when I can drive just as well. Remember Sarah Fanshaw?'

He laughed and groaned at the same time. 'How can I ever forget her?'

One of the things Betty had always liked about Lauren was her ability to give as good as she got – though she had to admit that in the years she'd known her, she'd never seen her lose her temper like that – and being lectured by a woman young enough to be her own granddaughter had been galling.

Her own granddaughter? Yes, she did have one, and although she'd denied it she could see the resemblance between Katie and Charlie. There was resentment in her over that. She'd always wanted a grandchild to fuss over, and Charlie had kept Katie hidden from her. How could he have been so mean and unnatural? If she'd watched Katie grow up from babyhood she might have felt differently about her now. But to have a teenager foisted on her, and one with a bun in the oven, at that, was just not fair.

But was she jealous of Katie, as Lauren had suggested? Of course not, she thought uneasily. Lauren knew exactly where to stick her fork in to get a reaction from her. As for Katie, the crafty little chit was winding Lauren around her little finger. Leave the girl Charlie's money? No way. If he'd wanted Katie to have anything he'd have left it to her in his will.

But then, he hadn't made out a will, since he hadn't expected to die at his age. If there was anything of value to be salvaged from this mess the court would probably award it to Katie, anyway. But not the key to the storage facility. Charlie had given that to her, and whatever he had stashed there, it must have some value for him to have kept it a secret. When the fuss had died down, somehow, she was going to find out what was in it. She would leave it to Lauren, whether she wanted it or not!

After the car drove away she watered the plants in the conservatory, put on her straw hat and fetched a fork from the potting shed. She began to loosen the long strands of grass that were attempting to strangle the rose bushes. Despite being weed-ridden the roses still bloomed, pink, yellow, orange and white. Most of the heavy flower heads drooped towards the ground on thin, short twigs that should have been pruned off several winters ago.

She cut a bunch for the cottage. The perfume was heady, the sun warm against her back as she clipped them from the bushes. There was a rose bowl in her room, cut crystal, and with holes to stick the stems through. The arrangement looked nice when she finished, a bouquet of fragrant colour to sit in the centre of the little table under the window.

When the cats stood up on the window sill and meowed she told them, 'If you want to go out the door's open.'

She felt tired, as she often did of late, and wondered about it. She didn't want to take a nap yet. Lauren had cleared some of the rose beds, but she'd promised herself she'd lighten the load. Going back out with the cats in attendance, she was surprised to see a man bending over the flowerbed.

'Who are you?' she asked.

The old geezer must be deaf, Betty thought, when he didn't turn.

She advanced on him, fork held at the ready, crinkling her eyes against the glare of the sun. She'd forgotten her sunglasses. Sweat dotted her forehead and she felt a bit dizzy.

The old man stood up, turned and smiled at her. 'I'm Harry Simpson. The roses need pruning.'

One of the cats gave a yowl and streaked back towards the house. The other one followed. The daft buggers couldn't make up their minds whether they were coming or going.

'I know they do. But they'll have to wait until they've finished blooming.'

'Ah . . . yes, of course they will.'

She said, 'Do I know you?'

'I live here.' His voice had a vagueness to it. 'They put me in a home, you know.'

'Who did?'

'My daughter and her husband.'

'I'm sorry.' There was a pain in Betty's chest and she found it hard to take a breath. 'Look, I can't stand here talking. I'm not feeling well and I've got to rest. You get on back to that home you live in. You can visit me another time.'

She turned away and stumbled towards the door. When she closed it the man was gone. Flicking the switch on the radio she went and lay on her bed, her heart thumping loudly in her chest. She was perspiring all over. After a while the pain eased off. 'Thank God for that,' she whispered, and wondered if she should tell Lauren she'd had a queer turn. No, she'd only fuss and make her see a doctor. The worry of the last couple of weeks had upset her, that's all. All she needed to do was rest.

Closing her eyes, Betty smiled. She'd known a James Simpson once. He'd taken her up west, dancing at the Hammersmith Palais, with him in his Sunday suit. Then Sid had come on the scene, as cool as a cucumber in his Teddy boy suit, complete with curled lip and quiffed hair. Like a fool she'd fallen for him immediately. A useless git he'd turned out to be, though.

She would have been about a year older than Katie was now

when she went out with James, but more innocent. She'd worn her hair in a ponytail, and the latest fashion, a circular skirt in a green paisley design that she'd bought from Marks and Spencer, over a stiff net petticoat. Her sweater had been lime green and her waist cinched in with a white elastic waspie belt.

James Simpson had been the first boy who'd kissed her. They'd been shuffling round the dance floor in a big circle, moving to a foxtrot played by the Lou Praeger band, for no rock and roll was allowed in the Palais at the time. The mirrored ball had been sending glittery reflections over the crowd. The long imagined kiss had been a disappointment – wet and dribbly, and his mouth had tasted of tobacco.

It had been James who had started her off smoking. At that age it had seemed sophisticated. She'd given it up five years ago, when she'd moved in with Charlie and Lauren. Charlie had never smoked, and he wouldn't allow her to smoke in the house – said the smell got into everything. Popping out of doors every half an hour for a fag had not seemed worth the effort, especially when it was cold.

Oddly, Sid had never smoked, and he was a real good kisser, and good at the other stuff, as well. Always at it, he was, and she wasn't the only one he was at it with! Charlie had turned out to be his father's son all right. Both had been drinkers, as well, but while Charlie liked wine, Sid had sculled a nightly tot of whisky and had guzzled down his ale by the bucket. Sid's liver had been as hard as a piece of leather when he'd died, the doctor had said. Served him right!

Her Charlie had given her a home with Lauren not long after. Mind, he'd sold her house and had borrowed the proceeds. A shame about the old geezer in the garden. Still, it wasn't her problem, and if Harry Simpson had found his way here, so he could find his way back to where he lived now. Not that she'd mind if he came again. She liked a bit of company.

As for Lauren, at first she'd thought she wouldn't get on with her daughter-in-law, but although they'd had the odd argybargy, she'd come to like her.

The cats came out of hiding and climbed stealthily on to the bed. She said when they snuggled together behind her knees, 'Keep your fleas to yourself if you want to stay there.' Kneading the bed covers they began to purr in unison.

There was something comforting about living here. She'd thought she'd never get used to the quiet here, but it had only taken a few days. The peace of the place seemed to seep into her body, which was filled with lassitude.

She smiled when an Andy Williams song came on the radio. Now there was a hit from her youth, and his voice was as soothing as cough syrup.

Betty began to softly sing along with him, '*I'm loony about you . . . you dragonfly.*'

'*Bu-utt-er-fly,*' he sang.

'Same difference, they both have wings,' she said, as she drifted into sleep.

Seven

They'd had a swim. Katie Parker was at the far end of the small strip of beach, sketch book in hand and preoccupied with what she was doing.

Beside him, as sleek as a seal, Lauren lay on her towel, her shapely legs pointing towards the sea. Her toenails were painted in the same pink pearly varnish as her fingernails. She wasn't sleeping, but her eyelids were closed and now and again he saw the gleam of her eyes behind the quivering sweep of her dark eyelashes.

Theo was very aware of her. Propping himself up on one elbow he gazed down at the flawless skin of her face. 'Be careful you don't burn.'

Her eyes opened and met his, sparkling and blue, as though they'd been flung from the depths of the sea. He mourned their loss when she reached for her sunglasses and said, 'I was thinking. There's something I want to ask you, Theo, but I don't quite know how to.'

He nodded, non-committally.

'Because of your position, do people often ask you to do them favours?'

'That was an unexpected question.'

'Do they?' she insisted.

'Of course. I'm also offered bribes or other inducements.'

'How do you handle it?'

'It depends entirely on what it is. It's possible that the person requesting the favour will be charged if the favour is likely to pervert the cause of justice.'

'But if it were a confidential matter, what then? What if a crime had been committed against someone and there might be some evidence—'

He placed his finger over her mouth. 'Stop right there, Lauren. Under some circumstances, perverting the cause of justice can carry a life sentence.'

She took his finger away. 'And what if somebody quite innocent might be ruined if the crime was to go to court.'

He gave a long-suffering sigh in the face of her determination. 'Is this about something Charlie Parker has done?'

'I wish it were, because he can no longer be hurt.'

His mouth dried. 'Not you, Lauren. Please don't tell me you're implicated in this affair.'

'Lord, no,' she said sharply and her glance went to Katie. 'This is something else altogether. And anything I tell you will be in the strictest confidence.'

'I can't promise that, Lauren. I'm not a priest, and I've sworn to uphold the law.'

'I'm not going to ask you to break it. I just want your advice, really.'

The good thing was that she hadn't yet let go of his finger, and her own were curled gently around it. The bad thing was that he'd allowed her to back him into a corner. He adjusted his hand so it was holding hers, but his heart was filling with dread. 'Go on.'

'I suppose you've noticed that Katie is expecting a baby.'

His heart gave a relieved leap. Definitely unexpected. 'I hadn't, I just thought she was a little on the plump side. You know . . . teenage stuff.'

'She doesn't know who the father is. She was drugged and raped by three men. Two of them were young . . . the third was Brian Allingham.'

His eyes sharpened, but her nails were digging into his hand with the tension she was experiencing, so he knew she hadn't finished.

'Brian videotaped the assault on her. Then he paid the boys off . . . then he . . . he . . .' Tears came to her eyes. 'Katie had never been with a man before.'

'If she can identify the men they can be charged. The video—'

'We know this, Theo. What Katie wants is for the video tape to be found and destroyed. She doesn't want it to be copied and sold to the porn merchants, or turn up on the Internet. And at the moment she intends to give the baby up for adoption.'

'And you want me to find the video. Is that it?'

She nodded.

He groaned. 'There are thousands of them, Lauren. Even if I found it, it may have already been distributed.'

'Will you try? Brian said he was going to call the video "The Rape of the Virgin".'

'Very original,' he said drily. 'Does Katie know you were going to ask me this?'

'It was her idea. She was too embarrassed to talk to you herself.'

'I can't just destroy evidence if I find it. The man needs locking up. We need proof so he can be charged and convicted – and we need Katie to stand up in court and tell her story. If I find the tape and we can identify those young men, the least she deserves is to know that they can be punished. But I'll need her help to nail them.'

'I know what you need, Theo, and I won't even try to put any pressure on you. But neither will I pressure Katie. She's desperate at the moment. We've arranged for her to see a psychologist who's experienced in rape counselling.'

Theo caressed her tense knuckles until they relaxed, then lifted her hand against his mouth and kissed the palm. 'I'll go and talk to Katie in private.'

'Be gentle with her. Her feelings are very fragile at the moment, but she's hiding behind defiance.'

'When the occasion warrants I can be sensitive to the needs of others.'

'I know, I've experienced it. I'm sorry to bring this up on your day off.'

He leaned forward and kissed her, the contact jolting him into the realization that he was going to get this woman into his bed, whatever the consequences. 'It hasn't spoiled my enjoyment of the day.'

'Must you go back tonight?'

When he raised an eyebrow she laughed and reached for her

tabard. 'It wasn't a proposition . . . not with two other women in the house.'

'Damn!' he said with faked annoyance and was about to suggest a hotel when she smiled, as if she'd read his mind. He supposed he was easy to read, at that.

'Some other time, Theo. We both know it will happen. Let's get to know each other first, mmmm?'

He wished she hadn't said that. He turned his back on her, pulled his jeans on with his tee shirt over the top. He prowled down to the damp sand left by the retreating tide, examining shells and pieces of seaweed, his arousal kept under control by the unforgiving denim, until it subsided.

A growl reached his ears and she said, so he could only just hear her, 'You have a fantastic bum, Theo.'

The woman was going to make him play the game before giving him his reward. She'd be all the more enjoyable for waiting, he thought, grinning to himself.

Katie looked up and saw him coming, her face a pale oval. In his job he'd seen hundreds of faces with the same expression – wary, worried and a bit scared, as though they'd searched their minds to remember if they'd broken the law, and failing to come up with a crime, had begun to suspect bad news.

Be gentle with her, she's fragile, Lauren had said.

Of course she was fragile. Three men had taken her innocence. They'd held her down, opened her up and laughed as they'd exposed her. Then they'd ripped her apart, and enjoyed the ruination of her. Brian Allingham had taped the act, his intention to sell the crime against the girl as entertainment to members of the public who needed to feed their sickness.

Anger began to burn in him. He'd said his need to prosecute wasn't about Katie. It was. He wanted her to have the courage to stand up for herself. If she could do it, then others would come forward, then others. Eventually they would find Brian Allingham. He'd be brought back home to face a dozen charges, found guilty and buried.

She stood as he approached her, but she was poised and tense, as though she wanted to run from him. He didn't blame her. He stopped a little way away from her. 'Lauren has told me about your troubles.'

Her eyes left his face and she gazed down at her foot, shuffling the sand into heaps and obviously embarrassed. There should be a woman officer trained in counselling talking to her. Women were better at this. They understood the feelings of a rape victim. He could only do his best.

'Don't be ashamed, Katie. You were set up, and it's not your fault.'

'Can you find the tape?' she asked, in a small voice that wrenched at his heart.

'I'll try. But I'll be truthful, I can't withhold it as evidence. You know, as the victim of a crime you can apply for compensation.'

'I just want it to go away.'

'What's happened won't go away, not even after your baby is born.'

'I'm going to give it away. I won't know who its father is, and I'll always wonder?'

'You'll know if we can catch the men who did this to you. DNA testing will take care of that. Whatever your intentions regarding the future of the baby, if you stand up and fight for your rights, and those of your child, you'll feel better about it, and about yourself.'

'I'll never feel better . . . I feel so dirty.'

'You must try not to think that way. And you'll never know if you'll feel better unless you give yourself a chance to. Don't let these bastards get away with what they did. Lauren will stand by you. She's worried about you, you know.'

Katie smiled, her young face illuminated by her emotional connection to Lauren. 'Lauren's lovely, she's the only friend I've got.'

She could do much worse than Lauren, who would never let the girl down. The grandmother was a bit of a dragon though. Stepping closer, he took her hands in his. 'You don't count me as a friend, then?'

'You're a cop.'

'That doesn't mean I can't be a friend. Because I'm a cop I can help and advise you in ways that Lauren can't.'

Her eyes went to their joined hands, then to his face. 'You're gone on Lauren, aren't you? I knew it right from the beginning. You couldn't take your eyes off her. That's why you're helping me, so you have an excuse to see her.'

'Not entirely. Although I like Lauren a lot, I also like you.' He chuckled. 'Was I that obvious?'

She nodded. 'If something happened . . . say, you had a row and didn't like Lauren any more. Would you still be my friend?'

She badly needed one. 'Katie, my dear. I'm really not offering my friendship because of Lauren, even though it might stand me in good stead. I'm offering it to you, and I won't abandon you for any reason, unless you no longer want me in your life. Would you like to think about it . . . discuss it with Lauren and your grandmother if you like, and perhaps with your counsellor when you see her.'

She shook her head and took a deep breath. 'I've been thinking about it while I was sketching. It's up to me to make the decision, isn't it?'

'At your age it never hurts to have advice from someone older.' He grinned when she made a face at him. 'However much we resent it. But yes, ultimately it will be you who'll decide the course that your life will take. I promised Lauren I wouldn't put any pressure on you, so I'd like you to think it over first. He took his wallet from his back pocket and extracted a card. You can call me on my mobile any time.'

'Thank you, Detective Sergeant Ransom.'

Only for now, he thought. There was a vacancy coming up in the department and he was expecting his inspector's rank any day. 'My friends call me Theo.'

'Thank you, Theo, then.' She gave a faint smile, then a breathless giggle. 'I never thought I'd ever have a copper as a friend, especially one as old as you. It feels odd, as though I should be on my best behaviour while you're around.'

He gave her a pained look. 'Believe it or not I'm only thirty. I was also a teenager once. So was Lauren and so was your Gran.'

'My Gran? Oh, my God . . . she's such an old tartar. She used to sell fish for her father when she was a girl, and she went through the war and all that stuff. Said she slept down the underground when the Germans bombed London.'

'She's had a hard life, and needed to be tough. It becomes a habit.'

'I suppose it does. You're quite good at figuring things out, aren't you?'

'It's part of my job.'

'Lauren is too, only it's more to do with . . . I don't know how to describe it. Feelings I suppose.'

'Women's intuition?' he suggested.

'Yes . . . she can smile at me, or squeeze my hand when I'm upset, and I know she understands. It makes me feel better.' She looked slightly embarrassed. 'Here, I've got something for you.' She plucked her sketch book from the rock she'd been sitting on, tore a page from it and handed it to him. It was a likeness of Lauren's face.

'You've caught that dreamy expression she has in her eyes sometimes. It's very good. Thank you.'

'One day I'm going to take lessons.'

'Surely the best lesson is to practise the art. In the meantime, you can sign your name on it, like most artists do.'

'I'm not a real artist . . . not yet.' She went a bit pink at the thought as she signed her name, as if she was an impostor. 'There . . . is that all right?'

'Perfect. Keep it nice and flat in the book, and you can pop it into my bike pannier when we get back, so it doesn't crease. I'll find a frame for it when I get home.'

'Have you got a nice home?'

'I'm living in a warehouse flat. I bought it when I first started work, with the help of a legacy. It's central and it's handy, but not very homely.'

'Do you have a car?'

'I find the bike more convenient in London for private use. It's cheap to run and easy to park. Cars come with the job.'

He held her hand as they walked back along the sand and said casually, 'Do you think you'd be able to sketch pictures of the men who committed the crime against you.'

Her forehead crinkled in thought. 'I might be able to. But won't they be on the tape?'

'I doubt it . . . at least, not their faces. Allingham wouldn't have wanted them to be able to witness against him.'

'I'll think about it, see if I can remember. Don't forget I was drugged. I can remember what was happening, but the details are blurry.'

'Of course. There's no rush.'

'They hurt me, you know. Afterwards Brian dumped me in the alley like I was just a piece of rubbish. I kept being sick, and he kept giggling. Then he went off and left me there. I think he'd taken something. I hope the baby isn't his. I'm sorry, I think I'm going to cry.' The forlorn sob she gave nearly tore his heart in half.

He brought them to a stop. Feeling like he was her execu-
tioner, for there was no way he could prevent the girl from
being hurt further over this, Theo slid his arms around her and
pulled her gently against him. 'It's OK, Katie. It's OK. You
should have told your mother.'

'I daren't. My mother . . . she wasn't the type you could tell
things to. She liked Brian and his wife. They used to go club-
bing together when my dad was away. Sometimes I thought
they, well, you know . . . shared *everything*. They used to call
me the little rat.' Katie cried a little bit, then sniffed and light-
ened her mood with, 'Lauren will be jealous if she sees you
hugging me.'

'You think so . . .?'

Looking up at him through teary eyes she managed a watery
laugh. 'Are you kidding? Anyone can see she's nuts about you.'

'I think it's the other way round.'

'Do me a favour, will you? When we have tea, pretend that
you believe Lauren made the chocolate cake, even if it looks
like a bought one. She's got a bet on with my grandmother and
I don't want the old crab to win.'

His glance went over Katie's head to where Lauren stood.
When she smiled at him he grinned like the besotted idiot he
was. He thought he might have fallen in love.

'Nice cake,' he said later when he was seated astride his idling
bike. It was nearly dusk, the trees were dark, spreading shapes
beginning to merge with the sky. He wouldn't get home until
well past midnight, and had to be up at six.

'You know, Theo, you've mentioned that about ten times.'

'That's because I enjoyed it. It's the best chocolate cake I've
ever eaten.'

'Definitely overkill.' Her giggle was a delight. 'All right, I
confess. I bought it, as you well know. When I learn to cook
a decent cake I'll personally deliver it to you.'

'Make that sooner rather than later.' He slipped an arm around
her waist and he pulled her a little closer to him. 'I've had a
wonderful day. Thank you for everything, Lauren.'

'You've won a fan in young Katie.'

'And in you, I hope.'

'You really don't need to promote yourself. After being
almost married to Charlie for four years I can spot a fake a

mile away.' A low humming laugh reached his ears. 'I've enjoyed today, too. Thank you for sharing it with me.' She leaned forward and kissed him, her lips claiming his with enough passion to send his pulses pounding. Blood raced in his ears when she withdrew her mouth. 'Nice, very nice. Can you do that again?' he said.

She laughed as she fitted the helmet over his head. She closed his visor and took a step back. 'I could, but I won't, since I want to get to sleep tonight. It's time for you to go home, Theo Ransom. Watch out for the hedgehogs, they're all over the place at this time of night.'

Standing at the gate Lauren listened to the twin exhausts of his bike bubble away into the distance. She wished she was sitting behind him, her arms around his waist and her face hugged against his back.

The air was a soft, but slightly humid caress, and it was filled with flying insects. Bats began to swoop. She couldn't remember when she'd enjoyed a day so much. 'Goodnight, Theo,' she whispered before going back indoors, the cats following after her.

Betty was sewing something together when Lauren got back inside the house. The radio was playing rock and roll.

Katie came down the stairs in her pyjamas, jiggling her hips in time to the music. Grabbing Lauren's hands she swung her around. Then Betty was on her feet too. Turning the music up she joined in. Giggling and laughing they all twirled around, then clutched each other's waists to form a line. They weaved round the table, kicking their legs up when room allowed. Finally out of breath, they fell into the chairs nearest to them when the music ended.

'Would anybody like a cup of tea?' Lauren said, when they stopped laughing.

'I'd like some Ovaltine,' said Betty, picking up her stitching again. 'I'll be getting into my nightclothes in a minute.'

Katie stood. 'Me too please. It helps me sleep. I'll make sure the downstairs windows are closed and locked while you're doing that.'

'Then we'll all have it.'

Just as she carried the tray in Katie's mobile began to ring. Katie gazed at it, her expression wary and her eyes worried.

'Would you like me to get that?' Lauren offered.

Katie nodded.

'Yes?'

There was some heavy breathing followed by, 'Remember what I did to you Katie? I'm going to do it again one day. I'm watching you.'

'Get off the line and leave Katie alone, you pest.'

Betty made an exasperated noise in her throat, plucked the phone from her hand and shouted, 'Listen you scabby excuse for a disease, come anyway near my granddaughter and I'll feed your knackers to my Rottweiler while you're still attached to them. Bugger off! Got it?' She flipped the phone on to the chair. 'Don't you worry, Katie love. I'll buy you a new telephone with a new number the next time we go out – one of those fancy ones that take photographs of the people ringing you.'

Lauren and Katie exchanged a glance, then grinned at each other.

Betty bristled. 'What's so funny?'

Lauren ventured, 'I think you've got the wrong idea about those phones.'

'And you haven't got a Rottweiler,' Katie added.

'I could always buy one from the kennels if need be.' Giving a huff of laughter Betty threw the garment she'd been sewing over to Katie. 'Here.'

Katie held it up. It was a baby's matinee jacket in pale yellow. Wonder came into her eyes. 'It's so tiny.'

'Babies are small. Even so they're hard work to bring into the world. If you ask me it would be more comfortable if we laid eggs and sat on them.'

Katie giggled.

'Well . . . do you like it?'

'It's lovely.' Tears came into Katie's eyes. 'But I won't need it.'

'Maybe you won't, girl, but it's not for you, is it? While I'm alive no great-grandchild of mine is coming into the world with nothing to wear. It's going to be hard enough for this kid not knowing where it came from. It's going to have a full outfit of clothes to start life with, and you can help me choose them. I'm not having people say that we don't care.'

Katie went to stand before her, and said, her voice a painful whisper, 'Do you care?'

'All my life I've had to be tough, and I'm not one to show my feelings easily, Katie.'

'But that doesn't mean that you don't have any, does it?' Katie's words were almost a plea.

'Of course it doesn't. It just means that I'm sparing with them.'

'Can I hug you, then, a sort of thank you?'

Betty sighed. 'I suppose so, but make it quick. I want to drink my Ovaltine before it gets cold.'

It was an awkward, stiff sort of embrace, like a sculpture where the creator had captured everything but the tender emotion of the moment. A pat on the back from Betty signalled the familiarity was over.

It was sad that Katie could look so happy with the small ration of grandmotherly attention she'd been afforded, Lauren thought. But then, look how Betty had flown to her defence on the phone. She was sure Betty would grow to love her granddaughter if she'd take off her armour long enough to get to know her. At the moment she felt like shaking Betty. But at least Katie was holding her own. The girl had a way of sneaking her way into the affections when you weren't looking.

Katie was already asleep when Lauren went to say goodnight, her teddy bear keeping watch over her from the bed head and Tiger curled up against her feet. If she and Charlie had produced a child . . . a daughter, she'd look a bit like Katie, Lauren thought. But she was thankful now that Charlie had been responsible about it, even if he'd been a cheat and a liar about everything else.

Despite her calm demeanour, being told she'd been duped for all those years had embarrassed Lauren, and the deception had wounded her more than knowing Charlie was dead. His actions had hurt them all. She trampled on the anger that began to rise in her. It wouldn't help to rage about what couldn't be undone. Besides, there was nobody to aim the anger at but herself, and there were other people worse off.

She kissed the girl's cheek, and whispered after she'd switched off her bedside lamp, 'Sleep tight, Katie, girl.'

After she went to her own room Lauren stood in the dark and gazed out of the window. The sky was a clear and ancient darkness with a wisdom that went on forever, time marked by stars stepping into infinity. A ghostly sliver of a moon smiled down at her.

She smiled in return. The night had a magic to it and she hugged it tight inside her.

A fox barked cautiously.

Theo would be a third of the way home now, she thought, purring through the night on his motorbike. The thought of him coming all this way to see them had warmed her.

'Take good care of yourself, Theo,' she whispered into the night. 'I don't want to lose you, too.'

Eight

The dinner invitation from Samantha Bamford had arrived just two days before on an expensive card with Grantham Manor embossed in gold next to an outline of the house.

Lauren was trying to decide between her favourite midnight-blue trouser suit and an eye-catching red dress that Charlie had bought her. She gazed at the invitation. Dress wasn't stated, an obvious oversight. And since she didn't want to catch anyone's eye . . . She hung the clothes back in the wardrobe and took out her little black dress, accessorizing it with a diamond brooch and ear studs. Out of habit she stroked a little *Hot Couture* at the pulses in her throat and at her wrists.

Charlie had bought her the perfume. 'It's Givenchy, proper French designer stuff. Only the best for you,' he'd said. Suddenly she missed having Charlie to escort her. Despite his faults, for most of the time they'd lived together he'd been pleasant company and a good mixer. How could he have done this to her?

She hardened her heart. How? It was because she'd repre-sented something Charlie aspired to. If he'd confessed about his first wife she'd have waited for him to get a divorce and would probably have still married him. She'd been in love with him then – though boredom had set in within two years. Because the perfume reminded her of Charlie it suddenly lost its attrac-tion for her.

'Damn the devious bastard!' she said to her reflection.

Katie appeared behind her. 'I can only imagine you're talking about my dad.'

'Sorry, Katie. I was having a private conversation with myself, a moment of exasperation. You weren't meant to overhear it.'

'I get angry when I think about my dad, too, though I don't really mean it either.'

Katie's smile told Lauren the girl was pleased she'd found something they shared in common, so she didn't correct the assumption.

'You look nice. I wish I had long legs like you. And you smell lovely.'

Taking the stopper from the scent bottle Lauren dabbed it behind Katie's ears, then replaced it and handed the bottle to her. 'There, you smell lovely too, now. Keep the rest of it. And you do look all right, Katie. Once you've had the baby you'll slim down and feel less of a lump. Did you want me for anything specific?'

'That horsey bloke rang.'

'Horsey bloke . . .? Oh, you mean Daniel. What did he want?'

'He said he'll pick you up for the dinner. He'll toot his horn when he gets here.'

Lauren picked up her clutch bag and checked the contents. Money, handkerchief, keys, a small packet of tissues, notebook and pen. 'Oh good . . . that will save me having to drive in the dark.'

'You don't *like* him, do you?'

'Yes, I do quite. He's all right.'

'He's good looking, but he's not hot, like Theo.'

'Hot?'

'You know exactly what I mean . . . *hot!* Like if you trickled water on his stomach it would sizzle. *Splissssssssssssh!*'

'Ah, I see . . .' Lauren grinned as her imagination pictured the interesting scene. 'I have to admit that Daniel's probably not that hot. But he's a good conversationalist and good company.' She slipped into a pair of strapped silver sandals with high heels. 'Do I look all right?'

'Just perfect.' Katie sighed and picked up the invitation. 'I wish I was a fly on the wall. I bet this Samantha Bamford will go green with jealousy and chuck up into the nearest pot plant when she sets eyes on you.'

Lauren burst out laughing. 'Katie Parker, I believe your grandmother is being a bad influence on you. Behave yourself.'

She was rewarded with Charlie's cheeky smile. 'I'll wait up, then you can tell me all about it.'

A car horn honked.

Lauren kissed the girl on the cheek, and even though she doubted that Katie would stay awake that long, she said, 'You do that.'

Lauren felt a little strange when they pulled into the forecourt of Grantham estate. Apart from some patches of repaired stonework, it still seemed the same as when she had left it.

Inside was a different story. The panelling had been restored, as had some of the tapestries that had adorned the hall, though close inspection revealed that they were woven copies. Little brass posts supported red velvet ropes in front of the pictures and the furniture. There were notices saying don't touch the exhibits, and arrows pointing this way and that.

Lauren's grandfather and grandmother were on display. And there was her father, thin and aesthetic looking, his gentle features unlike the ruddy bucolic complexion of his father, but more subdued, like that of his mother. He was the type of man nobody would see in a crowd. In the painting Lauren was seated on his lap, her head against his chest, her thumb in her mouth. Her hair was brushed into dark curls. She'd been about three. His free hand rested on the head of a glossy red setter.

Her mother was up there too, beautiful and brittle, leaning on the piano. Her mouth was discontented, her eyes penetrating and watchful. *Portia. Lady Bishop* was inscribed on a brass plate.

Her glance went back to her father. 'Hello, Pa, I've missed you,' she whispered when Daniel turned to greet someone, and his blue eyes seemed to gaze into hers and his smile widen just a fraction, as if they were sharing a secret. She wanted to cry.

'Lauren, this is Samantha Bamford.'

She turned towards her, the current mistress of Grantham, a smile automatically coming to her face. Samantha had a carefully contrived sort of beauty. Her face had a lasered translucency to it, her shoulder length hair was artfully curled and streaked with a soft honey blonde. Her figure was perfect. Pale breasts cleared her bodice to a dangerous degree. She obviously spent a great deal of money to keep herself looking this good.

Lauren was glad she hadn't worn her red dress, for although there was more material in hers, the one Samantha wore was a flaunting gold satin – a dress that made its own overwhelming statement. They would have competed horribly for attention.

Hazel-green eyes darted over her when Daniel introduced them. Her voice was so carefully enunciated that it was painful. 'Miss Bishop, how nice to meet you. Daniel has told me so much about you.'

'It's nice to meet you too. You've done quite a lot of work on the hall, I see. It looks marvellous. You have quite a flair for furnishings.'

'There's so much to do here, but I feel it's my duty to preserve our heritage, and we can afford it. It's a shame to allow a building such as this to fall down. I have to run it as a business, of course.'

Obviously the woman hadn't heard of death duties.

'Daniel tells me you hope to be employed here.'

'I do need to find employment of some sort. If not here, somewhere else.'

Daniel's arm came around her waist, his hand resting lightly on her hip. She resisted the slight pressure that would draw her against him. 'Don't let Lauren go, Sam, old girl. She'd be an asset . . . what better than having a real live lady to usher people around the ancestral heap.'

'I'm hardly a blue blood, Daniel.'

'Lady Lauren Bishop. Yes . . . I can see it would give the place some tone.'

'Actually, I have no title. As the daughter of a Baron I'm simply referred to as Miss Bishop.'

'You mean you don't get to inherit the title?'

'The title is passed down through the male line, and at the moment is classed as extinct. If I ever have a son he might like to claim it though.'

'Well, as long as he doesn't think he's entitled to have Grantham Estate back.'

'I shouldn't think so. Besides, most of the land has been sold off over the years, and without the income from rents and such the upkeep would be too much for most people. Even my father was forced to sell off land to pay the inheritance tax.'

'Ah, but I'm running Grantham House as a business, as well as living here. Although it took a lot of money to restore the areas I wanted to initially open to the public, it's beginning to pay for itself.'

'Whereas, to me Grantham is the home of my ancestors, the place I grew up in.' Although she didn't say so, running it as a business would have been considered vulgar by her father, who'd much preferred for himself and the title to gently moulder away into obscurity, much to her mother's disgust.

'Some of the house dates back to the sixteenth century. Sir Hubert Bishop, one of the earlier barons, was a gambler, you know. He lost the estate to his best friend at the card table during the Napoleonic wars, and was then killed in battle. The man who won the estate from him married the daughter of the house, took the Bishop name as his own and was awarded the title.'

'I didn't know that.' Samantha's eyes narrowed in on Daniel's hand and she frowned slightly. 'Daniel, why don't you go and find Greg while I talk to Lauren alone. We'll join you in a moment or two.'

'I can offer you employment at weekends,' she said abruptly, as soon as Daniel had gone. 'And I have another project in mind. I intend to write a book on the history of the place, just a thin, illustrated volume – something to sell to the customers. Stories like that one you've just told me would be perfect. I've succeeded in getting a grant from the arts people to pay for a historian, and half the publication costs. My husband will give me the rest.'

'But I'm not a historian, and they'll want you to use one recommended by them, surely.'

'I don't want someone who will talk over my head and confuse me with dates. You're an expert as far as this place is concerned, and they can't dispute that. I also know of your circumstances, Lauren. You need money.' She dropped her careful diction. 'Hell, we all need money, and this will be well paid while it lasts. You need a job and I need you.'

Lauren was suddenly struck by enthusiasm for the project. 'I do like the sound of the project. I think my father would have approved.'

'Good. Can you use a computer?'

'I can open a file and write letters.'

'Then you can open a file and write stories. OK . . . I'll provide you with a laptop, and I'll draw up a contract.'

'We haven't actually talked money yet, Samantha.'

'Mrs Bamford,' the woman said gently. 'I'll be your employer and you'll have to remember that, Lauren?'

The woman certainly knew where and how to draw a line,

but two could play at that game. 'Of course you will, Mrs Bamford . . . if I decide to take up your offer. I'll need to see the contract first.'

A spark of irritation flared in her eyes. 'It will be a standard contract, and I wouldn't advise you to wait too long if you want to work here, Lauren.'

Lauren decided to pull rank. 'As I said earlier, Mrs Bamford, if we are to be formal, I'm addressed as Miss Bishop.' She smiled as Daniel came back with a muscular looking man in his late forties.

'This is Greg Bamford, Lauren, Samantha's husband and managing director of Bamford electronics. Greg, meet Miss Bishop, who grew up in Grantham House.'

'An honour to meet you, Miss Bishop. Call me Greg if you would.'

'I'd like to. I'm Lauren.' They shook hands.

'Has Lauren taken you up on your offer, Sam?' Greg said, pushing an easy smile towards his wife.

'*Miss Bishop* hasn't decided yet. She wants to see the contract. I've offered her the standard.'

Mildly, he said, 'I don't usually interfere with your business, Sam, but I've told you before. You don't stint on staff who come with the right qualifications. Tell you what, I'll write up Lauren's contract myself . . . make her an offer she can't refuse.' An approving smile came Lauren's way. 'You're quite right to insist on reading it first. Have your lawyer look it over, too. Give me a ring at work if there's anything you'd like to discuss, and he slid his card into her hand.'

Samantha pushed through them, as snappy as a starving gold-fish. 'We're neglecting our other guests. Let's go in, shall we? Daniel!' she called out sharply, and he left Lauren's side to hurry forward and offer Samantha his arm.

Greg watched them go, then said, 'Sam's nose is out of joint.'

'Is it?' was all Lauren said.

'She finds herself at a disadvantage.'

'I can't imagine why.'

'One thing you're not, is stupid. Don't pretend you are, Lauren. Sam's outclassed. She knows it and she doesn't like it.'

'I have no control over the way I was brought up, and Mrs Bamford wasn't obliged to invite me to dinner. I don't think we'll get along, I'm afraid.'

'Of course she had to invite you. Everyone expected her to. You'll get along if you put your mind to it. Samantha flares up quickly, but she rarely holds a grudge, and she admits to her mistakes once she recognizes she made one. Work for her and I'll make sure that you're well compensated.'

'I'll think about it. Money isn't everything.'

'Don't be a fool about money, Lauren. It opens doors.'

'Sometimes it opens the wrong doors and they slam back in your face.'

'Now you're talking about your own situation?'

It sounded as though Daniel had been talking out of turn about her. 'You don't know anything about my situation.'

'I know everything about it. I made it my business to find out. Besides which, I read the papers.'

Disconcerted, she gazed at him, annoyed by the lack of privacy she was being afforded. 'I'm not about to discuss my business with a stranger.'

'Your past is not going to go away in a hurry, and hiding here won't stop you from being discovered. Before long somebody will discover the Lauren Parker/Bishop connection, or the papers will be tipped off. Then the journalists will swarm over the place like wasps round a lemonade can. You can't blame them, it's their job.'

'I'm well aware of that, Greg. But there is more to this than you know. Other people need to be protected at the moment – people who can't defend themselves as well as I can. I'm not going to be manoeuvred into doing what other people want me to do, just to fulfil the curiosity of the public. When and if I go public, I intend to choose the time and place.'

'If it gets so you need a place to hole up in, I'm sure I can accommodate the three of you.'

'Thank you, Greg, that's nice to know.'

He gazed approvingly at her. 'Tell me when you're ready. I know people in the magazine business and will be able to broker you a good deal for an exclusive story. Normal commission, of course.'

'Do you never stop trying to make money?'

He wasn't offended by her question. 'Never, it's my hobby. We'd better go in now, there are several people waiting to re-acquaint themselves with you. At the risk of sounding like the butler, the drawing room is this way, Madam!'

'Ah . . . exactly where it used to be when I lived here,' she said drily.

He looked at her, then raised an apologetic eyebrow. They both laughed.

A few minutes later they were in the drawing room. There was a hush when they walked in, then a man detached himself from his companions. 'Miss Bishop . . . Lauren. How wonderful to see you again after all this time.'

'And you, Reverend Andrews.'

'I believe you've rented Blackbird's Nest. How long are you here for?'

'I've taken a six-month lease on the cottage.'

Mrs Andrews pushed forward, a large beige bow decorating the left hip of her large beige dress. She elbowed her husband in the ribs. 'Oh goody. Ask her then, Henry?'

'Ask me what, Mrs Andrews?'

'Ask her, Henry? Go on.'

'All right, dear.' He smiled at his wife, then coughed nervously. 'When we heard you were back in the district we thought we'd ask you to open the indoor fête in November. It's to help raise money for the poor at Christmas.'

'Of course, I'd be delighted. Where's the fête being held, in the church hall?'

'Mrs Bamford has kindly offered us the use of the entrance hall, here at Grantham.'

And Samantha Bamford was expecting to be asked to do the honours by the look on her face – as so she should have been. But Lauren could hardly retract her acceptance now.

'Well, I hope to see you in church on Sunday. If I'd known you were here I'd have visited you.'

Her former piano teacher, Averil Perkins had been hovering, and took advantage of a pause to say, 'Ah, Miss Bishop . . . do you remember me?'

'Yes I do, Miss Perkins.' Daniel had been wrong about hardly anyone knowing her, she thought.

Samantha drew her aside later, when the guests were beginning to thin out. 'I owe you an apology. I'm a bossy cow who likes her own way. I thought you were having a go at me with that Miss Bishop stuff. I do want you to work here, so please don't judge me on tonight.'

'You don't have to apologize, Mrs Bamford. The formal

address is correct protocol, but you were right, I was having a go at you.'

'Then can we cut out the crap and use first names?' When a husky laugh left Sam's throat, Lauren joined in.

'It might be a good idea. I'm sorry about this fête thing, I didn't realize it was being held here when I accepted. It's always been a family duty to open the fêtes in the district.'

'Oh, it doesn't matter, since I've got a rush of coach trips booked in for that day. I thought it might help sales if the fête was held here this year. It's for a good cause. Little things seem to take on a great importance in the country.'

Including opening the fête, something her father had always taken for granted. 'I could go down with a cold on that day if you like.'

'Don't you dare. If you decide to work for me you'll be flat out showing the visitors around as soon as you've made the speech. You have to keep them moving, and by the time the tour is over they're ushered into the tea room.' She shrugged. 'Next year perhaps it'll be my turn.'

'Yes . . . who knows where I'll be then.'

Daniel took her by the elbow. 'Time to go home, Lauren.'

'It was a wonderful dinner, Samantha.'

Greg came up behind them. 'I enjoyed your company, Lauren. I'll get that contract to you as soon as possible.'

'Thank you. Goodnight to you both, then.'

Samantha seemed to take it for granted that Lauren would work for her.

As it turned out she was proved to be right, for the contract was as good as Greg had promised.

Nine

'Congratulations, Detective Inspector Ransom.'

'Thanks, guv, the extra pay will come in handy.'

'Any more on the Parker case?'

Theo shrugged. 'I'm following a new lead. I'm going through the videos at the moment.'

'A constable can do that.'

'I'd rather do it myself.'

'Reason?'

'I'm looking for a specific video.'

Kevin Crane leaned back in his chair and gazed at him. 'There's already enough video evidence to convict Brian Allingham when we catch up with him.'

'I know. This is a rather delicate matter. I'm doing it as a favour for someone, in my own time. It could lead to more serious charges if I can play this lead right.'

Interest sharpened his senior's eyes. 'Should I know about who this favour is for?'

Dragging in a deep breath, Theo shrugged. 'I don't see why not, since I know you can be trusted to keep it to yourself. Charlie Parker's daughter was drugged at a party at Brian Allingham's place, and pack raped by a couple of young thugs. I believe Allingham videoed the event before he had a go at her too.'

'Ironic, really.'

'But sad. It was an out and out crime. Katie Parker was still at school when this happened. She had nothing to do with her parents' business, and whatever the score was between Allingham and Charlie Parker she didn't deserve to be punished for it. She's hardly more than a kid.'

'Was the assault reported?'

'No . . . it was five months ago. The girl is pregnant and didn't tell anyone until recently.'

'So there's no physical evidence that a rape took place, just her word against Allingham's. Do you believe her?'

'Yes, I do. There will be evidence if I can find the tape, or the rapists. She's reluctant, she just wants the tape to be destroyed. All the same, if I can get hold of the tape I think she'll agree to witness against the young men, who in their turn might be persuaded to drop Allingham in the shit.'

'Have you offered the girl the tape?'

'No, but it won't be the first time evidence has been buried deep enough to never see the light of day again.'

'I see . . . where is this girl?'

'Holed up in a country cottage with her grandmother and

Lauren Bishop.' He gave a faint smile. 'I've never seen anything like it. They should be at each other's throats but they're all supporting each other. Charlie Parker's mother is a tough old bird, but Lauren handles her, and holds them together, I think.'

'Lauren?'

'Lauren Bishop. She's Charlie's former wife . . . the illegal one. She's gone back to using the name she was born with. She's really something.'

A suspicious pair of brown eyes gazed into his. 'That smile of yours says you're on the hunt. Are you involved with the woman?'

'Not yet . . . but I'm working on it. Lauren Bishop is a honey.'

'You're getting close to putting your job on the line, Theo. Don't drop a bollock and allow your balls to govern your brain . . . not with a possible witness. You're a good copper, Theo, one of the best. It could fuck up a future promotion.'

'I'll take that risk. As for the rest, I'm still thinking along the lines of a private detection agency. I have all the contacts.'

'When you've decided, let me know. I might feel like a change of employment. There are too few jobs at the top and too much competition. I wasn't cut out to be a politician.'

'If I could get a partner it would come about much sooner. Think on it seriously, Kev. You could be your own boss. Better still, discuss it with Rosie. She thinks I'm the best thing to come along since sliced bread.'

'Rosie needs her head examined if she thinks that. Though if you nail that douche-bag Brian Allingham, I promise I'll think seriously about it.' Kevin grinned as he picked up his pen. 'Get out of here, Theo! I've got work to do. Come over for dinner. We'll celebrate, and it will give the kids someone to beat up apart from me.'

'I was going to look for the video. It's called "The Rape of the Virgin".'

'Along with a hundred others.' Kevin's eyes darkened. 'Is there truth in that title, d'you think?'

'In Katie Parker's case, so I believe.'

He nodded. 'I'll get one of the women constables to sort out all the videos and DVDs with that title. It'll narrow things down a bit.'

Theo nodded. 'Thanks.'

* * *

A week later, Theo still hadn't found it.

He flopped into his armchair when he got home, hung his legs over the arm, punched in Lauren's number and gazed out over the city while he waited for her answer. He imagined her running down the staircase and snatching up the receiver.

'Lauren Bishop.'

Her voice was a delight to his ears. 'Hello Lauren Bishop . . . how are you?'

'I'm fine.' She gave a breathless sort of laugh that caressed his ear. 'You?'

'I'm fine too. Perfect, actually.'

'Good. I prefer extremes to half measures. I've been offered a job at Grantham House, showing visitors around and helping the owner to write a short history of the place.'

'And will you take it?'

'I need employment and it's well paid. I know the background of the place better than most. So yes, I think I'll take it. Why have you called?'

'I wanted to hear your voice. Why else?'

Laughter in her voice she told him, 'You're a real boost to my ego, but now you've said that I'm about to be afflicted by *struck dumb*.'

'You mean *dumbstruck*.'

'Do I? Yes, I suppose I do.'

'I've been thinking about you a lot.'

She laughed. 'How long is a lot? Once a week . . . every day?'

'Every second of every minute of every damned day . . . and night,' he thought to add.

'Really?' she purred.

'Really.'

'Flattery will get you everywhere, Theo. You should phone me more often, I love calls like this.'

'I've just been promoted to Detective Inspector.'

'Congratulations, Sherlock. I'm proud of you. I'll open a bottle of wine and drink your health. I was looking for an excuse to open it. Better still, we could drink it together sometime. I'd prefer that.'

He grinned from ear to ear. 'Can we talk?'

'Yes, Katie and Betty are in the garden.'

'I've been looking for the tape. No luck so far. The good

thing about this is that it might not have been copied. Allingham might have it with him, or hidden it. I don't suppose you'd know if he had a storage place outside the home anywhere . . . a rented garage or something. Or even if Charlie had, come to that?'

'I take it that was the real reason you phoned.' He could hear a touch of hurt in her voice.

'Then you'd be wrong, Lauren. You asked me to do Katie a favour and I'm doing it the best way I know how. I can't work in the dark.'

'Sorry, how dreadfully churlish of me. Of course you can't. I know nothing of Brian Allingham's affairs, though. We didn't mix socially if I could help it. Charlie didn't like him much either towards the end. I felt . . .' She hesitated.

'Felt what?'

'This will sound like nonsense, but about six months before he died Charlie became worried about something, and angry if Brian was mentioned. He was usually an easy-going man, and I got the feeling that Brian had some sort of hold over him.'

Theo held female intuition in great respect. 'It's not nonsense. The very fact of your existence would have given Brian the upper hand, even grounds for blackmail.'

'I think they had a fight a few weeks previous to the accident. Charlie came home with a bruised face and knuckles. He said he wanted to break off the partnership. Brian Allingham had brokered a deal without his agreement, he said, and it could end up as business suicide if he didn't get it sorted out. He didn't say what it was and he wouldn't discuss it.'

'I wish you'd told me this before, Lauren. Think back . . . how many months ago did this fight take place?'

He heard her counting under her breath, then she murmured, almost to herself, 'It was early spring. He didn't usually bring his work worries home, and it wasn't like him to let anything bother him.' Her voice strengthened. 'It was just before my birthday, March. He didn't invite the Allinghams to the restaurant. I wondered about it and he said they'd gone abroad. But they hadn't.'

'Two weeks later Katie was attacked. It's possible the motive was revenge.'

There was a moment of silence, then she offered hesitantly,

'You think it happened because Brian Allingham wasn't invited to my birthday? Isn't that a bit trivial? I'd hate to think—'

There was no way he was going to allow her to shoulder any blame. 'No, nothing so petty, I'm sure. I'm looking past the obvious. I think there's more to this – something bigger that caused the argument in the first place – something that needed safeguards in place, so that Charlie would keep quiet and have to go along with whatever deal Allingham had set up. It has to be bigger than porno.'

'That's why you asked me about the garage?'

'Uh-huh. Let's leave it for now. I'll allow it to ferment in my brain a bit. When can I see you again?'

'I'll be working during the day at the weekends now. I'll be available on Monday through to Wednesday.'

'Damn, I'll be working then. I'll get down when I can, if that's all right with you.'

'It's more than all right. Ring me any time you like. I love hearing from you. I'm sorry I was so touchy before.'

'Considering the circumstances, I don't blame you. In the meantime, keep a look out for the parcel I sent you.'

Her voice became animated and curious. 'A parcel? How exciting, what's in it?'

'I'm not telling you.'

'I hate being teased. If you were here I'd throw you on an ant's nest.'

'If I was there I'd kiss you senseless.'

'Would you then?'

'Absolutely.'

She gave a little gurgle of laughter. 'You know, Theo, I rather like the sound of that.'

'You're only saying that because you're safe at the moment.' He growled with frustration. 'Lauren Bishop, I love you.' He hadn't meant to blurt it straight out like that. Now she'd want marriage, kids, and a house in the suburbs – everything he'd avoided so far, and wasn't ready for, in fact. He felt vulnerable, as though he'd exposed himself to ridicule. 'I'm sorry . . . forget I said that. It was spur of the moment.'

'I can't promise you that, Theo,' she said softly. 'It's the nicest thing anyone has said to me in a long time. Don't worry, I won't expect a ring on my finger and a house in the suburbs on the strength of a throwaway remark. Goodnight.'

The woman was a witch. She'd read his mind. He managed to squash a strong urge to tell her he loved her all over again. He might have to re-evaluate his future if this kept up. 'Goodnight.'

If you were sensible you'd never see her again, he told himself as soon as he'd hung up, and he looked around the proportions of his sparsely furnished flat. There were two bedrooms, one with an en-suite the other with a dressing room, and a separate bathroom. Downstairs was a kitchen, and a dining room incorporated into the lounge area. The flat looked out over the river. He'd built in some bookshelves which also accommodated his desk and computer. The warehouse block had the added bonus of off-street parking, secured inside a wall with wrought-iron gates.

He frowned. A flat on the river wasn't a place in which to bring up babies. There were too many unguarded spaces. It could be made safe, he thought, and grinned. Love kept changing his perspective of things. It would turn him into a handyman if need be – after all, he'd done a good job of painting Lauren's ceilings. Then again, he could sell the warehouse flat at a vast profit and buy something bigger with a garden – somewhere out of London perhaps, but within comfortable reach.

'How many babies do you want, Theo?' he said out loud. 'This is a fine pad, right in the thick of things and you don't want to get rid of it yet, d'you? Besides, you don't know if Lauren wants babies. Also besides, Lauren might want to have a say in the matter. Besides which, she might say no. End of conversation.'

'Besides—'

'Shut up with the besides, will you? In answer to your first question, as it happens I want two children, at least. A boy followed by a girl. If I only have one child he'll be lonely growing up and he'll start talking to himself when he's an adult – just like his father does. Definitely the end of this stupid conversation now.'

The tide was going out and a barge was heading downstream in the fast flowing water. The sky was flecked with clouds tinted sunset pink and yellow on their undersides. Shadows lengthened to paint cold, pewter slabs upon the water. Most of the bustle had gone from the day. He'd never noticed the poetic quality of his surroundings before.

Truth was, Theo knew he'd never felt so alone before. There had been women, nice women, but he'd never met one he'd wanted to settle down with, nor even shack up in semi-permanency with. Now, the emptiness of his bachelor life crowded in on him.

He went to the kitchen, took a meal from the freezer and placed it in the microwave. Pouring himself a glass of white wine he slid one of the DVDs he'd brought home with him into the player. A woman in a tight black corset shook her overblown accessories at him. More of the same in the second one. The third one featured a daisy chain of mixed gender all joined together and engaged in the sexual act with their nearest neighbour. He failed to appreciate the merit of mass copulation. Porn had much of a muchness to it.

Theo preferred the type of women who had a modicum of modesty about them. It made the chase more satisfying and the eventual conquest sweeter. He breathed a sigh of relief when he played the last video in the box, while eating something tastelessly fragrant on rice at the same time. He thought it might be chicken.

His mother would have a fit if she saw these films. Sarah Fanshaw was on a lecture tour in America at the moment. She was highly sought after as a speaker by the women's colleges. His father was back in Oxford. On a whim Theo rang home.

'E. J. Ransom.' It was an affectation his father had adopted several years before, after one of his students had referred to him that way. It stood for Elgar James.

'Hello father, it's Theo.'

'Theo? Ah yes, Theodore,' he said vaguely, then became all bluff and hearty as if he'd just recognized who he was. 'How are you, my boy?'

'I'm well. I've just been promoted to detective inspector.'

'Good . . . good.'

'How are you keeping, father?'

'I have a bit of a cold. I hate summer colds, they always seem to linger. I think the germs multiply in the warmer air.'

Long ago Theo had learned that if he agreed with his parents it avoided having to listen to a long lecture on the whys and wherefores of the matter. 'Yes, I suppose they must.'

Theo heard a woman's voice in the background and his father whispered, 'It's my son. I'll just be a minute.'

'I thought mother was still in America,' he said.

'Yes, she is. It's the housekeeper.'

'I didn't know Mrs Sharp lived in.'

'No, of course she doesn't . . . this is a different housekeeper.'

'Rather late to be working isn't it? It's ten thirty.'

'Really, Theo. Who I entertain and when is my business. After all, I've never interfered in your life.'

Surprised by his father's sudden testiness Theo gazed at the phone in his hand and allowed a grievance to slip out. 'You're quite right, Father, you never have interfered, except when I wanted to think for myself. My apologies. Goodnight.' He hung up.

A few minutes later the phone rang. 'Look here, Theo, I'm sorry if I sounded sharp. It's just . . .?'

'There's no need to explain. I understand.'

'No you don't understand, since I haven't told you. Your mother and I are no longer together. We weren't going to tell you. We wanted to spare your feelings.'

'Spare my feelings? Good God! You do realize that I'm thirty years old and no longer an adolescent.'

'Thirty? Are you? Of course . . . good grief, how time flies. You must meet Andrea one day.'

'Your *housekeeper?*'

'Well, no actually. My fiancée. You'll like her.'

'I'm sure I shall. Congratulations, Father.'

Theo rang his mother a little later, using her first name, as he'd been instructed to since childhood. 'Sarah. I've just spoken to my father. He told me about the split. I'm so sorry.'

'I'm not. The older men get the more pathetic they become. He's living with a woman, one of those mature students who've raised a family, and who imagine that the portion of brain still left operating in their skulls will absorb a university education.'

Her mother was at her venomous best and he cut her down. 'That remark wasn't worthy of respect. I thought you were the champion of women.'

There was a short silence, then she said. 'So did I, until I realized I was actually anti-men rather the pro-women.' Her voice rose to a strident pitch. 'Your father's floozie is only forty-five, eighteen years his junior. I don't suppose your father told you about me? No, he wouldn't have. He's always been so stuffy about such things.'

'Such things as what? Actually, he hardly mentioned you.'

An aggrieved sniff reverberated against his eardrum. 'I'd better tell you myself then. I've met somebody else, a psychology professor. I'll be staying on in America.'

'Ah, I see. I've got news too. I've just been promoted at work.'

'That's nice, dear. A good school always helps to further a career, even if one wasn't a particularly academic student,' she said absently.

Theo defended himself with the truth. 'I didn't do too badly at school.'

It was as if he'd never spoken. 'My affair embarrassed your father. He could have understood it if I'd left him for another man. He knew about Trudy, of course, but he didn't suspect that we were an item – or if he did, he wouldn't have expected me to come out.'

'Come out?' he said stupidly.

'You know exactly what I'm getting at, Theodore . . . Trudy and I making our love for each other public knowledge. Surely I haven't shocked you, as well, have I?'

'A little.' He was actually as shocked as hell, and he felt like hitting back. 'I thought all that feminist stuff you spouted when I was growing up was bullshit.'

'Bullshit!' She sounded scandalized. 'I thought I'd brought you up better than that, Theo. It sounds as though you've turned into a mere male after all.'

As an insult, it was lame. 'I'm afraid I have, mother. I'm unashamedly male in my ways and my thinking is definitely *mere* when compared to your intellect and that of my father. If that's a disappointment to you, tough. You can blame it all on my masculine genes.'

There was a moment of silence, then she said, 'You know, Theo, even though I didn't want the responsibility of children I grew quite fond of you. You were such a dear, ordinary little boy, one without complications. Now, you seem to have grown horns and a tail.'

He couldn't remember his mother admitting she'd felt anything for him before, or sounding so genuinely wounded. 'No, I haven't. All I've done is grow a full set of male hormones, as per my genetic blueprint. I act and feel like a male, and see no reason to pander to your way of thinking because of it.'

'When put like that I can appreciate your reasoning. I'm sorry if I failed you in any way. I've never pretended to be maternal, but I did my best.'

It might have been better if she had pretended. 'Oh, you were all right, a no-fuss mother. My friends were scared of you. When I told them you were a genuine witch it stopped me from being bullied.'

She chuckled. 'Perhaps it's best that you do know what's going on. When you meet Trudy, I'm sure you'll like her.'

He gave her the same answer as he had to his father. 'I'm sure I will. Drop in next time you're in London. I'm still living in the same place.'

'That ugly warehouse building?'

'It's improved since your last visit,' which if he remembered correctly was about seven years previously.

'Keep in touch, dear. Thank you for being so understanding, which is more than your father is.'

Understanding? Theo had been too stunned to utter a coherent sentence, but at least he'd managed to avoid a lecture. Good God! His mother was in a relationship with a woman called Trudy, and his sixty-plus father was engaged to be married to a woman eighteen years younger than himself. Everyone had heard of parents having troublesome children, but he'd ended up with troublesome parents, even though he was proud of them in his own way. Come to think of it they'd always been troublesome. Shaking his head in mock puzzlement he thought with genuine amusement and his tongue firmly planted in his cheek, *Whatever is the world coming to Sherlock?*

Sherlock? Damn you, Lauren Bishop. Nobody else would get away with calling me that.

He made an effort to be kind. 'Nobody raises an eyebrow at such relationships these days. I wish you all happiness with um . . . Trudy, wasn't it? Goodbye, Sarah.'

'Goodbye, Theo.'

The news of his promotion hadn't attracted much of a reaction, he thought wryly, as he put down the receiver. He laughed. He hadn't expected one . . . it was par for the course.

'Flour . . . chocolate . . . sugar,' Lauren muttered, making a face. 'All the ingredients for a chocolate cake, in fact, with a recipe and a cake pan included.' Opening a bag of smarties Theo had

added for decoration, she ate a handful then passed the bag
around.

'I told you he'd cotton on about that shop-bought cake,' Betty
said triumphantly. 'You owe me a fiver.'

Katie grabbed a silver object from the bottom of the box.
'It's a key with a label on it. Cubitt Wharf, Isle of Dogs.' The
other side of the label had the rest of Theo's address on it.

'He expects me to deliver it as well as cook it,' Lauren splut-
tered. 'What a damned cheek!'

Betty grinned. 'I like the way that man goes about things.
He knows what he wants. Stop eating those smarties, else you'll
end up with a rear end like mine.'

'God forbid,' Katie muttered under her breath.

'I'll make the cake on Sunday night and take it to him on
Monday. Now let me see. I can take a train to Waterloo from
here, then get the dockland line to the Island Gardens' station.'

'You've got it all worked out then,' Betty said.

'I just happen to know the area.'

Katie chipped in, after exchanging a grin with her grandmother, 'We'll see you on Tuesday or Wednesday, then.'

Lauren felt her cheeks heat and she mumbled, 'I'll be home
on the same day. If Theo's not in I'll leave the cake and come
straight back home. You see your counsellor on Tuesday, and
I have to shop for the week on Wednesday.'

Katie picked up her bag. 'Stop being so pathetic. I'm seventeen in a few weeks time, all grown up. I don't need you here
for my counselling. After all, it's not as if you're my mother
or anything. Besides, it's private, like them practising Catholics
who go to confession. I'm off now. I promised to do a bit of
cleaning for old Mr Dunne.'

Betty's hands went to her hips. 'Don't you overdo it working
for some old geezer you hardly know. You've got that baby
you're carrying to think of.'

'As if I need reminding. Besides, it's only a bit of ironing
and dusting and I want to pay him back for letting me have
the bike cheap. I promised I'd clean his glass cabinet for him
today. He's got some lovely china and stuff that used to belong
to his wife. He bought her an ornament for every wedding
anniversary, and has over forty of them. They're so pretty, ladies
in historical dress. You should come up and visit him, Gran.
His cottage is not far, about a mile.'

'And most of it uphill. I'd be worn out when I got there.'

A grin spread across Katie's face. 'I could give you a lift. You could sit on the carrier at the back of my bike.'

'And a right Nellie I'd look with my legs apart, my skirt flying in the wind and my drawers showing. What's more, that's an old-fashioned bike and it would probably collapse from shock.'

Lauren began to laugh. She enjoyed it when grandmother and granddaughter got along like this. They were more alike than either of them realized.

'Tell you what, young Katie,' Betty called out as the girl headed for the door. 'I'll treat you to some driving lessons for your birthday. And I might buy you a car to run us around with. Not a fancy new one, mind.'

The girl turned, her eyes shining and her face breaking into a smile. 'Honest?'

Betty nodded. 'But first you've got to get your provisional licence. I'll ring up some local driving schools and find out what they cost. I reckon there will be a book with all the road rules and things in.'

Rushing back to her grandmother, Katie threw her arms around her in a hug. 'Thank you, Gran.'

''Ere . . . pack it in, will you. I've just ironed my blouse and you're creasing it. Get off with you.'

'I'm popping out to the post office; is there anything you need?' Lauren said to Betty a little later.

'Yes, a birthday card for Katie in case I forget when the time comes.'

'We'll have to give her a little party. I'll look around for a nice present for her. We can invite John Dunne and the vicar to tea, and Eve, her counsellor.'

Betty grimaced. 'That's a nice birthday for her, innit? We'll sit around sipping tea like a herd of genteel pensioners with our pinkies crooked. Let's take the girl out to dinner and a show somewhere. She must be fed up with hanging around here all the time. I know I am.'

'Then come into the shopping centre with me.'

'No, I can't be bothered. I'm going to ring around the driving schools and see what's needed. Then I'm going to tidy up the conservatory.'

'The driving lessons you offered Katie for her birthday was a nice gesture.'

'Don't you go reading anything into that, mind. It was for my own comfort. Now you'll be working I might need someone to run me around from time to time. And anyway, she won't be able to take the kid on a bicycle when it's born.'

'But she said she's going to have it adopted.'

'Yeah . . . well, we'll see about that, won't we? Saying it is easy, but carrying it out is a different matter altogether. It can't be easy to give away your own flesh and blood, can it?'

Lauren said softly, 'Betty Parker, you're an old fraud. You want her to keep the baby, don't you?'

Betty sniffed. 'It ain't none of my business what Katie does with her own kid . . . though if I'd been allowed to know the girl when she was growing up, things might have been different for both of us. At least she'd have had someone to care for her when she was left alone.'

'She's got someone to care for her now . . . us.'

'Speak for yourself, Lauren. That was your decision, and you made her care your responsibility, not mine. Charlie and that Higgins tart made it clear that Katie didn't need a grandmother.'

'I'm disappointed that you feel that way. If you had known Katie when she was growing up you'd have fought tooth and nail to be a grandmother to her.'

'Be that as it may. I wasn't allowed to know her, was I? When I think what Charlie has done to us all . . .' She wiped a tear from the corner of her eye. 'I don't know what he was thinking of . . . I really don't. Oh, I know he had a few troubles when he was young, but I was so proud of what he'd become. My mother always said, "Pride goes before a fall" and she was right.'

'Charlie has no say in the matter now. Katie is—'

Betty banged her cup down in the saucer. 'Stop interfering. This has got nothing to do with you. You're not even related to us.'

Lauren knew Betty was lashing out to relieve her feelings, but nevertheless, it hurt. 'Let's not start the day with an argument,' she said calmly.

'Right, we won't, though if you ask me a good argument would do you good. You're a cold fish – no passion, Charlie said, and he was right. No wonder he had another woman on the go.'

It was hard not to bite at that. Charlie had been a selfish lover who, when he bothered her at all, had always left her wanting. It was obvious now that he'd married and deceived her because he wanted her money and liked the idea of who she was. 'Let's face it, Betty,' she heard herself say, 'in your eyes no female would have been good enough for Charlie – not even his daughter.' Picking up her purse she stalked away from Betty, anger festering in her as she slammed the door behind her.

A few moments later she rang the doorbell.

Betty opened the door and glared at her. 'Got something else to say, have you?'

'Yes, I've forgotten my keys.' Betty's belligerent attitude tipped Lauren's anger into fury. She'd catered to this woman for long enough. 'And what's more I feel the need to inform you that my personal relationship with your son is none of your damned business. From what you've learned of Charlie lately you must have cottoned on to the fact by now that your son was a liar, a deceiver and an all round . . . *turd!* Nothing he said could be taken at face value, and he couldn't be trusted. I was considering divorcing him when he died. And if you damned well say anything like that to me again I'll divorce you instead, and you can find yourself somewhere else to live.'

'Hah, the worm has finally turned, has it?'

'You might be well advised to remember it.' Lauren stalked off again, knowing she'd be late for work if she stayed any longer. Already she was feeling guilty for shouting at Betty. And stupid. She didn't usually lay down the law.

This time it was Betty who slammed the door behind Lauren.

Inside, a lump of soot dropped down the chimney, shattered in the grate and peppered the rug.

'Now look what you made me do!' Betty yelled.

Ten

The argument had been frustration vented, nothing more and nothing less, Lauren thought – but still it sat heavily on her shoulders. She didn't like an atmosphere of dissent. It reminded her of her childhood when her mother did a duty visit. Lauren had always been scared that her mother would take her away from Grantham, as she'd often threatened. Portia had been inclined to find fault with everything.

'Look at your hair; it needs trimming, and such a dreadful dark colour. And for goodness sake stop *slumping*, Lauren. It's most unattractive. I can't imagine how I gave birth to such a lump of a girl.' On perusal of her school reports, Portia would shake her head and say nothing but a soft, 'Oh dear.'

She threw off her memories as she headed towards Grantham, slowing down as she reached Daniel, who was riding a fine-looking chestnut mare towards the bridle path. He indicated that she stop, and she gazed out through the open window at him. 'I can't chat for long, I'll be late for work.'

'Come riding with me this evening, Lauren.'

She gazed at the chestnut, a beautiful creature who gazed back at her and snickered softly. She reached out to stroke her silky neck. 'I haven't been on a horse for ages.'

'All the more reason to get your backside on the saddle.'

She nodded. 'About seven then . . . will that do?'

'I'll have Gemma saddled for you. She's a well-behaved mare who will give you a good ride without being too challenging. How's the job going?'

She smiled, for she had Daniel to thank for her present employment. 'It's odd being back at Grantham, knowing it belongs to someone else, but I'm quite enjoying it.'

'You're getting on with Samantha all right, then?'

'Of course. She doesn't bother me much.'

'And Greg?'

'On the occasions I've run into him he's been very pleasant.'

'Glad to hear it,' he said. 'I'll see you later.' He tipped his cap and moved off.

The day was uneventful with six coach loads of people booked in to keep her busy, as well as people in cars.

'They're staying for lunch, which will bring in some money. I must get some souvenir ware made. I was thinking of playing cards, drink mats and paper openers with a picture of Grantham and the family crest on. What do you think?'

Like her father, Lauren wasn't very commercially minded, but she said what was expected of her. 'Yes, I imagine they might do well. You might go in for some mugs as well, and some cheap and simple canvas bags with Grantham Hall and the phone number. It would act as an advert as well as a souvenir. You can't use the Bishop family crest on anything, though.'

Samantha grunted as she gazed at an elderly woman climbing down from the coach. 'Why ever not?'

'You have no entitlement. You bought the house, that's all. The crest belongs to my family.'

Samantha didn't look at all pleased. 'You can grant me a licence or something, can't you?'

'I'm afraid not. My father wouldn't have liked it being commercialized.'

'The way I look at it, the baron's long dead, and what he doesn't know can't hurt him.'

'I'm sorry. It's out of the question.' She walked stiffly away from Samantha's unfriendly stare. She didn't need another argument.

The rest of the day passed uneventfully. Later, it was as if the disagreement with Betty had never happened. Betty had cooked Lauren her favourite curry. It was followed by a crumble made from apples picked from a gnarled and ancient tree in the garden and cooked by Katie with Betty's help.

When Lauren praised the pudding and asked for a second helping, the girl smiled proudly at Betty.

Lauren wondered what the pair of them did all day, then realized how clean and tidy the cottage was, and without any input from herself. A semblance of order had been restored to the garden, too. Betty looked tired, Lauren thought, the dark smudges under her eyes a telltale sign that she was not sleeping well. But it was no use saying anything to her because Betty would bristle and dismiss any notion that she might be ill, and they'd already had one row today.

After tea she changed into jeans and a sweater and dug out her old riding boots. She imagined Daniel would have a hard hat she could borrow. 'I'm going riding with Daniel.'

'What shall I tell your man if he calls?' Betty asked.

Lauren dismissed the blush that crept under her skin. 'Theo is not my man.'

Katie giggled. 'If you don't want him I'll take him off your hands.'

Betty managed a disapproving huff. 'That one's a whole heap

of man to manage, missy. You've had enough trouble with men as it is.'

Katie's smile faltered. 'That wasn't my fault. I was a victim, my counsellor said, and not all men are bastards. Eve said the memory of the assault will never go away, but it would be a mistake to blame all men. Theo's lovely, and he listens to me when I talk. I like him.'

'He's too old for you, ducks.'

'I know that, silly. He's more like an uncle. I'm thinking that I might testify against those men if they catch them. It might stop them from attacking somebody else.'

Lauren offered, 'I'll stand up with you in court if it comes to that.'

'Oh, there's no need. Eve, my counsellor will be there with me if I decide to go ahead.'

Lauren felt hurt that she could be dismissed so easily by Katie now. 'I'm off then.'

Betty cracked, 'Bring me back some horse shit to put on the roses. I'll tell the copper you've gone riding with Daniel if he calls, shall I?'

'If you would.' Lauren considered for a moment. 'Tell him I'll return his call when I get back.'

Katie followed her out to the gate. 'I want to tell you something.'

'What is it, Katie?'

'I heard that Samantha Bamford is getting it on with Daniel Mather.'

Shocked, Lauren gazed at the girl. 'You shouldn't listen to gossip. Who told you such a wicked thing?'

'John Dunne. He said Daniel was carrying on with the mistress of Grantham Hall, even though she was twenty years older. His wife left him when she found out, but that was years later.'

Now Lauren felt even more shocked. Twenty years older? Lucy was younger than Daniel, and the pair seemed fond of each other. Surely not?

There came a short, sharp memory of herself going to the stables to see a newborn foal, of two people in the straw, of them pulling hastily apart and adjusting their clothing.

Then later, her mother shaking her back and forth and threatening her if she told her father what she'd seen.

'You've been spying on me you sly little wretch. I'll lock you in the deepest cellar if you tell. You'll never be found in the darkness and nobody will hear you cry for help except the ghosts, and they'll frighten the wits from you before the rats and spiders eat you alive.'

Her heart began to beat a hard rhythm inside her chest and she felt like crouching in a corner and hiding her face in her arms. But she couldn't, because the garden had no corners dark enough to shield her from the fury of her mother's devastating scorn.

Katie's eyes widened. 'You've gone pale. Are you all right?'

Sucking in a deep breath Lauren fought off her panic to return to normal – if normal was absorbing the fact that her mother had been the one to enjoy a close relationship with Daniel. She'd not considered such a thing before. It was as if her brain had decided she was mature enough to dissemble the clues it had stored and was now able to cope with the news. How inconvenient of it. She didn't know why she'd felt such an initial shock, after all she would not hesitate on embarking on an affair with . . . Theo, say. Neither of them were married to other people, though.

But she'd once thought she was. Sometimes she still felt married, and she tried to remember exactly when she'd fallen out of love with Charlie.

Had she ever been in love with him? It didn't feel as though she had, now, and only a fool would feel guilt over the situation. It was simple. She was a grown woman with the hots for a sexy, delicious man. She should enjoy the situation.

She smiled and her voice strengthened. 'I'm fine, really, Katie. Don't fuss. I do want you to promise not to repeat what John Dunne told you. He's an old man whose mind has begun to play tricks. He's got mixed up with something that happened in the past, and I know the person he's referring to. It simply isn't true, and even if it was, repeating such a thing could cause considerable damage to Samantha Bamford's marriage, and it could get you into serious trouble.'

'Sorry, Lauren. I promise not to repeat it to anyone. I just thought you ought to know what people are saying, in case he makes a move on you as well.'

'He wouldn't. Daniel is a gentleman and . . . he was a *friend* of my mother, and that's who John was referring to.' There, she'd said it, accepted it even, though she'd forced out the last part.

Katie's mouth twisted into a grimace. 'I'm sorry. It just goes to prove that there's no such thing as a gentleman.'

Taking Katie's face between her palms, Lauren gently kissed her forehead. 'You're too young to be so cynical, my love.' But she knew she was lying to herself and Katie was right. Daniel *was* just a man, and a not very honourable one at that to cheat on his wife. She wouldn't be at all surprised if he didn't make a play for her. If he did she'd just have to put him firmly in his place.

But as it turned out Daniel didn't even look at her the wrong way. She enjoyed the exercise the ride afforded her and found that her riding ability hadn't been impeded by the absence of practice, except the muscles in her thighs and buttocks had begun to complain bitterly. A soak in a warm bath would fix that.

As they rode back into the courtyard a teenage girl came from the stable building to greet them. Her hair was long and dark, and she was wearing jeans and a cropped top that left her waist bare. Her dark eyes were glittering and sharp as her glance went from one to the other. Sulkily, she said, 'Hi, Daniel.'

Daniel said in a slightly dismayed sort of voice, 'Hello, Pippa. What are you doing here?'

The Bamfords' daughter, Lauren thought, for the girl looked like Samantha.

'I thought it was the evening for my riding lesson.'

'That's tomorrow. Is Tony with you?'

The girl shrugged. 'No. When my brother realized we'd got the wrong evening he sloped off to see if the badgers are active. He'll be back for me soon. I wanted to stay and see the horses. Gubbins appears to be a bit off-colour.'

'He's strained a tendon so is feeling sorry for himself and sulking. Seeing you cheered him up no end, I expect. You're his favourite girl.'

The girl smiled and said with more enthusiasm, 'I gave him my apple.'

'Gubbins would have liked that.' Daniel nodded. 'I'm afraid I can't give you a lesson now. I have things to do . . . though you might like to stay and have a glass of lemonade with Miss Bishop until your brother comes back.' The smile he offered Lauren contained a plea. 'You will stay, won't you Lauren?'

Seeing the hero worship in the girl's eyes Lauren nodded

and held out a hand to the girl. 'I don't believe we've met before. I grew up at Grantham Hall.'

'How do you do, Miss Bishop, I'm Phillipa Bamford. You can call me Pippa if you like, everyone does. You live in Blackbird's Nest, don't you?'

'Yes, I do.'

'It must feel cramped after living at the hall.'

'Anything would be cramped after living at the hall. Do you like living there, Pippa?'

'Oh yes, Tony and I have terrific fun exploring it when we're not at school. We found some old clothes in the attic. And sometimes we dress up and get into the roped-off areas, and we sit at the tables or lie in the beds and pretend to be dummies. Sometimes we move slightly, or allow our eyes to move, to scare the visitors. They're never quite sure whether they see us move or not.' The shrill peal of laughter she gave invited a reply from one of the horses. 'Don't tell the parents, will you?'

Lauren gave her a conspiratorial grin. 'I'll keep a lookout for you next weekend.'

'We've heard there's a secret passage in the house, but we can't find it. Do you know where it is?'

'I've never heard of a secret passage at Grantham. There's a set of servants' stairs that lead from the staircase landing to the old kitchen in the basement. It's on the house blueprint, and was designed to allow the upstairs maids to go about their work without being seen by the household and the guests. My great-great-grandfather had a linen cupboard built in front of the doorway at the kitchen end.' He'd needed to discourage one of his sons from visiting the female staff when they were supposed to be working, her father had once said.

'Will you show me how to get into it, Miss Bishop?'

'Call me Lauren. I will if your father and mother say it's all right. They might want to make sure the stairs are still safe.' Though they'd been made of stone, she recalled, so she couldn't see why they wouldn't be safe.

'I'll talk to them about it tonight.'

The girl had become quite animated, and when her brother came for her she was bubbling with excitement over the servants' stairs.

Daniel smiled when the pair left. 'Thanks for staying, Lauren. She's a nice kid, but impressionable, and has a bit of a thing going for me, I'm afraid. It makes me nervous.'

Charlie Parker and Brian Allingham would have made a meal out of Pippa Bamford's hero worship. The sudden thought sickened her. She hadn't been very worldly herself when she met Charlie, a legacy of her sheltered upbringing. She must have appeared naive to Charlie at the beginning, and before the indifference had set in. She'd been wearing blinkers in the beginning, not to have noticed what was going on under her nose.

'It was the least I could do, Daniel. Thank you for the ride. I enjoyed it.'

'The horses enjoyed it too. We must do it again. Come anytime, Lauren. I usually ride out at the same time each evening.'

'Thank you. I might, at that.'

'Have you heard from your mother lately?' he said at the car when she was clipping on her seat belt.

'Not recently,' and she couldn't help asking, 'Have you?'

'Me?' He shrugged and his eyes drifted away from hers. 'Portia would hardly contact me. I haven't seen her for years.'

'No, I don't suppose she would,' and suddenly she wanted him to know that she was aware of what had happened. 'My mother has never been the type to take hostages . . . was it worth it, Daniel?'

He gazed at her silently for a few seconds, then understanding dawned in his eyes. There were no excuses, no apology forthcoming. He just shrugged and said quietly as he closed the car door. 'No it was not. I lost more than I gained. Goodnight, Lauren.'

He was not a man to discuss his conquests, and for that she felt respect as she drove home. Daniel was a nice man who'd paid the price for his mistake. He deserved better.

Eleven

Shortly after breakfast the next morning, Lauren's mobile rang. Her heart leaped as Theo came into her mind.

'Lauren Bishop.'

There came a chuckle from the other end. 'Is that what you're calling yourself now? Well, I suppose it came as a shock to discover you weren't exactly who you thought you were, Mrs Parker.'

A spark of dread flickered to life inside her. She said faintly, knowing full well who it was, 'Who is this?'

'Come on, Lauren, you know exactly who.'

'It's Brian Allingham isn't it?'

'And the lady is awarded the first prize.'

'What do you want?'

'The money Charlie owes me to start with – or return of the goods.'

'I don't know what you're talking about. There was a little money in the safe which belonged to me. The house and contents have been seized. When the police have finished with it the bank intends to sell the property and the car to cover the mortgage and loans.'

'Don't give me that, Lauren. Charlie owed me two million for my half of the deal.'

She gasped. 'Two million! Don't be so ridiculous. Look, I don't care if you believe me or not, Brian.' She took great satisfaction in saying, 'You and Charlie were the biggest pair of cheats and liars that I've ever met – and you're worse, considering what you did to Katie.'

There was a short silence, then he said cautiously, 'What exactly did I do to Katie?'

She'd been stupid blabbing it out, and reminded herself not to mention the result. She bit her lip and mumbled, 'I think you know, Brian. I want that video you recorded.'

'Which video are you talking about?'

She spelled it out for him. 'The one where Katie was assaulted.'

There was a sharp intake of breath. 'So the brat ratted on me, did she. Well, Lauren my dear, it seems to me that we're in a position where we can barter.'

'I don't barter with criminals.' Besides which, she didn't have a clue what money Brian was talking about, or where it could be.

'Let me put it this way, Lauren dear. Unless you come up with the money or the merchandise I'll circulate that tape of Katie.'

'What merchandise?' she cried out in panic. 'I don't know what to look for.'

'Oh, you poor, dumb little cow. I don't know what Charlie saw in you, I really don't. What d'you think you should be looking for?'

'More tapes?'

'Don't be stupid, darling,' and his voice hardened. 'Something that would have brought in a fortune for Charlie and me. That was the price he agreed to pay for getting out of the partnership.' His voice settled into a whine. 'I've got to get it back, Lauren. There are people after me, people I made promises to – and they're not very friendly.'

'Perhaps you should put yourself under police protection,' she said with as much sarcasm as she could muster.

'Such wit, Lauren. You won't feel like laughing when the villains knock on your door – and they will if you don't come up with the goods. I'll make sure of it.'

The penny suddenly dropped and she whispered. 'Are you talking about drugs? No, not Charlie . . . he wouldn't.' But yes, he might, she thought. He'd dealt in drugs as a juvenile Theo had told her. She must find out where Brian was ringing from. 'Where are you, Brian?'

'Don't be stupid. I'm not about to tell you that. The police would have cottoned on to you by now. I'll ring you in a few days. Don't tell anyone I called, else those thugs I talked about will pay you a visit . . . and you won't like it.'

'Except you don't know my address. And if I don't find your goods, what then, Brian? They'll come after you, so you're in the same boat. I'd guess they might find you in Spain. As I recall, you had a property there.'

He laughed. 'Keep guessing, darling. By the way, how is Dorset looking at this time of year?'

Her eyes narrowed. It was a shot in the dark because he knew she'd been born and brought up here. Summoning up some courage she gave a light laugh. 'I'm miles away from Dorset.'

'A chicken always goes back to its roost,' he said, then laughed and hung up.

Lauren wondered if she should call the police. Next, she wondered why she was even asking herself such a thing. *Drugs!* That was a heavy scene, even for Charlie, who'd professed to loathe anything to do with drugs. She must think everything through.

'A chicken always goes back to its roost!' she muttered.

The phrase refused to leave her mind for the rest of the day, which was busy with several coach loads of tourists. She warmed to her job as she guided them through the selected route around her childhood home, carpeted now, which gave an impression of luxury, and she fed the tourists with information and little snippets of scandal about her ancestors.

She posed for photographs under her parents' portraits then began the next tour, smiling when she saw Tony in a faded red uniform. He was seated at a table reading a book, wearing a false moustache and pair of round glasses. Pippa in a maid's outfit had just set a cup down in front of him. The pair were as stiff as ramrods. They were very good.

She ad-libbed for their benefit. 'The uniform dates back to the Crimean War. It belonged to Sir Edward Bishop, who had the reputation of being a womanizer.'

'Dirty old bugger, these blue bloods are all the same,' a man muttered to his wife.

She embellished the tale for his benefit. 'Sir Edward died of a fever. It's been suggested that he had a son by a housemaid he fell in love with, and the boy was adopted at birth because his wife had been unable to bear a child of her own. The boy succeeded to the barony after his father's death, but nothing was found in the records to suggest a discrepancy in his blood line.'

'What happened to the maid?' someone asked.

'She eventually became the housekeeper. Sir Edward gave her a pension when she retired, and a cottage on the estate free of rent for life. She outlived him by six months.'

'Not much of a legacy then.'

Somebody giggled. 'I'm sure Sir Edward winked at me. He's very handsome.'

All eyes had turned to Tony, whose eyes reflected laughter. He was having difficulty maintaining his pose and it was a marvel that he could stop himself from blinking, she thought.

'They're very good dummies, they look almost real,' someone said.

A woman went nearer to the barrier and stared at Pippa. 'I'm sure that maid wasn't smiling before.'

'You'll be seeing ghosts soon, Babs,' her partner said.

'Talking of ghosts . . .' Lauren led the party away before the Bamford siblings collapsed into laughter. 'One of the ladies of the house died in childbirth and her spirit has sometimes been seen in the ladies' library to those who are sensitive to such things. As we move into the room you may feel a sudden drop in temperature. Don't be alarmed by this.' Actually, the room had always been cool, due to the fact that it was on the north side, and it had always attracted draughts for some reason. The chimney was built in the wrong place, her father had told her. 'Lady Marguerite's portrait can be seen over the fireplace . . .'

When they reached the hall a man requested a photograph. 'Would you stand under your father's photograph please, Miss Bishop. I believe he was the last of the Barons.'

'Yes, he was, the male line came to an end on his death.'

Her father had never shown any disappointment in the fact that she'd been born a female. A gentleman in every sense of the word, he'd loved her unreservedly and had guided her with gentleness and love. She'd done no wrong in his eyes, while in her mother's eyes she'd never been able to do anything right. Still, it was no good worrying about that now.

She watched the man leave after he'd thanked her. She couldn't remember him being one of her party, but vaguely remembered seeing him talking to Samantha Bamford earlier.

Odd, she thought, then forgot about him as the second coach tour gathered around her with expectant eyes. She stood under her parents' portraits and smiled, for Charlie had once told her that a smile went a long way with the punters. 'I'm Lauren Bishop, daughter of Portia, Lady Bishop and the late Baron, Sir Alexander Bishop. Welcome to Grantham Hall.'

All eyes went up to the portraits then back to her. Comparisons were made. She smiled again. 'For security reasons the only photographs allowed in the interior of the house must be taken right here in the entrance hall. Now, if you'd all like to follow me . . .'

That evening she rang Theo and left a message on his answering machine. As a result she spent the evening in suspense, waiting for a return call that never came.

It was 2 a.m. when the soft buzz of her phone brought her awake.

She wondered if it was Brian again and said cautiously, 'Lauren Bishop.'

'Hello, Lauren.'

Theo's voice flowed like warm honey against her ear and her heart lifted. 'I'm glad it's you,' she said sleepily, and smiled. 'What are you doing?'

'Talking to you. I've just got home from work.'

'Poor you. I wish I was with you.'

'So do I. I'm sorry to ring you so late.'

'It's better than not hearing from you at all.' She heard Katie stir, pulled the covers over her head and said. 'I might sound a bit muffled. You're under the blanket with me.'

He chuckled. 'Just where I'd like to be.'

'Would you, Theo? Why?'

She could hear laughter in his voice when he said, 'Are you kidding? Or is this an invitation to indulge in a dirty phone call?'

She giggled. 'It wasn't an invitation, but it's a splendid idea of yours. I've never had a dirty phone call. It will be a new experience, so carry on. Talk dirty to me.'

'I've never made one before.'

'There's always a first time. Pretend you're under the blankets with me. What would you be doing?'

'Oh God,' he groaned. 'It's more like, what *wouldn't* I be doing.'

'What would you do first?' she urged.

'You know, Lauren, this is going to give me the biggest hard-on in history. First, I'd kiss you.'

Her own temerity surprised her when she purred, 'Where?'

'Everywhere. I'd start at the top, probably just in front of your ear, the place where you have that cute little freckle.'

She touched it with her finger tip, genuinely surprised. 'You've noticed that I have a freckle there?'

'Just a tiny one . . . from there I'd kiss your eyelids then map my way around your face and kiss your mouth.'

'You sound like a cartographer. Can't you be a little bit more romantic? What would I be doing?' she said, feeling a rush of pleasure imagining his lips nuzzling against her skin.

After a moment of silence he groaned. 'This is doing me no good at all, Lauren.'

'It is me. I feel . . . sort of wicked!' She could hear his breath whispering against her ear and almost feel the brush of it against her face. 'Go on, Theo,' she prompted. 'There's something so sexually furtive about what we're doing that I'm coming out in goosebumps.'

'You're a witch, Lauren. Right now I'd like to open your thighs and slide my tongue right inside you.'

'Detective Inspector Ransom!' She felt a shock of erotic pleasure that melted her core and mewed with the pleasure the thought of him doing exactly that brought her. As a way of making love this wasn't perfect, but it added excitement to their relationship. She had no doubt that when they got together it would be explosive.

Huskily, he said, 'How do you feel now?'

She told him. 'Hot . . . I feel really hot. I've never felt like this about anyone before, Theo Ransom. Imagine my hands around you . . . sliding, caressing, my mouth over yours.'

'You've got me firmly by the balls,' he whispered, and she knew he'd reached a point of no return.

'I know,' she said. 'Goodnight, Theo, my love. Sweet dreams.' It was an effort to cut him off, but for her own sake, she did. She was covered in perspiration, and there was a fiery ache in the pit of her stomach. She threw off the covers, bathing her body in the cool night air streaming through the window. She laughed with the delight of it, lowering her voice to a quiet chuckle when she remembered the time.

Lauren drifted off to sleep with the warm glow of arousal still lingering about her. It wasn't until morning that she remembered she'd forgotten to tell him about Brian's phone call.

Waking late, she scrambled out of bed and into her clothes. She raised the ire of Betty, who'd cooked her a proper breakfast, by snatching up a piece of bacon and washing it down with a cup of tea.

Katie came downstairs still in her nightdress, and bleary-eyed. 'You were talking and laughing in your sleep last night. It kept me awake.'

Lauren's eyes widened and colour seeped into her cheeks. It was hard to keep her words casual. 'Oh, what did I say?'

'I didn't catch the words, they were all muffled, 'cepting you did call out that hunky detective's name a couple of times.'

'Theo?' she said carefully.

Betty grinned. 'How many other detectives do you know?'

Katie sent a grin towards Betty and said, 'Theo . . . Theo, my love, wherefore art thou, Theodore?'

'I didn't say that.'

'No, you said in a shocked voice, "Detective Inspector Ransom!" Then you began to laugh.'

Lauren's blush deepened as she remembered that moment. Flustered, she said, 'I must have been dreaming.' Gazing at the clock she changed the subject. 'Goodness me, look at the time. I'll be late for work.'

'Goodness me,' the two said together, then burst into laughter.

Brian phoned again when she was walking towards her car. 'This is just to let you know I mean business. You have one week in which to find the merchandise, Lauren. If not, my companions might visit you at that ancestral heap of stones you work in.'

He hung up before she could utter a word, leaving her shocked and shaking.

After Lauren had gone Betty and Katie exchanged a grin.

'Dreaming, my arse,' Betty said practically. 'I heard her phone ring, and I bet you did too, you little tart. The very idea, listening in to Lauren's private conversation. And don't try and deny it, your ears are still flapping, Miss Nosy Parker. What else did she say to him?'

'Now whose ears are flapping?' Katie giggled. 'I didn't hear any more. I think she ducked her head under the blankets because it was all muffled. She was on the phone a long time though, whispering and laughing and making funny noises.'

'I bet you anything you like that she'll be making that chocolate cake and visiting the hunky Theo in London before too long.'

'Do you think they're in love?'

'I think they're hot for each other – and Charlie's not even cold in his grave yet.'

'A lot he cared. Look at the way he treated her, marrying her when he was already married then spending her money. Even though he was all right to me, I know that was wrong. Dad was a con man, and worse.' She gazed at her grandmother with sadness in her eyes. 'You don't really blame any of this on Lauren, do you? It was my father who was at fault. He cheated on all of us. Lauren has done her best to look after us. I wish *she* was my sister, and I want her to be happy.'

Betty had to admit that the girl was right. 'Of course I don't blame the duchess. She's a nice girl, despite her hoity-toity background. Not everyone would put up with having to live with their mother-in-law, but she was always good to me.'

'What will we do if she marries Theo?'

'We'll manage. We'll find our own place to rent and the three of us will look after each other.'

'Three?'

'Me, you and the baby.'

Katie opened her mouth, then shut it again. It was a waste of time arguing with her grandmother, whose ability to twist reason was inexhaustible. She'd already made her mind up to what she was going to do, and nothing and nobody was going to stop her.

At Grantham Hall people were arriving by the car load, and a great queue of people stretched from the hall down through the door and across the driveway.

The Bamford family was called in to help manage the extra crowds, Tony and Pippa were utilized in the tea rooms, clearing tables. The size of Lauren's groups seemed to double in number, and they listened to her with greater intensity, their eyes fixed firmly on her face. Cameras flashed left, right and centre in the Hall. She found it all slightly unnerving.

Samantha Bamford was pleased with the crowds. 'You'll have to talk them through the tours faster so we can fit a couple of extra ones in. I hope this keeps up until the end of summer. It will put us on the map and I can get the souvenirs manufactured over the winter.'

By the end of the day Lauren was exhausted. She pulled to the side of the road when her mobile rang, hoping it wasn't Brian again. It wasn't, it was her mother.

'Have you seen the papers?' Portia Demasi screeched. 'How could you do this to your own mother? Have you no pride?'

'Pride?' A yawning pit of dismay appeared in Lauren's stomach. 'Mother? What are you doing telephoning me after all this time? I don't even know what you're talking about.'

'I'm talking about your face being on the front of the tabloids.'

'Oh, my God,' she groaned. 'Surely not again.'

'And that dreadful hair cut looks so cheap.'

'Do be quiet a moment, mother, I'm trying to think.'

'Think! You should have thought before you married that . . . *bigamist!* I told you that marrying out of your class would be a mistake. Well, all I can say is good riddance to him. Just don't come to me for help.'

'I wouldn't dream of asking you for help.'

Her mother wasn't listening. She began to dress her down in her usual manner. 'Your father would turn over in his grave if he knew what you were doing. A common tour guide in your former home? How could you?'

'I needed to earn some money to live.'

'So, not content with making a fool of you, the man also stole your money from you. What have you got in your head for a brain, Lauren? Cauliflower?'

Just at this moment she wouldn't be at all surprised, for her temples were throbbing. 'Do shut up, Mother,' she hissed.

'Pardon me? Remember, Lauren, this is your mother you're talking to.'

'You wouldn't know what it's like to be a *mother.* Go and practise being an Italian aristocrat. You might succeed, where you failed at being an English one.' She cut her mother off halfway through an outraged yelp and flicked the phone to off. She felt jittery with nerves, as she usually did after an encounter with her mother, yet strangely pleased with herself that she'd stood up to her at long last.

Driving to the nearest garage she bought herself a paper and stared at the picture of herself on the front page. Her mother had been wrong about the hairstyle. *Bigamist's 'other' wife run to earth at her former home.*

Apart from the close up on the front page, there was one of her standing under the portrait of her father. *The second Mrs Parker has been identified as the Hon. Lauren Bishop, daughter of the late Lord Bishop and Portia, Lady Bishop.*

No wonder her mother had been steamed up.

Lauren skimmed the article, remembering the man who'd taken her photograph talking to Samantha Bamford. There was a lot of information about Grantham, about the electronic magnate Greg Bamford buying it from her mother, and the irony of the daughter working there – the daughter who'd married a bigamist and brought disgrace to her family name.

'All I did was fall in love and get married,' she whispered in despair, and gazed at a small head shot of Charlie, her heart giving a wrench, for she saw now what she hadn't seen before. Charlie Parker had resembled her father, except his dapper neatness was contrived where her father's had been part of him.

'I hope you're enjoying the damage you inflicted on us. You were an idiot to get involved with drugs,' she railed at him.

White-faced, she returned home, half expecting to see a posse of reporters camped in the grounds. There were none. Flinging the paper on the table, she rang Grantham Hall.

It was Greg who answered. 'Samantha's gone out. Is there anything I can help you with, Lauren?'

She went straight into the attack. 'Have you seen the papers?'

'Yes, of course . . . excellent publicity. The takings quadrupled today. I told Samantha that you'd be worth every penny of your wage.'

Quietly, she said, 'You mean you exposed me deliberately?'

'You did agree to be part of the publicity. It was in your contract. I must admit I didn't expect you to give them so much information about your personal life though.' Lauren had the feeling that Samantha, annoyed by her refusal to allow her to use the Bishop family crest, had caused this mischief deliberately.

'I didn't give them any information at all,' she said flatly. 'I didn't even know it was happening. Why do you think I moved here? It was to get away from the publicity . . . and it's not just me involved. I've made myself responsible for my former husband's mother and daughter, both of whom have their own issues to deal with over this.'

'I'm so sorry, Lauren, but the bigamy thing wasn't your fault.'

'I'm well aware of that. You don't understand, Greg. There's more to this affair than the bigamy issue. By revealing my whereabouts you've put us all in danger. Charlie Parker and his partner were involved in criminal activities we didn't even know about.'

There was silence for a few moments then he said, his voice contrite, 'Lauren, I'm so sorry, I had no idea. Look, if anyone asks for your address I won't tell a soul, and I'll make sure Samantha doesn't either. And if you like I'll fix up some security around the cottage. Infrared cameras, lights and a direct line to my place. I can even fix you up with a security alarm, phone tap and a dog.'

The anger she felt, lessened. 'That's kind of you, Greg, but the damage has already been done. I'll say yes to everything except the phone tap and dog. Animals are such a responsibility when one has to rent, and we've already got two cats.' She remembered her shrinking treasury and sighed. 'You must let me know the cost.'

'Since we're the cause of your latest troubles there will be no charge. I'll install it myself, then dismantle it when you vacate the cottage. Sorry, love. I imagine Samantha gave out the information. She probably thought it was a good idea at the time.'

Greg sounded so penitent that Lauren forgave him, and her qualms about their lack of safety fled. 'You won't give my phone number out to anyone either, will you?'

'Not without your permission. I know it's unlisted. Look, there's still a few hours daylight left. I'll come down and make a start on it. I can get the cameras and security lights in this evening, at least. I'll have to put some cables in for the alarm system, and might have to do some rewiring first.'

'Then you must stay for dinner.'

'Suits me, since Sam and the kids have gone into town to take in the latest film.'

Betty, who'd been unashamedly listening to the conversation put her hands on her hips, then shrugged and wandered off towards the kitchen.

Katie had been glumly reading the paper. She sank on to a chair when she finished the article. 'We won't have to leave here, will we? We've just settled in.'

'I shouldn't think so.' But still, Lauren was worried. Even if the press decided that the story had played out, Brian's threat was still a valid one. Now he knew where she worked, he might send those men after her if she didn't discover what he was looking for.

'Who was that on the phone earlier?' Betty asked.

'Nobody . . . it was no one. A wrong number.'

'You never could lie, your eyes go all funny. It was Brian Allingham, wasn't it?'

'What makes you think that?'

'The look on your face, as though you had a rotten stink up your snout.'

She supposed she should tell them since they would be in equal danger. 'It *was* Brian. He said that Charlie had something he wants.'

'Did he say what?'

'Drugs, or the money from the sale of them. He was talking an amount of two million pounds as his share.'

Betty's face turned red and she said faintly, 'How much?'

The three of them gazed unbelievingly at each other, then Katie said, 'Oh, God! What are we going to do?'

'Don't you worry, we'll manage,' Betty said fiercely, and putting an arm around her, drew her granddaughter close against her.

'There's more,' Lauren told them. 'Brian said there are men threatening him. Dealers I imagine. He says he has Katie's tape, and he'll only exchange it for the money, or if I tell him the whereabouts of the drugs.'

'You'd better report this to that detective feller of yours.'

'I thought about it, but I can't risk it. Brian said he'll tell the dealers about us if I inform the police.'

A little moan came from Katie's mouth.

'I'll find out,' Lauren promised. 'I still have my house key, and if Charlie hid anything at the house it will still be there.'

'But the police have already searched it.'

'It's a big house, I expect they missed some places. After all, they were only looking for specific items at the time . . . videos, not drugs or large amounts of money.' There had been twenty-five thousand pounds in the safe, she thought uneasily. That had taken up quite a bit of room, so how large a container would four million pounds need? The money would probably fit into a large suitcase, and so would the drugs. 'I'll search the house from cellar to attic – and the garden shed, as well.'

Betty rolled her eyes. 'Sometimes you're as naive as a new born babe. D'you think the cops haven't already done that. How do you know they haven't found it and are watching the place, waiting for someone to make a move?'

'Theo would have told me.'

'Those crims might be watching the place as well, or Brian Allingham.'

Lauren made a joke of it. 'Then they'll all be milling about watching each other like passengers catching trains at Waterloo station, and I'll see them.' She felt a twinge at the thought that Theo might not trust her, though he'd have grounds not to now if he found out what she was about to do. 'How would they know about the drugs, anyway?'

'They have ways and means – informers and phone taps, gossip and stuff.'

'You've watched too many episodes of *The Bill*.'

Exasperation lodged in Betty's face. 'You can be stubborn if you like, and I can see you're not going to listen to sense. I'm going to say it anyway. Don't blame me if you get captured by villains and sold into prostitution overseas. Ask that tame DI of yours what goes on in the underworld.'

'Apart from Orpheus attempting to free Eurydice, you mean.'

The reference was lost on Betty, and when the woman gazed at her with uncertainty, Lauren felt sorry that she'd made the remark. She softened her voice. She shouldn't have mocked Betty when the woman was only concerned about her safety. 'Sorry, Betty, it was a flippant remark. Tame is certainly not a word that can be applied to Theo.'

Would he have had her phone tapped? Certainly, he'd known her number, and at almost the same time as she'd had it connected. Picking up the receiver she listened, but heard only the dial tone. She said, 'Theo, if you're listening in, I want you to know that I'll never forgive you if you've been spying on us.'

Katie's giggle earned her a frown from Betty. 'It's not funny. You're going then?'

Lauren nodded. 'If I can't find anything, then I promise I'll contact Theo tomorrow and tell him about the phone call.'

'Then there's nothing more to be said.'

'That's right, and please don't discuss this when Mr Bamford comes to fix up the security system. I don't want anyone to know where I've gone, and I'll be back by the morning.'

The pragmatic Betty gave her a nod. Katie just chewed on her lip and looked worried.

Twelve

It was one thirty when Lauren reached her former home. She took the precaution of driving round the block several times, smiling because the cloak and dagger stuff seemed slightly ridiculous.

Apart from the usual cars parked along the side of the road, all was dark and quiet. The calm before the storm, she thought, for there was an ominous humidity to the air, which was charged with electricity. Now and again a gust of wind stirred in the trees lining the road.

She parked in the same spot in the driveway that she'd used for the past five years. Oddly though, she now felt like an intruder, especially since there was a FOR SALE sign poking out of the hedge.

There was no moon, it was hidden behind clouds. Then a wind came from nowhere to claw at the leaves of the trees and shrubs with a rattling suddenness. Lauren started. A faint glow from a lamp further up the street provided her with a modicum of light. As if it had been waiting for her to step out of the car, as she headed for the house the sky opened. Rain dropped out of the roiling clouds in a heavy deluge.

The door to the house was recessed into a deep porch, into which no light penetrated. She felt a slight atmosphere of menace as she approached and chided herself for being so stupid. Nobody was going to jump out at her. Nevertheless her heart began to pound as she inserted the key into the lock, using the small light on her key ring to guide her. The lock opened with a loud click, the sound almost buried when lightning snicked through the air, and thunder rumbled.

Almost too late, Lauren remembered the security alarm and hoped it was no longer armed, for she had no control on her key ring. Holding her breath she counted to twenty. Nothing. With a sigh of relief she pulled the door shut behind her.

She stood for a moment, her back pressed against the door, taking her bearings. The house smelled stale and felt alien to her, as if it knew she'd never liked it and was now rejecting her. When her eyes had adjusted she switched on the torch she'd brought with her.
The battery was low, for the light kept fading.

'Get some new batteries from the kitchen,' she whispered and groped her way into the shining space. Lightning turned the kitchen into daylight, each flash making her nearly jump out of her skin. The cupboards were bare. She'd have to make do with the light she had. 'Now, where to start,' she whispered. Upstairs, and work her way down would be best.

It was a big house, especially when compared to the cottage.

She went through every bedroom, through every cupboard and drawer, looking for she knew not what. Nothing! Not even the personal stuff she'd been forced to leave behind. She wondered what had happened to it.

Going into the upstairs hall she gazed speculatively at the hatch leading to the roof cavity. She found the pole, levered the cover back and brought down the metal staircase that had been concertinaed into the roof space, with one fluid motion. Her teeth gritted when the metal screeched alarmingly. The mechanism needed oiling.

Climbing the ladder she swung her beam around the cavernous space. When a flash of lightning was followed by a loud, rolling clap of thunder that echoed deafeningly in the roof space, she found it hard to ride it out. Her feeble torch light revealed nothing, not even a cardboard box. Charlie always said that anything stored in the roof was a fire hazard.

'It wouldn't be half as much a hazard as you proved to be Charlie Parker,' she said out loud. 'Look at the mess you've left us all in. Where did you hide the drugs? Or have you already sold them? If so, where's the money? Certainly not in the bank account.'

She made her way backwards down the staircase and swung it back into position. Poor Charlie, what a fool he'd been, she thought. And she'd been a bigger fool for marrying him. If it hadn't been for the accident that had killed him she'd still be living here – still be supporting the farce of being Mrs Charlie Parker – still wavering about divorcing Charlie.

'Drugs,' she said out loud, and shivered, wondering where else to look for them.

There was a noise downstairs, a scuffing sound.

She froze, her ears straining. There was nothing else to hear, but she had a sense that someone was waiting for her in the darkness.

'Jack the Ripper, perhaps,' she said out loud, hoping her own voice would give her courage. Then she wished she hadn't said anything at all, because fear grabbed at her, making her weak.

She sat on the top stair, staring down into a pit of darkness as though it was hell, a sick feeling in the back of her throat as the storm gradually retreated. But she couldn't stay up here indefinitely. Clicking on the torch she glanced at her watch. She'd been in the house for an hour already, and had got exactly

nowhere. Charlie must have a hidden compartment somewhere
. . . under the stairs, perhaps. She made her way quietly down,
illuminating each step she took. It would be just her luck to
fall and break her leg or something.

When she reached the bottom stair her wavering beam fell
on a pair of black boots standing side by side a little way into
the hall. She frowned as she stared uncomprehending at them.
Charlie had never worn black boots in his life. Her beam trav-
elled upwards. The boots had legs inside them, black clad in
leather. Her torch failed, leaving her in darkness.

Legs! Adrenalin bolted into her like a zag of lightning that
had been left behind, salting her tongue. When a faded flash
illuminated the hall she thought she saw a man standing there
and her heart nearly failed her. Immediately she thought,
Charlie's ghost! She gave a cry of fright and threw her torch
at the intruder.

Ghost or not, he grunted in pain as a dull thud against his
body told her she'd scored a hit. Then the torch fell to the floor
and rolled back and forth. The light supply returned and the
narrow beam of light painted a stripe that moved back and forth
across the walls.

She should have run, but she was paralysed to the spot and
her legs refused to move. In fact she was trembling so much
that they could hardly hold her upright. Then her wrist was
grasped in a strong grip and she was turned, her arm held
loosely against her back. At the same time an arm snaked
around her front to pull her backwards and pinned her against
a muscled body. When the hand left her wrist and clamped
over her mouth, her knees turned to water and she gave a
frightened little moan.

'Got you!' Theo whispered gently against her ear.

Her relief was absolute and everything inside her seemed to
sag. Nerves instantly shredded, Lauren gave a sob, and began
to cry. Theo turned her against him then. Moving into his arms
she held him tight, mostly as a prop, because she was as angry
as hell with him. Yet her heart pounded against his chest, and
she buried her face into his neck.

'You scared me . . . I hate you, Theo Ransom,' she snuffled.

'It serves you right,' he said without a shred of sympathy in
his voice. 'I'd be quite within my rights to charge you with
breaking and entering, plus assault of a policeman.'

'I didn't break in, I had a key,' she argued. 'And I didn't assault you.'

'Technically, you did both. The house has been resumed by the mortgagee, and where d'you think that torch hit? Another inch and I would have been emasculated.'

His aggrieved voice brought laughter bubbling up inside her. She sneaked a conciliatory kiss against his jaw. 'That would have been a shame. I'm sorry, Theo. It was a purely reflex action. How did you know I was here, anyway?'

'I rang you tonight. Katie answered the phone and she was worried sick about what you were getting up to. Why didn't you tell me about the phone call from Allingham?'

He was stroking his fingers through her hair now, it was quite dreamy and relaxing. 'I was going to, tomorrow, when I'd found what I was looking for.'

'Which is what, exactly?'

'Specifically . . . illegal drugs or a large amount of money.' She gazed up at him in the darkness. 'Do you know that the personal things I left behind have gone? Everything! Not that I want anything that relates to Charlie Parker, but there was other stuff, photograph albums and things.'

'It's in storage. It will be returned to you eventually.'

'You're very thorough,' she told him stiffly. 'Did you know about the drugs?'

'It's my job to be thorough, and no, I didn't, though I suspected there was more to this case than was apparent. Now it's just stepped into the realms of major crime. You could be in danger, especially since that article appeared in the paper today.'

'You don't think I invited the attention of the press, do you? My employer thought the connection between myself and Grantham Hall was a good idea for publicity for her business. Unfortunately, it backfired on me because the newspaper put two and two together. Her husband has just fitted some security at the cottage to make up for it. Do you really think I'm in danger?'

'If drugs are involved, yes . . . but not from anyone but Brian Allingham, since he now knows where you work, thanks to that newspaper article. His bank accounts are frozen, so he'll be getting desperate for money.'

'I can't imagine Charlie being involved in drug dealing.'

'He was certainly involved. We've been following a paper trail.

Six months ago he took out a personal loan, using this house as collateral. Brian Allingham did the same thing with his property. Charlie placed the money in several separate bank accounts up and down the country. It totalled half a million dollars, which is a lot of drugs in anyone's language, since it would have a street value of at least six times as much. He closed the accounts a month later, all on the same day, and was paid out in cash. There's no record of what he did with that cash. Now my guess is that he paid for a drug consignment with it.'

'So, I'm looking for drugs, not money?'

'You *were* looking for drugs. Now you're not looking for anything. You're going to go home and leave everything to the police. I'll put a trace on your phone line. If Allingham rings again we might be able to locate him.'

'What if those men come after me?'

'An educated guess tells me there are no men. It was a simple transaction. Charlie seems to have paid for the consignment – and something that large would have come across by boat I'd imagine. We'd know if there was a new batch of drugs in circulation. The dealers don't wait. It's broken down into smaller lots and sold down the line as soon as possible. The money Charlie borrowed has gone somewhere. My guess is that he and Brian intended to launder the proceeds from the sales through the video store. Though as it is, there isn't room for any more scum to float on that particular pond. Charlie wouldn't have had time to get the stuff out on the street before he died. And Allingham wouldn't know if Charlie had actually bought the consignment. I'm surprised at that. It sounds as though they didn't trust each other. Allingham's beginning to panic, so he's going to take risks.'

'Do you think Charlie was involved in the abuse of children?'

'In the sense that he was dealing in child porn, yes. The films themselves originated abroad, mostly from the Philippines. He wouldn't have been active in the original crime.'

She shuddered. 'Buying and selling them is just as bad, because it contributes to the crime.'

Theo nodded, not bothering to encourage her need to exonerate her former partner in some way. 'Charlie Parker was a ball of slime,' he said dispassionately. 'You're better off without him.'

'I know . . . but I feel soiled just by the thought of knowing someone who dealt in this stuff.'

'There's nothing you can do about it now, so don't let it drag you down.'

Everything Theo said was common sense. 'What can I do about the publicity?'

'Ride it out. Eventually they'll find something else to write about. By the way, you forgot to mention that you were a blue blood.'

'My father had a minor title, that's all. I think the responsibility of it weighed him down sometimes.'

'In what way?'

'Oh, I don't know. People expect you to live up to it, and it sets you apart.'

'I can see that it would. What did your parents think of your association with Charles Parker?'

'My father was dead by the time I married, and my mother disapproved. She regarded him as totally beneath us.'

'She was right. He's a sordid piece of work.'

'My mother was a model before she married my father. He was her second husband. Her first was the seventies political writer, Ellis James.'

'He disappeared in Vietnam, didn't he?'

She nodded. 'So I believe. My mother and I have absolutely nothing in common. She'd probably disapprove of you too, just on principle.'

'That's not important, as long as you approve of me.' He grazed a finger across her cheek and touched against her mouth, locating it. He followed it up with a kiss, his mouth so tender against hers that he left her aching and breathless. How this man could kiss!

She attempted to snuggle up to him but he wouldn't let her. 'You're going home, right now, Lauren. As it is you won't get there until dawn. No more nocturnal raids. You tell me everything when it happens and you behave yourself.'

'Must I go home?'

After a momentary hesitation he said regretfully, 'Yes, you must.' Closing the house door behind them he escorted her to the car. When she was seated behind the wheel he held out his hand. 'I'm confiscating the house keys.'

As she removed them from her key ring and placed them in

his hand she remembered something. 'By the way, I think Brian might still be in the UK.'

'What makes you say that?'

'He said that chickens always come home to roost. He was referring to me being in Dorset, but when I asked him if he was in Spain, he laughed, and I had the feeling he was applying it to himself, as well. Of course, I hadn't seen the newspaper article then, and neither had he.' She shrugged. 'I feel like the biggest of fools for being taken in by Charlie. How did my life become such a mess?'

'Stop being sorry for yourself. Most of us are vulnerable to being conned at one time or another.' Stooping, he kissed her through the open window then tweaked her nose.

She had a sudden thought and said enthusiastically. 'You know, Theo, if I tell Brian I've found the drugs I could arrange to meet him. Then you could follow us and arrest him.'

'I'll tell you this for free, Lauren, and you'd better believe it. This isn't a game. If you even think of taking matters into your own hands again I'll put you over my knee and tan your backside for you.'

'You're irresistible when you're being assertive,' she cooed.

He gave a ghost of a chuckle. 'The next time I see you I'll expect you to be carrying a home-made chocolate cake.'

'Will you, indeed? By the way, I enjoyed the smarties.' She started the engine of her car and smiled at him. 'What's more, you're awfully good at making filthy phone calls.'

His teeth were a gleam of light in the darkness as he grinned. 'You're leading me astray, but that's something to look forward to in the future.'

Sober now, she gazed at him. 'What's between us . . . it's not . . . faked, is it? I'd hate it if I was being used as a means to an end, just because I'm susceptible to you.'

'Is that what you think . . . that I'm faking it?'

'It's crossed my mind,' she said truthfully.

'You might as well know that it crossed my mind too at the beginning, since it was obvious we were attracted to each other. But you'll have to use your own discretion on whether you're going to trust me or not. Remember though, trust works two ways.'

'In my experience, it doesn't always . . . but my action tonight did nothing to help matters, did it?'

'No, it didn't, but it was very informative.' He tipped up her chin and kissed her again. 'I still adore you, Lauren Bishop. I also know a delaying tactic when I see one. Go home. I'll contact you in a day or two.'

He'd told her again that he loved her, but in the same throw-away fashion as before. He'd also given her some food for thought, she realized as she drove away.

Lauren followed the tunnel of light made by her headlights. The roads were empty, except for the occasional lorry rumbling past. Rain slicked the roads and gushed into the gutters, now miniature streams in the built-up areas. In the country the water gathered in the shallow ditches, spilling over to orange glaze the tarmac in the low lying areas. The storm had retreated leaving the occasional grumble, like an old man digesting his dinner.

She arrived home in fast time, just as dawn laid a faint yellow light across the horizon.

The gate squeaked a protest as she pushed it open. She'd been tempted to oil it until she realized that it would serve as an early warning that somebody was coming. Nevertheless she winced as she closed it behind her with the same result, hoping it didn't wake Betty and her granddaughter.

She was halfway across the lawn when she was suddenly bathed in a strong light. Damn! She'd forgotten the new security system, and felt like an intruder caught in its beam.

As she put her key into the lock the light went off and a song thrush began to sing in the trees.

The door wouldn't open. Getting hold of the knob with both hands she tried to shake it back and forth, then swore. Nothing would budge the damned thing.

The two cats weaved around her ankles, making her jump.

Braving the light again, she picked up a small stone and threw it through Katie's bedroom window. 'Katie!'

When Katie's tousled head appeared at the window the kittens began to noisily claw their way up the trellis that supported the clematis.

'I can't see for that damned light. Who's there?' Katie shouted threateningly.

'It's me, Lauren, I can't get in. The door seems to be glued into the frame.'

'It's got bolts on it now, remember?'

'Well, you should have left it unbolted until I came home. I can't open the door from the outside, so will you please come down and let me in.'

'Theo said he'd look after you and I expected you to stay with him. D'you know what the time is?'

'Yes, I do. Now, will you stop acting like my mother and open the damned door. I'm tired and I want to sleep for a couple of hours, at least.' Lauren was about to stamp her foot when Katie's head disappeared from view. A few moments later there came the sound of bolts being pulled back.

'Did you find it?' Katie whispered.

'No, and Theo read me the riot act. Thanks to you he threatened to put me over his knee.'

When a soft giggle came her way, Lauren smiled. 'I'm going to bed. Rouse me at eight if I'm still asleep.'

When she fell into bed she heard the thrush again. Then, just as she closed her eyes she heard another bird . . . then another. It was the dawn chorus.

'Noisy creatures,' she groaned and pulled the blankets over her head.

Thirteen

There was no doubt in Lauren's mind that Samantha had leaked her business to the papers. There was a new notice up in the entrance hall. No photographs allowed!

When they next met, Samantha had a strained look on her face, and the atmosphere between them was charged. Lauren found it hard to be civil to her until Samantha broke the ice.

'I'm sorry,' she said a little later.

'So am I, since it put me in a spot,' Lauren said briefly. 'Did Pippa and Tony tell you about the servants' stairs. I promised I'd show it to them, with your permission.'

She nodded. 'Greg has found the catch, and it's safe. He's going to remove the dresser. I was looking at the security films, and noticed that the kids are messing about in the exhibits.'

'They're just having fun.'

'The other guide has complained about them. I don't want them to be a nuisance to my employees.'

'They don't bother me, really, and the tourists enjoy it. Pippa and Tony are very good.'

'I noticed.' Samantha managed a smile. 'They're good kids most of the time. I'll tell them it's OK to do it on your shift. Did they get the clothes from you?'

'There are several trunks of clothing in the attic, they would have got them from there. Much of it is moth-eaten and mouldy. You might be able to restore some of the costumes and put them on show, though.'

Samantha nodded. 'I really am sorry about that article. You'll forgive me, won't you?'

Until the next time, Lauren thought.

'I don't want you to leave because of it. People like you.'

Remembering her generous salary, Lauren nodded non-committally then moved forward to greet her first coach load. It turned out to be a busy Saturday and she was looking forward to some time off. She'd decided she was going to make Theo's cake and visit him in London.

Only one reporter managed to find her way to the cottage door that evening.

'Leave her to me, at least my dial hasn't been wrapped around the fish and chips lately,' Betty said, as Lauren and Katie concealed themselves behind the flowered curtains.

The girl was young and full of herself. 'I'm looking for a Miss Bishop. I believe she lives hereabouts.'

'It ain't me. I'm Mrs Church.' Betty picked up the hose and began to water a flowerbed. 'That Bishop woman, she's up in yon graveyard, I reckon.'

'Hardly, else I wouldn't be looking for her.'

Closing one eye, Betty made a gargling noise and began to twitch. The hose swung about and dowsed the woman.

Giving a scream the woman headed for the gate, brushing the water from her suit.

'Sorry, love,' Betty called out to her. ''Tis the twitches, see. The water brings it on. Hydrophobia the doctor said it is. Caught it from a dog bite. You never know when the twitches are going to come over you. Miss Bishop, was it?'

The woman turned to gaze at her, a question in her eyes.

'There be several Lord and Lady Bishops in the graveyard. And there's a Miss Bishop as well. Ethel, her name was. Died a hundred year ago. Reckon she's nothing but mouldy bones now, so not much use to you, aye? Who did you say you worked for?'

'The Trumpet Times,' the woman said sarcastically, which put Betty off not at all.

'My Sidney had a bugle once. He could play the last post, and Boogie Woogie Boy from company B on it. He got his lip stuck in the mouthpiece and had to go to the 'ospital.'

Katie stuffed her face in the curtains and dissolved into giggles.

'Wait a minute!' Betty said triumphantly as the woman got into her car. 'There's a Miss Bishop who lives over Dorchester way. Come to think of it, it might be Blandford. Or Wareham, mebbe. Then there's Miss Bishop who owns the fish shop. Poetic that is, if you say it fast and run it together . . . it sort of rhymes. *Missbisshhopownsafisshhop*.' Waving the hose Betty advanced on the hapless reporter. 'Hang on, Miss. I think I know who you're looking for.'

The car window was quickly wound up. 'Get fucked!' the reporter mouthed from the safety the glass offered her, and made a rude sign.

'Tsk, tsk! Manners, young lady.' As the car drove away Betty cackled with laughter. 'Of course, it could always be the Miss Bishop who lives right here. I'll tell her you called, shall I?'

Lauren was glad when the weekend was over. Her legs ached and she was sick of smiling at people. She washed her hair, then, filling the bath with warm water she added some salts and climbed in. It was a nice, deep bath. The water covered her body up to the neck, and a folded towel made a comfortable head rest.

She'd slopped several coats of white paint over the walls and Katie had painted a scattering of poppies on it. The rusty toilet cistern and pipe was now pillar box red, with a bright blue ball swinging at the end of a yellow chain to act as a hand grip. On the window sill a red geranium bloomed, courtesy of Betty. There was a shelf for shampoos and lotions as well as a narrow set of metal shelves she'd bought to keep towels, soaps, flannels and other things on.

She closed her eyes and relaxed, until Greg came into her

mind. Just before she'd left Grantham he'd handed her a laptop to start work on the history pamphlets. 'I'll fix you up with a separate email address through the business, if you like. You can use your own private password to get into it.'

'That won't be necessary.' And since she wasn't being paid to work in her time off, she said, 'Most of the family records are kept in the library. If you leave the laptop there I'll talk to Samantha so she can rearrange my tour guide duties to incorporate the writing. I can't do both at the same time.'

Greg had appeared taken aback for a moment, then he shrugged. Had he but known it, Lauren had remembered that Greg's business was electronics and, despite being offered her own password, Lauren decided not to use the computer for private emails. She didn't know if she could trust him after the newspaper article.

After she'd soaked the weariness out of herself she assembled the ingredients for Theo's chocolate cake. With advice from both Betty and Katie, the result was better than she'd hoped for. After the other two had gone to bed she decorated the offering with the few smarties remaining in the packet. It looked delicious.

She stored it in a plastic container, then packed an overnight bag and placed it in the lounge. As well as clothes, there was a sealed envelope from Katie for Theo.

'It's some drawings I promised him. Tell him I'm sorry they're not better, but it's the best I can do.'

'I will.'

Tomorrow, she'd drive herself into town, leave her car in an overnight car park, then take the train.

Lauren had felt exposed when she'd alighted at Waterloo. But she'd quickly realized that a squad of newspaper photographers hiding behind every rubbish bin in case the bigamous widow of Charlie Parker walked by, was highly unlikely. She also realized that unless she was extremely unlucky and ran into a former acquaintance, nobody would give a damn who she was or where she was going.

There was a faint touch of autumn in the air. Although still warmed by summer the trees were beginning to look tired and displayed the first offering of yellowing leaves. The long drawn out twilight had shortened slightly.

Winter would bring new life with Katie's baby. What a hard way to start life, being unwanted. She couldn't blame Katie for her attitude. Being assaulted in such a manner must be terrifying as well as soul-destroying. Easy to say that the baby wasn't at fault, which it wasn't. Lauren admired Katie. The girl possessed such courage. But now and again she stared into space, an expression of such utter despair in her eyes that Lauren ached for her. She just hoped that the infant was adopted by people who would give it love, despite its beginning.

Lauren wondered if her own mother had expressed dislike for the child she'd carried, perhaps that dislike had been absorbed by her and that's why they didn't get on. Mothers should love their children, she thought. She would love hers if she ever had any.

She shook off her faint feeling of depression as she left the train and crossed Manchester Road then into Saunders Ness Road. She found Theo's flat easily enough, situated as it was on the top floor of a square building built from biscuit-coloured brick. It was what it was, a converted warehouse without any pretension at being anything else. It was stamped all over with small, evenly spaced square windows.

The view across the river to the Millennium Dome was breathtaking.

She went up to the fifth floor, rapped at the door, then getting no answer let herself inside. She was in a hall. Most of the doors were open. Immediately in front of her was a kitchen large enough to eat in. Open double doors to her right led into an L-shaped lounge. To the left was a bedroom, and she guessed there was another one behind the closed door.

The cake container had been carried carefully in a hessian bag. She placed the cake on a plate in the middle of the kitchen table. It had sunk slightly in the middle, but she'd levelled out the sink hole with butter cream, so it didn't really notice.

She explored the rest of the sparsely furnished flat. It was more spacious than she'd imagined it would be from the outside. Each bedroom had its own bathroom, and there was a dressing room attached to the one that was being used.

The phone rang. She smiled when Theo's voice smoothly cut in. 'Theo Ransom speaking. I'm otherwise engaged, but leave your number and I'll ring back when I can.'

The caller said, 'Lauren, if you're there I'll be home in a couple of hours if nothing else comes up. Make yourself —'

She sprinted across the room and snatched the receiver up. 'Theo?'

'You *are* there.' She could hear the smile in his voice. 'I had a feeling you'd come up to London today.'

There was the clatter of an office going on in the background, telephones ringing, laughter and people talking.

'The invitation was irresistible. I've brought your cake and was about to leave it on the table and go home again.'

'Go home without seeing me? That's cruel, when I've missed you so much.'

'You're such a charmer,' she purred.

His voice lowered to a whisper. 'It's the absolute truth.'

She pitched her voice to match his. 'Why are you whispering?'

'Because two nosy coppers have just sat on my desk, flicked on the speaker phone and are listening in. Why are *you* whispering?'

'Because you are. I thought I'd better humour you.'

When a cheer went up, she laughed. 'Isn't there a law about eavesdropping?'

Darkly, he said, 'Not in this nick, obviously.'

'I'll see you later, Theo,' she purred for the benefit of his companions.

'Make yourself at home, darling,' somebody said in the background.

'I've already kicked off my shoes.'

There was a scuffle followed by a mumble of voices, then Theo said, 'Don't mind those oafs. I've got to go, Lauren. See you later, I'm looking forward to it.'

She looked forward to seeing him, too. Inside, she churned with a mixture of excitement and nerves.

She laid the table for two with wine and candles.

Hours later, when she was too ravenous to wait any longer, she cooked a frozen meal for one, took a shower in the navy-blue and white bathroom then slipped into the white cotton nightie she'd brought with her and went to bed. So much for the seduction of him she'd planned.

It was 2 a.m. before Theo let himself in. There had been a particularly brutal killing – a man had been set upon by a gang of youths who'd broken into an Indian restaurant. A knife had been used.

It had been harrowing, since the man's wife and two children were present in the restaurant.

Theo had been lucky. There had been evidence from a camera in the street, as well as one inside the restaurant. They'd rounded the perpetrators up in record time and they were being detained until it could be ascertained who had actually stabbed the man. The knife was still missing, but hopefully it would be found in a nearby alley or dropped down a drain.

He took a quick shower to rid himself of the crime, which still filled his nostrils, then in his bathrobe went through to the kitchen. There was his cake, slightly lopsided, and with a heart made from red smarties pressed into the top. Two wine glasses stood by it. He cut himself a slice, washing it down with a glass of milk. He noticed the champagne in the fridge as he put the milk bottle back in.

He drew a thick yellow envelope towards him and opened it. From Katie . . . the drawings he'd asked her to do. They were a jumble of eyes, noses and mouths – one with a chipped tooth, and a blank forehead with a straight fall of dark hair. There was a drawing of a hand with a word spelled across the knuckles. 'Now, what have we here?' He stared at it for a moment. SNUG it said. His eyes narrowed and he said softly, 'A tattoo. Good girl, Katie.'

He smiled then and took out the champagne. Time to put work behind him. He went to the bathroom to clean his teeth, and from there he wandered through to the bedrooms, wondering which one Lauren would have used.

She was in his bed . . . a good omen.

He sat on the side of the bed and gazed down at her, so vulnerable in sleep, her hand curled against her cheek. She looked so peaceful that it was a shame to wake her. But he would wake her! Leaning forward he gently kissed her.

Lauren opened her eyelids a chink and gazed at Theo through her lashes. He was seated on the side of the bed in the dim light from the hall, gazing down at her.

She grinned with pleasure at the sight of him. 'Hello, Theo darling.'

There was a smile in his voice when he drew his finger down her nose and said,'Hello sleepy, you're in my bed.'

'Isn't this where you want me to be? I can move into the spare room if you like. What's the time?'

'Yes to the first, I don't like to the second, and after two o'clock to the third. I'm sorry I'm so late.'

'It can't be helped in your job. How was the cake?' she said, and jumped when he popped the cork from the champagne.

'The best I've ever tasted.'

Propping herself up on the pillows she took the glass he offered her. 'Here's to your promotion Detective Inspector Ransom. I'm sure you deserve it.'

Swallowing her drink she gave a little shudder at the tart taste. A tiny belch slipped out. She stretched like a cat, making pleasurable noises. 'I feel quite comfortable in your bed.'

'You won't be comfortable for much longer.'

'Is that a promise?' Her hands went to the belt tied around his waist and pulled it undone. He finished his drink in a hurry and set the glass next to hers on the bedside table.

His mouth brushed against hers and he chuckled when she said, 'You taste of toothpaste as well as champagne.'

'It was either that or chocolate cake.' Shedding the garment he slid into the bed beside her. 'Let's get rid of the nightdress. Put your arms up.'

Obediently she did as she was told. Pulling the garment over her head Theo trapped her inside it while he stooped to kiss her stomach.

Her stomach hollowed, the muscles tightening as she swooped in air. She grabbed him by the hair, bringing his head up before he could move any lower, wriggling and laughing. He growled, then pulled her nightie off and threw it into the corner. Fitting his hands around her buttocks he drew her against him and gently held her there.

Light from a street lamp outside painted the planes of his face in shadow and light. The hollows of his eyes gleamed and his mouth was a scimitar of a smile. Theo's taut body was everything Lauren knew it would be – all of it rampantly male.

She wriggled closer, kissed his mouth and laughed when he grew hard against her. 'That's quite an advertisement.'

He pulled back a little, propped himself up on his elbow and gazed down at her, his free hand on her hip, his thumb gently caressing. 'Am I dreaming?'

'You're not.' Taking his hand in hers she kissed the palm, then gently nipped the fleshy base of his thumb.

He groaned, 'You'll never guess how much I've wanted this. Don't touch me this first time, else I'll burst.'

Lauren found her hands pinned, then Theo gently rotated her from her side on to her back and kicked the covers away from their bodies. When his head dipped and his tongue curled to paint the hardening nubs of her breasts she gave a soft gasp. His fingers entwined with hers against the pillow and he took her mouth with his in a deep, exploratory kiss.

Oh, God, she thought, every inch of her was so incredibly needful now that she didn't know where to start. And he had her hands pinned.

She liked her hands pinned, the feel of his palms pressing against her palms, his fingers dovetailed into the spaces between hers, the tips curling into the vee-shaped openings so the slightest of pressure was a caress of such eroticism that it raced through her body to alert each nerve end. She felt helpless to stop his plunder, knew that her strength would be powerless against his.

There was no sense of force about this. All she had to do was move her hands to free herself, but she didn't want to yet.

She hooked her foot over his calf, gently rubbed it. His tongue stroked into her mouth and touched against hers. He freed her hands and she threaded her fingers through his hair as his mouth shifted down to her breasts, then in a few minutes, lower still.

She had never experienced love-making so personal, so intense. But she knew what to expect, hadn't he told her over the phone in erotic detail. Yet when his breath touched against the moist centre of her, she gave a little sob of anticipation.

He placed a hand under each hip, lifted her slightly, parted her thighs and slid gently inside her. A little yelp left her mouth. It was extreme pleasure, like a shaft of ice stroking against an over-heated centre so they melted together. She remembered what Katie had said about a drop of water sizzling against Theo's skin.

It was she who was sizzling, though, and that turned into a molten heat. She gave a little cry as she experienced a kind of release. Immediately he was on his knees inside her spread thighs, his hand fumbling in the bedside drawer. She dared close her hands around his testicles and stroke the taut, silky skin. His penis stood up proudly.

'Any more of that will prove to be your downfall,' he said thickly.

She took the rubber from him, rolling it snugly along his shaft as if she was used to it. Immediately he pushed inside her, filling her slickness completely. His hands slid under her behind, his mouth covered hers and filled it with little rushes, timed with each thrust.

Excitement grew in her again and she whispered his name against his ear with each thrust. She wanted him closer so slid her legs up around his waist and locked him inside.

Giving a grunt of approval his stroke quickened, then he lost any semblance of control and began to thrust hard, fast and strong into her. His release came a few seconds after hers and all the urgency went from them. They collapsed in a heap together, limp and spent.

Lauren giggled and Theo chuckled. He kissed the end of her nose. 'That was definitely worth waiting for.'

'You didn't wait long, I was a pushover.'

'So was I, you shameless hussy. Will you stay tonight?'

'I'm here tonight?'

'I mean tomorrow's tonight.'

'Oh, I thought you meant today's tonight. Is it tomorrow already? Yes, I suppose it must be. All right, I'll stay tonight.'

Theo sighed. 'You know, Lauren, you're the damnedest woman for mixing me up.'

There were a few moments of closeness in their new intimacy as they gazed at each other in the dim light. Then a wide grin crossed his face and he ruffled her hair with his hands. For no reason, they both began to laugh.

Theo's stomach rumbled. 'I'm hungry,' he said unnecessarily.

'So am I. Will chocolate cake and champagne do us for between courses, d'you think? I read somewhere that it's good for the libido.'

He chuckled. 'My libido is suffering from an over-abundance of lust at the moment. But by all means let's indulge ourselves. You can go and get the cake while I visit the bathroom.'

Cake, champagne and lusts were all consumed satisfactorily before the night was over.

*   *   *

'You look like hell, and you're late,' Kevin said.

'Only twenty minutes.' Theo chuckled, remembering Lauren lying asleep amongst the crumpled, cake-crumbed sheets, her mouth and body smeared with chocolate. When he'd taken a last lick at her she'd smiled in her sleep and said, 'You can't go. You're under arrest.'

'I didn't get much sleep last night.'

'Like that was it?'

'You'd better believe it.'

'Well, keep your mind on the job, Theo. Those thugs you brought in last night are armed to the teeth with lawyers and social workers from the Community Legal Service, all demanding their rights.'

'Perhaps they need reminding that the dead man had rights, too.'

'The knife was found this morning. Kitchen variety, taken from the restaurant that belonged to the victim.'

'Fingerprints?'

'The handle was wiped clean.'

'Par for the course.'

Kevin grinned. 'The good news is that the kid who wiped it held it by the blade to do so. We have a thumb and forefinger, and there's blood under his nails. The bad news is, he's only thirteen years old. He comes from a decent home, has no juvenile record and does OK at school. His father and the family lawyer are coming in for the interview. Do it by the book, Theo. Get him interviewed, charged and bailed. A confession would be good. Whatever the outcome he's going to get nothing but a slap over the wrist. We can't hang about on this one.'

'What about the rest of them?'

'Straightforward breaking and entering. Two of them have turned eighteen so will be charged as adults. Both have got records as long as your arm so will do some heavy jail time.'

Theo got a break. The lad's father was an old-fashioned type who believed in children facing up to their crime and taking the punishment. Theo had the feeling the kid had taken too much heavy-handed punishment in the past when he lost his defiant air and began to snivel. He hadn't meant to kill anyone. He'd got in with a bad crowd and the break-in had been an initiation. The victim had lunged at him with the knife, and he'd grabbed it from him and turned it back at him. His confession was typed and signed.

'Self-defence?' the lawyer suggested.

Theo charged the kid with manslaughter and handed him into the keeping of his father. If the lawyer thought he could prove self-defence he could fight it out in court.

His sergeant had taken care of the other juvenile. Theo picked up the files of the remaining two – both adults.

One was Colin Smith, known as Smithy. The other was Carl Winchester, who answered to Guns. They had long records, petty crime mostly, starting off with vandalism, graffiti, car theft, driving without a licence. Then there was shoplifting, through to minor drug infringements, drunk and disorderly. It went on and on. Both were members of a right wing organization. Both had already done a stretch in juvenile prison. Theo wondered how they'd enjoy sharing a cell with the heavies.

Their lawyer came. He smiled at Theo. 'What is it we're looking at?'

'Both were involved in the same group break-in which led to the death of a man. Both men have juvenile records.'

'Did either of my clients have anything to do with the killing?'

'Not directly, as far as we can tell.'

They were an unlovely pair with shaved heads, dirty teeth, foul mouths and tattoos. Winchester had his street name tattooed on his fingers. When Theo gazed at it he remembered Katie's drawing. SNUG she'd spelled out. She'd been under extreme stress at the time. What if she'd mistaken it for GUNS?

Elation filled him.

A few hours later he watched the pair of them swagger from the station. They wouldn't be free for long. When this case went to court they'd be given a stretch. He'd wait, piece his facts together and then, with Katie's help would hit them with the sexual assault charge.

He felt no sympathy for any of them. He kept that for the man who was killed while trying to defend his premises and family.

'All in all a good day's work,' Kevin said. 'Fancy doing a TV interview?'

'No, you can accept the accolades for my hard work all by yourself. I want to get home early. I didn't have time for breakfast or lunch and I'm starving.'

'I've heard that bloodhounds work better on an empty stomach.'

'No . . . that's a sheepdog.'

'Maaaaaah!'

'Goodnight, Bo-peep.'

Theo couldn't get home fast enough. There was a delicious smell of cooking coming from his flat when he let himself in. What's more, Lauren was there to greet him, dressed in blue jeans and a plain blue shirt with the sleeves folded back. It was too big for her, probably because it was his. There was a warm smile on her face, a slightly abashed expression in her eyes, as if she'd recalled the abandoned enjoyment of their intimacy the night before.

He winked at her, and a delicate blush tinted her cheeks, as if she'd been a virgin bride on her wedding night. What had her love life with Charlie Parker been like if one night in his own bed could cause such a reaction in her? She hadn't seemed that experienced in the nuances of love-making, but once he'd led her into it she'd been wild.

'You have pretty blue eyes,' he said. 'Like bluebells.'

'Yours resemble a hunting hawk, only better.'

'I thought hunting hawks had reddish brown eyes.'

'I did say yours were better.' She slid her arms around his neck and kissed him, her mouth parting under his for the few moments of greeting. He felt like Saint George might have done when returning home after slaying the dragon – and enjoyed the feeling.

The smell of dinner set his juices flowing and he sniffed hungrily at the air. 'What's cooking?'

'A lamb roast.'

He laughed.

Fourteen

When Lauren went back to work the tension between herself and Samantha had eased. The coaches still kept coming, and cars with locals who had discovered Grantham Hall as a nice little country run on Sunday with a cream tea at the end of it, came in a steady stream.

There was now a security alarm installed for the lower half of the cottage, so they could have the bedroom windows open at night when they slept, but they had locks installed on the sashes, and the windows were not open wide enough for anyone but a small monkey or two cats to climb through.

Autumn was painting the leaves in orange, red and yellows. The occasional leaf drifted to the ground, but as yet the shedding off of summer was light. Samantha took over two of Lauren's tours, and she'd started work writing a potted history of her ancestors. There was plenty of material in the family archives, including one or two scandals to add pepper to the pot.

Pippa and Tony had reluctantly returned to their respective schools.

Katie was in her sixth month, and could no longer be mistaken for anything but pregnant. She took to driving like a duck to water.

Lauren hadn't seen Theo for a couple of weeks, though he'd phoned her on a couple of occasions. She wondered if he'd regarded their time together as a one-night stand. Then she wondered why it mattered to her when she'd blatantly let him know how attractive she found him. She had gone to him, not the other way round. She'd led him on. She hoped he didn't think she went to bed with every man she considered to be attractive.

Chocolate cake! Who would have thought it would turn out to be so sensual.

In the cottage they hadn't been long in bed one night when the phone roused her. It was the landline, she realized. Her mobile was on charge and she wondered if it was Theo.

Betty had got there first. 'Who is this?' she shouted, then banged the receiver down and shrugged. 'It must have been a wrong number. Bloody idiots ringing people at this time of night. The least they could do is say sorry instead of just hanging up.'

The clock said it was midnight.

Katie came down the stairs, rubbing sleep from her eyes. 'Who was that?'

'Wrong number.'

'I'm wide awake now. I'm going to make a drink. Does anyone want one?'

'Not me. I'm going back to bed.'

'So am I,' Betty grumbled.

Lauren had hardly got back in bed when the telephone rang again.

Katie took the call. 'Katie Parker speaking. No, this isn't Brook cottage, this is Blackbird's Nest, and no, we didn't order a pizza . . . at least, not tonight. That was last week.' There was a short pause, then Katie said, 'How did you get this number? Oh . . . it doesn't matter. I remember.'

Alarm prickled along Lauren's spine and she went down. 'How *did* they get the number?'

'We ordered a pizza for tea when you were away. I gave the number to them then. I thought it was my new mobile number I'd given them. I'm sorry.'

'No need to be. It's not much use having a landline if we're not allowed to use it. Goodnight, Katie.'

'Let's hope that's the last of the phone calls.'

But it wasn't. There was another one. The three of them gathered round the clamouring telephone and stared at it.

'Your turn,' Betty said.

'Lauren Bishop,' she said hesitantly. There was no answer, but the line was open for she could hear the faint sound of music. 'Brian, is that you?' she said cautiously.

The caller chuckled, then the phone call was cut off, as though a receiver had been hung up. It was unnerving. Lauren left the receiver off the hook, but the three of them got very little sleep for the rest of the night.

Lauren rang Theo early the next morning to tell him what had happened.

'Try not to let it rattle you, Lauren. You seem to have good security laid on. The phone calls might be unrelated. I was going to ring Katie. Is she there?'

'Still in bed after a disturbed night. I'll call her. Or I can give her a message.'

'Neither. I'll give her a ring on her mobile later. I've got something to tell her and it will afford her a bit of privacy to learn it directly from me, if you don't mind.'

'Why should I mind?' Lauren didn't probe any further, because Theo was right, Katie should be allowed some privacy. 'How are you, Theo?'

'Counting the days until I can see you again.'

Her heart began to ache and she felt like crying. He made it sound like she was precious to him. 'I was going to try and get up to see you next week, but in view of the phone calls I don't want to leave Betty and Katie alone here at the moment. Besides, Brian Allingham might ring me at any second. He'll want to know if I've found the drugs. I don't know what to tell him.'

'That you haven't found them. Tell him to give you a contact number.'

'I've tried that.'

As if on cue Katie's mobile began to ring. There was a sudden, angry yell from Katie. 'How did you get my new number? Don't think you're going to get away with this. I've had enough. I know who you are and I'm going to call the police and report what you did to me. You can tell Brian Allingham that, too.'

'Hang on, Theo,' Lauren said urgently. 'I think Katie just got another call.'

Katie's face was as black as thunder as she stomped down the stairs. She went into Lauren's arms and burst into tears. 'I'm sick of this, it's so creepy, and I'm getting scared of my own shadow. I hate them! I hate them! Isn't it enough that they did this to me, without them rubbing it in every five minutes.'

Lauren held her gently. 'Theo's on the phone, my love. He has some news for you. D'you want him to ring back.'

'No, I'll speak to him now.' She pulled some tissues from a box and blew her nose.

Betty came out of her room. She looked fatigued as she greeted them and headed for the kitchen.

'I'll go into the kitchen and help your Gran with breakfast while you talk to Theo. Call me if you need me.'

Katie's anger evaporated, leaving her feeling upset and vulnerable. 'Hi, Theo,' she said, trying not to sound too much of a drag.

'Hi, sweetheart. You're having a rough time of it from what I heard.'

A sob gathered in her throat. 'Why won't they leave me alone?'

'Because they're cowards who get their kicks from trying to ruin other people's lives. Putting the frighteners on you is an attempt to ensure your silence.'

'That's what *they* think,' Katie said.

'The good news is that I think – am almost sure, that I know the names of the men who assaulted you. I identified them from those drawings you did, especially the tattoo.'

'Who are they?'

'It would work against your interests if I told you that. At the moment they have other charges against them, which are unrelated to what happened to you. They should get some jail time for that. Later, I'm going to ask you to try and identify them from some mug shots.'

'What if I can't?'

'Then I'll have to try and get a confession out of them, implicating Brian Allingham if at all possible. If I can find the tape it will help.'

'And if you don't?'

'I won't charge them until I think there's enough evidence to make it stick.'

'How long would they be in prison for?'

'That would be up to the judge. They face about a year to eighteen months for the present charge. If they're found guilty of the sexual assault you were subjected to, I believe it carries an average sentence of about seven years.'

'And if they're not found guilty?'

'I can't answer that, and I can't guarantee that they won't be, but there's a better than average chance that they will if the case is presented properly. There's always a risk.'

'What about Brian Allingham?'

'It will be harder to prove he was actually part of the attack, unless . . .'

'Unless what?'

'It will strengthen the case if your baby's DNA matches his, but it won't prove it was rape. When we catch him he'll be given a hefty sentence as it is. Perhaps there will be more charges against him if things work out with this drugs thing. He may even go down for life.'

'If I go ahead with this I want him charged as well. If it wasn't for him . . . I hate him! I hate them all! If they hadn't kept ringing me to gloat I probably wouldn't have gone ahead. Now they've made me mad, so it serves them right.'

'OK, Katie love. I know it's difficult but I advise you not to do anything from an emotional standpoint. You might regret it.

Think it over. Weigh up the risks as well as the benefits. Talk about it to your counsellor and take her advice. She can ring me if she needs to.'

'Thank you, Theo. You're really nice.'

'Well, that's between you and me, so don't tell anyone else. I'm a copper and have a reputation to uphold.'

Katie managed a smile at that. 'Do you want to talk to Lauren again?'

'I do, but haven't got time now. You can do something for me, if you would, though.'

'What?'

'Tell her I love her.'

'Oh, Theo, that's so romantic . . . she's really gone on you, you know.'

But Theo was gone too.

The baby inside her began to move. It felt weird. Her hands covered the swelling as it pushed against her palms. She imagined it in black boots with a shaved head, a tattoo of a swastika on its forehead and rings in its nose. She shuddered that this *thing* had been forced on her. What a way to be created – in hate. No, not even that, for they'd had no reason to hate her. They'd treated her like she was nothing, just some piece of rubbish. They'd assaulted her for the fun of it . . . or because Brian Allingham had paid them. And he'd raped her because the sight of what had been going on had excited him. He was a dirty old man, and she wanted him to pay for that. Once they were made to pay she'd feel better.

Oh yes. They needn't think she was going to wallow in self-pity for the rest of her life. She was going to unload the kid, then forget about them. It would be like it never happened.

'You wait, Brian Allingham,' she muttered. 'Theo will sort you out. I hope you never get out of jail.'

But for the first time she wondered whether it was a girl or boy she was carrying. She hoped it wasn't a boy because it might take after its father . . . whoever *that* was.

When she went through to the kitchen to give Lauren Theo's message, Lauren blushed, then shrugged. 'Don't get things wrong, you two. Theo doesn't mean he loves me in a profound sense. It just means that he values me as a friend.'

Betty gave a hoot of laughter. 'My God, you don't arf get your knickers in a twist with words. *Friend,* my arse! Judging by the smile you've been wearing since you came back from London it's more than that.'

'*Sizzle! sizzle!*' Katie said.

How much sizzle Theo possessed was going to remain Lauren's business, but she grinned. 'Oh, do be quiet, you two.'

Katie decided to tell Lauren and her Gran what Theo had told her. 'Theo wants me to think about it, so I'm going to talk it over with Eve the next time she comes. Then I'll decide.'

Betty had the sense to keep her opinion to herself on this occasion, but she grunted, 'Well, at least he's let you know what you're up against with those scumbags. And don't forget you have family.'

The slightly perplexed smile Katie offered Betty went unnoticed by her grandmother.

Lauren kissed Katie's forehead after she stood. 'Whatever you decide, you have my backing, and my help if you need it. Now, where's my bag? I've got to go to work. Be careful today. Keep the door locked while you're indoors. Ring me if anything untoward happens, and be wary of strangers.'

'As if we needed that advice from the duchess,' Betty said after Lauren had gone, and poured herself out another cup of tea. 'What are your plans for the day?'

'I intended to go to John Dunne's this morning. We'd planned to sort out some things for the church charity shop. He said his wife's clothes can go. And there's a whole pile of books and stuff. But I don't like leaving you here alone. Why don't you come with me, Gran? We can walk slowly so you don't get puffed.'

'I haven't got your energy, Miss. I'm going to clear up the breakfast things, then I'm going back to bed to catch up on last night's missed sleep.'

'I'll clear up if you want to rest. I'll try not to wake you when I leave, and I'll be back at lunchtime.'

'Don't forget to take your keys then.'

Charlie had done something right because Katie wasn't a bad little kid, Betty thought a little later when the need for a pee woke her. She still felt fatigued, but sleep seemed to elude her. She sighed as she got to her feet and headed into the bathroom. She might as well get dressed.

She'd just finished making a cup of tea when the doorbell rang.

She remembered just in time not to open the door, but gazed through the window. There was a lad in a crash helmet with a pizza box in his hands.

She opened the window a crack. 'I didn't order that.'

'Someone called Katie Parker ordered it over the phone. Is she in?'

'She'll be back in a minute.'

He held out the box. 'I can't wait all day, missus. D'you want this pizza or not?'

'Bring it to the window while I get my purse. How much is it?'

'Tell Katie I hope she enjoys it,' he said when she handed him the cash, plus a couple of shillings left over for a tip.

Betty closed the window and watched from behind the curtains as the lad left. Cheeky young bugger referring to Katie by her first name. He had a cocky walk to him. His balls must be squeezed tight in those stretch jeans he wore, she thought and laughed. From beyond the hedge a car drove off. Something struck her as funny about that, but she couldn't put her finger on it.

The pizza didn't feel very hot. She placed it on the kitchen cabinet. Tiger and Ginger jumped on the counter and sniffed at the box it was packed in.

She flicked at them with the tea towel. 'Get down you two. You know you're not allowed up here.'

But they jumped up again and were weaving around the box, purring deep in their throats, their eyes alert. She looked at the clock. It was gone noon. 'All right, we won't wait for Katie, and you can have some of mine. I'll cut off a couple of slices, put it on a plate and microwave it.'

The lid was taped each side. She used the knife to slice through it and lifted the lid. There in the corner of the box, whiskers twitching, was a rat.

Betty screeched at the sight of it and pushed the box away from her. The frightened creature jumped up into the air, then launched itself off the counter on to the floor. The pizza box followed suit, the contents spreading far and wide. The cats took off after the rat.

Picking up her skirt Betty stood on a stool and screamed while the trio chased around the lounge room. When they went up the stairs, she found the courage to descend from her perch.

She went into the kitchen and picked up the nearest knife, thinking: This isn't three blind mice and you're not the farmer's wife trying to chop off their tails with a carving knife. It's a rat, and you hate rats. She threw the knife into the sink. The rolling pin was a better bet. It would flatten the rat with one blow.

As she went back into the lounge the pain hit her in the chest, like a hand squeezing. She tried to take in a deep breath to ease it, but the pain moved down her arms and into her wrists.

'I'm having a heart attack,' she whispered.

She made it to the chair and sat there, doubled up, trying to breathe normally. Her pulse was pounding in her ears while she tried not to panic. In the opposite chair Harry Simpson sat, reading a newspaper.

How had he got in when the doors were locked? He must still have a key. She was glad he was here, all the same. 'I need an ambulance,' she gasped.

He gave her a smile, then rising, he walked towards the kitchen.

'I don't want water I need help, you useless article . . . I've got a bad pain in my chest . . . hey, the phone's in here,' she said.

Harry didn't come back. Everything seemed to slow down and Betty was damp with perspiration. Tiger strutted past her with the rat hanging limply in his mouth. Ginger followed after, making growling noises, his fur ridged around his neck like the mane on a miniature lion.

They sat in front of the door and gazed at her.

She gazed back at them, breathing harshly, and hoped Katie would soon be home.

'Thank goodness Katie got to you in time. You were lucky, Betty.'

'Call this lucky?' She was in a hospital bed, wired up to a machine that bleeped authoritatively. 'I had a heart attack. I can't even get out of bed for a pee?'

'It wasn't a heart attack. The cardiologist thinks it was a severe angina attack . . . a warning. Your blood pressure is sky high.'

'Well, all I can say is that I don't want to experience the real thing.'

'He says you've had these pains for some time.'

'Only because I told him so. What does he know?' She shrugged. 'All right, so I've had a few pains.'

'And headaches?'

'And headaches, and shortness of breath. And I haven't been sleeping well and my back itched last week and I've got ingrowing toenails. So what's new?'

'Oh, Betty, why didn't you tell me?'

'Because it wasn't any of your business, that's why. It's not as though I'm your mother.' Come to think of it she'd hate to be Portia Bishop, the cold bitch didn't deserve a daughter like Lauren. 'Besides, I didn't want to think about it, did I? If you're going to have a go at me wait till I'm better, I don't feel up to it at the moment.' Betty actually felt quite frightened and confused, but she wasn't going to admit to it. 'What are they going to do to me?'

'You're staying here over the weekend for tests. They need to get your blood pressure down. Then on Monday you're going to have an angiogram done to find out the extent of the blockage.'

'What's an angio whatsit?'

'The cardiologist explained it all to you. They thread a little camera through the femoral artery at the groin—'

'No! Don't tell me . . . I don't want to know.'

Lauren placed a hand over hers. 'It will be all right, Betty. They do lots of these procedures, and if they find a blockage it can usually be fixed. You'll feel much better afterwards.'

'Where's Katie gone?'

'She's in the waiting room. You frightened the life out of her.'

'Worse things happened in the war. I remember my mum telling me about a bomb dropping in the churchyard and sending a couple of coffins flying through the air. There were bones everywhere, like a bleeding charnel house. Kids are too soft these days.'

Lauren shuddered. 'And medical knowledge is much better advanced, so you can be thankful for that. Visiting time must be over. I'd better go now before I get kicked out.'

Betty clutched at her sleeve. There was something she needed to say. 'If anything bad happens to me you'll look after Katie, won't you?'

'There's no reason why anything untoward should happen to you, but yes . . . you know I will.'

Betty nodded, then looked around her and whispered, 'There's money in my sewing basket, hidden inside a pair of socks, lots of it. The plods missed it. Charlie gave it to me over the years, you know, and I never spent any of it. And my savings book is in there, too, and my jewels, and a small brown envelope with something in it. I decided to leave everything I've got to Katie, after all. I was going to make a will but I didn't have time.'

This negative train of thought from Betty needed to be discouraged. 'What am I supposed to do Betty, get out my violin? Where's the East End spirit you pride yourself on? You can make a will when you come home.'

'Hah! No sympathy from you, is there Duchess? You wait until you're sick and see what happens when there's nobody left on this earth who cares about you. And that Harry Simpson was worse than useless. He just walked off and left me lying there without a word. He's still got keys to the place, you know. How else could he have got inside. I looked across and he was just sitting there, reading a paper. He gave me the willies, I can tell you.'

'I'll ask Daniel to make inquiries. Do calm down, Betty. You're supposed to be resting.'

The nurse came in and took Betty's pulse, stuck a thermometer in her open mouth and gave Lauren an accusing look. 'Your grandmother should keep calm.'

'You should try a stronger sedative on her then.' Lauren kissed Betty goodbye and whispered in her ear, 'I'll visit tomorrow after work, Gran. In the meantime, behave yourself.'

The nurse made an exasperated sound when Betty removed the thermometer. She warned, '*Mrs Parker!*'

Betty ignored her. 'You won't leave Katie alone by herself, will you? That villain asked for her by name. The rat was meant as a warning.'

'Katie can come to Grantham Hall with me.'

As Lauren walked away Betty turned a fierce gaze on the nurse and said, 'All right, Florence Nightingale, let's get on with it. The sooner I can get out of this place the better I'll like it.'

'Will she be all right?' Katie said as the pair of them walked towards the car.

'We'll know when the tests have been done. The cardiologist thinks that a couple of the arteries in her heart may be partially blocked, which restricts the blood flow when she's under stress. He said that if that proves to be the case there's a fairly simple procedure to correct the problem. She'll have to change her lifestyle a bit though – go on a low fat diet, lose weight and exercise.'

When they'd settled themselves in the car she asked Katie, 'Did you see an old man? Betty said he was in the house when she collapsed, and he must have a set of keys to the cottage because the doors were locked. Harry Simpson, she said his name was.'

Katie's mouth fell open. 'Harry Simpson?'

'Yes . . . do you know him?'

'Noooo . . .' Katie grinned as she said cautiously. 'John Dunne told me that a Harry Simpson used to own the cottage we live in.'

'Ah, so he did. Now it belongs to his grandson in Australia. So Simpson senior could have a set of keys to the place.' Thrusting the key into the ignition Lauren started the car and began to back out of the parking space.

'That's not really possible. You see, Harry Simpson died about eight years ago, shortly after he was sent to that nursing home. Gran must have seen his ghost. Mr Dunne did tell me that his ghost had been seen at the cottage.'

'Are you trying to tell me that the cottage is haunted?' She remembered Daniel mentioning that it had a reputation of being haunted. But then, so did Grantham Hall, and in all the time she'd lived there she'd never seen anything even slightly resembling a ghost. That sort of stuff was nonsense . . . wasn't it? But Betty didn't imagine things.

'Yes it is haunted, I can feel it. Though I haven't seen his ghost myself, have you?'

Lauren gave Katie a quick glance to see if she was joking. The girl's eyes were as round as saucers. Come to think of it she sometimes had a spooky feeling, as if she was being watched.

As the meaning of it sunk in goosebumps ran up her spine. Lauren jumped and her foot depressed the accelerator. She shot out of the parking space and there was a sudden squeal of brakes followed by the sound of a horn, the screech of tyres and a tinkle of glass. Too late she stamped on the brake pedal.

'Creeping Jesus!' Katie whispered. 'You certainly know how to attract the cops.'

Lauren became aware of flashing lights. She drove back into the space she'd come out of and sighed when a man in a uniform appeared at the window.

'Are you all right, miss? You look as though you've seen a ghost,' the officer said with some concern.

'No, I haven't personally seen one, officer. But I've just learned that someone I know has. It startled me, and that caused me to . . .?'

'Back out of a parking space without indication or undue care,' he finished for her. 'Very ingenious, young lady. I'm Sergeant Curtis. Now, perhaps you'd like to turn off your engine and hand me your driving licence. Then you can blow in the bag in case that spirit you mentioned is still having a bad influence on you. I'll be able to arrest him once we've got him confined. Then we can take his statement and he can witness in your defence.'

Katie began to giggle.

Fifteen

'You did what!' Theo said, and began to laugh.

'Don't you dare laugh, Theo Ransom. Being fined for a traffic infringement was the end of an extremely upsetting day.'

'Tell me about it?'

'Somebody delivered a pizza with a live rat in it. When Betty opened it the rat jumped out. She panicked, and the stress brought on a severe angina attack. Katie found her when she came in and called an ambulance.'

'How is she?'

'Giving the hospital staff a hard time. She's out of danger and they're going to do some tests and decide on the treatment and a medication regime tomorrow. The thing is, Theo, the man was wearing a motorbike helmet, yet he got into a car when he left. And he asked for Katie by name. We think it might be the same man who's been making the nuisance calls, and it must be linked to that assault on her. First it was the phone calls. Now they know where we live. And then that awful policeman was so sarcastic when I told him about the ghost startling me.'

'What ghost was that?' he said quite seriously.

'The ghost of Harry Simpson. Betty's seen him twice. I thought Harry Simpson was alive when Betty mentioned him a couple of times, but when Katie told me he was a ghost I jumped. My foot hit the accelerator and I backed into a police car . . . rather fast. It was only a little dent. When I told the constable about the ghost he said if he caught the spirit in the breathalyser bag he could act as a witness in my defence.'

Theo chuckled. 'I think I smell a rat.'

'You're being perfectly horrible not to take this seriously.' She laughed anyway. She couldn't help it.

'I do take it seriously, believe me. Tell you what I'll do, my love. I'll have those thugs rounded up and they can spend the night in the lock-up. Will that put your mind at rest?'

'What if you can't find them?'

'I'll ring you if I don't. Didn't someone offer to put you up if needed?'

'Yes, but I really don't want to involve anyone else in this.'

'You do have security. I can only suggest that until this is over you park your car out of sight, then map out a route to it. Somewhere where you can get to it in a hurry if you have to escape. And plug the number of your local police station into your telephones. I'm going to alert them to what's going on and ask them to keep an eye on the cottage.'

She thought for a moment. 'There's an old Roman road on the other side of the copse. I could leave my car there. There's a track through. I don't know if I can find my way in the dark, though.'

'Leave a torch with your car keys in a handy place, and use some of that white ceiling paint to mark the trunks. Down near the bottom, where the torch will show them up.'

'All right.'

'Have you heard from Allingham, at all?'

'I would have called you if I had. Perhaps he's found what he was looking for.'

'We'd know if a large amount of drugs had been released on to the street.'

'How?'

'Mostly word of mouth. The stuff is sold off cheap at first, so there's usually an increase in drug-related deaths as a new lot of users are hooked. Then there's an increase in petty crime as new users try to find the money to support their habit. They become dealers, but snort, smoke, swallow or inject the product they're supposed to be selling, and get into debt. Then it's prostitution or crime, sometimes both. Many of the users end up on a slab in the morgue.'

She gave a small cry of distress. 'How can you stand it!'

'Because I have to. It's part of my job. But sometimes something good comes out of it to restore my faith in human nature.'

'Such as?'

'Katie . . . that's one gutsy kind of girl, just like her grandmother but not so raucous. You wouldn't expect someone like her to emerge unscathed from her background. But she did. Despite everything, she's strong. And she's not going to let what happened spoil her future. She has you to thank for that.'

'Me?'

'It was you who gave Katie support when she needed it. You accepted her unconditionally and you provided a buffer between her and her grandmother.'

'Betty's contrary by nature. She likes to be able to say, "I told you so" if something doesn't work out. It doesn't mean she doesn't care. Believe me, she does.'

'Then there's you, my Lauren. So capable, yet so defenceless. You trust too easily.'

His tender voice brought tears to her eyes. 'Are you worried about me, Theo?'

'You see more good than bad in people, and I'm too far away from you to be of much use if anything happens. Be very careful. If word of this shipment gets out there will be other people looking for it besides myself and Brian Allingham. The fact is, I need a breakthrough. And I want no more heroics from you, Lauren. No sneaking about in empty houses and garages in the middle of the night. No meeting Allingham behind my back.'

'I said I wouldn't.'

He sighed. 'I know what you said. But you don't always do what you say you're going to. You get ideas in your head and

are unaware of the danger you put yourself in. I must go. Close
your eyes for a moment. I want to kiss you.'

She could have sworn she felt his lips brush gently against
hers and she sighed. 'I think I love you, Theo Ransom.'

'I think you do, too. Take care,' he whispered, and was gone.

Theo made good his promise to haul in the thugs.

'On what charge?' Kevin said.

'I just want them off the street tonight.'

'Be careful the little darlings don't accuse us of harassment.'

'I'd like to kick their punk arses around the block. Sometimes
I wish they'd bring back the stocks. Betty Parker is hospital-
ized with heart trouble, brought on by the rat attack. Lauren is
so distracted that she backed into a police car outside the
hospital. Katie is holding on, but seems to be the victim of the
mischief. Both of them need a night of unbroken sleep.'

'Am I to take it that you think Allingham is at the back of
all this?'

'I'm sure he is. He seems to be lying low, or someone is
hiding him. There's something I'm missing.'

'Perhaps you'll find it in that box Constable Graham sorted
out for you. By the way I think the fair Davinia has the hots
for you.'

'Is that the blonde one with . . .'

Kevin held his cupped hands at arm's length and grinned.
'That's her. I think those tapes have given her ideas.'

'I was going to say with a Scouse accent.' Theo groaned at
the thought of Davinia Graham making sheep's eyes at him every
time he walked past her. 'Fortunately, the videos have paralysed
my libido.' OK, so he was lying! 'How many DVDs this time?'

'About twenty. She said they're the last.'

'Well, that's something.' He heaved up the box with an exag-
gerated sigh.

There was no tape of Katie Parker's assault. Theo could only
conclude that Brian Allingham had it, as he said he had. Or
perhaps it had never existed in the first place.

The next morning Theo got to work early. He made himself
a mug of coffee and hugged it between his hands as he took a
good look at the board.

Down one side was a picture of Charlie Parker and his wife
Jean. Katie was underneath. After a space there came Betty

and Lauren, her hair longer and with a couple of strands blowing across her face. Mentally, he blew her a kiss.

To the right of the board was Allingham and his wife, Carla. Carla was big on hair, which was several shades of blonde and unnaturally natural. Her skin was a burnt orange, applied with a heavy hand from a tube. Her eyes were spiked with black mascara and were as hard as nails.

'Frightening,' Kevin said from beside him, making him jump.

'What are you doing in so early?'

'I've got some paperwork to catch up on. I could ask the same of you.'

'I woke early and couldn't get back to sleep. Who else besides Brian Allingham and his missus was likely to know what Charlie was up to with the drug deal?'

Theo puzzled over it out loud, 'Look beyond the obvious.' Only one person occurred to him and he muttered, 'Monica Spencer?'

'Who's she?'

'Charlie Parker and Brian Allingham's receptionist. She's just a teenager.' Theo wrote the young woman's name on the board with the electronic pen. Monica's picture came up. She had dark eyes and was a bit on the plump side.

'Marvellous things those,' Kevin murmured. 'Saves paper.'

'Mmmm.' Theo's eyes sharpened in on Monica Spencer's photograph. She was a pretty girl. He dipped into the box, pulled out a DVD and smiled in satisfaction.

'What's that?'

'You'll see.' He slid it into the video unit and they watched it in silence. He stopped the film and zoomed in on a hand. 'Why . . . if it isn't one of my resident thugs,' he said. 'Monica doesn't look like a willing party. She's out cold. Someone has dubbed in the screams and groans, but it hasn't been edited properly. See that mirror on the wall, there's the back of the cameraman in it. There appears to be a ring on his little finger and he's going bald. If you listen carefully you can hear voices faintly in the background. The experts should be able to bring the details out.'

'You don't intend to show that to the girl, do you? The bastard has been very intrusive with that camera.'

'She's only seventeen. I'll take someone from the sexual assault unit and let them handle it.'

'Let's have a look at her statement.'

A woman constable had taken the statement from her. The girl was seventeen, and had worked in reception for nine months, ever since she'd got her diploma from the secretarial school she'd attended in Bristol. She wanted to be an actress, but her parents had thought secretarial work would be something to fall back on. She'd come to London to see if she could get into the theatre. She knew nothing of what her bosses had got up to. She didn't know about the first Mrs Parker or her daughter, but she'd met Lauren twice and had been invited to her birthday party.

She was a bit, well you know, stuck up, like a real lady. But she was nice to me. I was surprised that Charlie had married someone like her. When I told him she was too good for him, he laughed. He said she had class and he'd married her because he worshipped the ground she walked on and it was the only way he could get her into his bed at the time.

Theo winced at that. Monica Spencer had gone on to say that Mr Parker had been a generous, easy-going boss. He had been going to arrange for her to have a screen test with Mr Allingham. When asked about Brian Allingham she'd said she didn't know him all that well. He was more on the production side, while Mr Parker handled the distribution. But he was ever so nice to her when they met. She'd spoken to Mrs Allingham about becoming an actress. *I asked her if I needed to lose weight and she said that physically I had what it took to be a photographic model. She gave me a test to see if I was comfortable in front of a camera. She asked me to take my clothes off and took several photographs of me in a white bikini she gave me to wear.*

A white bikini had been ripped from the girl in the DVD, Theo thought briefly.

I think I fell asleep because I can't remember much. When I woke I was dressed, but I can't remember putting my clothes back on. I felt funny, sort of dizzy. Charlie told me off when I got back to work and asked me where I'd been for all that time. I told him about the test and stuff. There was a big row. He and Mr Allingham nearly came to blows.

Lauren had said that Charlie Parker had come home upset one night.

Charlie was furious. He ripped the film from the camera and exposed it. Mr Allingham said that I should be sacked for lying

*or made to apologize. I hadn't accused him of anything, and
I didn't want to lose my job, so for the sake of peace I said I
was sorry. He was nice to me, was Charlie. He said he was
going to buy Mr Allingham's half of the business, but to keep
quiet about it, and he gave me a pay rise. We began to go out,
night clubs and places. His wife didn't understand him . . .*

Theo groaned.

*Not that he'd hear a word against her. Charlie liked a social
life, you see, and they slept in separate bedrooms. He made me
laugh, said he knew some agents he could introduce me to. I
liked Charlie a lot.*

Charlie Parker had liked them young, but legal, Theo thought
with some distaste. Monica was seventeen, and star-struck. Both
men were predators. But while Charlie manipulated and
charmed his prey, Brian Allingham took what he wanted by
stealth and by force, and he added value to it by filming and
selling it.

He remembered Kevin was still there and looked up at him.
'What sort of boss would allow a junior receptionist to call
him by his first name, and discuss his wife's faults with her?'

'A boss who intends to get inside her knickers. He's going
for the sympathy angle.'

'Exactly what I thought. Charlie Parker was a busy boy. But
Allingham is an out and out villain. It sounds as though Monica
Spencer was given a date rape drug by Allingham. And it's
looking more and more as though Katie was assaulted out of
revenge.'

He wondered if Lauren had known about Monica Spencer.
Probably. But the marriage had been over as far as she'd been
concerned, so she wouldn't have let it bother her.

Kevin patted him on the shoulder. 'Don't forget it's your
evening for coming over to dinner. Be prepared . . . word has
got back to Rosie about your lady friend.'

'No kidding! How?'

'How do you think? Nothing stays secret in this nick for
long. You should stay away from her until this is over. For
Christ's sake, Theo, think about the harm this relationship could
do to you. The Parker woman could be up to her armpits in
this shit.'

'Her name's Lauren Bishop, not Parker. Now, I'm going to
tell you something that's for your ears alone. I'm like a pin to

a magnet. All the willpower in the world couldn't prevent me from seeing her. I've fallen in love. I'm going to marry her if she'll have me, and that's it.'

'You're playing with fire, friend.'

'I know . . . but I'm allowed some privacy in my personal life, and telling you is just a courtesy. I'm not looking for advice.'

'It would make sense if I took you off the case.'

'But you won't.'

'Why won't I?'

'Because you trust my instincts about people and you know I'll bring this case to a satisfying conclusion, whatever the cost to myself. And I'll find that drug stash even if I have to put my snout to the ground and sniff it out of its hiding place, myself.'

'Well, don't say I didn't warn you.'

'The worst anyone can do is suspend me. If that happens I'll resign and go into business for myself, and the first thing I'll do is take up where I left off. The next time Lauren comes to London we'll all go out to dinner and you and Rosie can have your curiosity satisfied. Now, go and get on with your paperwork like the good little policeman you are, Guv.'

Kevin groaned.

'We'll hire someone else to do it when we're PIs.'

'Tempt me, why don't you?' Kevin ambled off grumbling to himself.

Monica Spencer was holding something back. Her eyes shifted from side to side and she mumbled and kept taking deep breaths.

She lived in a bedsitter. The place was messy. Clothing was heaped up on the bed, shoes scattered around the floor. Monica picked up a pile of magazines from the table and moved them on to the floor with an apologetic look. 'Sorry, I haven't had time to clean, I've been trying to find work.'

Monica made them a mug of tea. Theo knew she was trying to gather her thoughts together. He didn't want her to. The more panicky she felt, the less likely it would be that she'd come up with a plausible lie.

The plain-clothes specialist sergeant who had come with Theo had skirted around the subject of sexual assault without success. Theo was getting impatient.

'Do you know the whereabouts of Brian Allingham?' he asked the girl bluntly.

Her eyes met his, skittered away.

'Before you answer I'll tell you that he's wanted for questioning over the sexual assault of a young woman. She was given a date rape drug and the assault was filmed for distribution via DVD.'

There was a worried look in the eyes that met his, but this time they stayed and she asked, 'Will he go to jail for it?'

'Quite possibly. We're still looking for evidence. It seemed to have gone missing.' He threw the DVD into her lap. 'It's similar to this DVD we found. It's a young girl who's wearing a white bikini. She's about the same age as you, and looks remarkably like you. There's a young man involved. He's known to us.'

'It *is* me, isn't it?' she said in a low, wobbly voice.

Theo made his questioning more sympathetic. 'Why didn't you tell us that you'd been sexually assaulted?'

Monica Spencer seemed to deflate, and tears came to her eyes. 'I wanted to, but I couldn't quite say it. I wasn't sure, you see.' She picked up the DVD. 'Can I keep this?'

'I'm afraid not. It's the only copy we have.'

Hope came into her eyes. 'It hasn't been distributed then?'

'Not as far as I can tell.'

'Can I see it?'

He looked enquiringly at the special sergeant. Pamela Roberts was a woman in her early forties. She was a comfortable woman with a motherly look to her. When she nodded, he said, 'I'll wait outside in the hall. Call me when you're ready, Sergeant Roberts, and I'll question Miss Spencer again.'

It wasn't long before he heard Monica cry out in distress, then she began to sob.

Monica's eyes were red with crying. She was reluctant. She said that she'd think about charging the two men with sexual assault.

'Has Brian Allingham threatened you, Miss Spencer?'

She nodded.

'Do you know where he's staying?'

'No, I don't . . . honestly.'

'Why did he contact you?'

'He wanted to know where Charlie stored things.'

'Did he say what sort of things?'

'No . . . but I got the impression it was about drugs. I caught Mr Allingham snorting once. He offered me some, only I didn't want to get into that sort of stuff.'

'Very sensible. Did Mr Parker deal in drugs?'

'No . . . at least, I don't think he did. He said he'd been involved with drugs when he was a kid and somebody had given him a chance to go straight. He'd never touched them since.'

Charlie Parker going straight? The man sold child pornography! Theo tried not to laugh. The girl was still young enough to believe a line dished up from a seasoned con man like Charlie. But still, it was consistent with what Lauren had told him, and believed.

'Monica. I have to ask you this. Did you and Charlie Parker share a sexual relationship?'

Her eyes rounded into saucers. 'Oh, no. Charlie was a real gentleman. He used to give me flowers and presents and we used to go out together. But he never attempted to lay a finger on me. He was trustworthy, and he was such fun. He made me laugh.'

There it was again. He'd even made Lauren laugh. Charliesque, she'd said of the bigamy, as though cheating on his wife – *on his two wives* – was some comedic talent Charlie possessed and could be forgiven for.

Well, Charlie might have been funny, but he was also a thieving bastard who didn't give much thought to others. He was also turning out to be an enigma, Theo realized. Women still liked him, even after he'd done the dirty on them.

'So what did you tell Allingham?'

'Just that Charlie didn't do drugs. He sneered something about Saint Charlie then warned me that I'd be in trouble if I went running to the police.' Her glance darted fearfully towards the door. 'He's got friends, and he might be watching the flat.'

'I doubt it. He was just trying to scare you. Are you sure you can't think of anywhere he might be hanging out?'

Monica thought for a minute, then said tentatively, 'This is probably nothing, but when he was on the phone I heard something . . . water splashing. I thought he might have been in the bath when he made the call, but then I heard the sound of an engine. The water became louder, as if waves were slapping against the side of a boat. I think the engine noise might have been a boat going by.'

Theo smiled at her. 'You're an observant girl, Miss Spencer. I'll make sure the tape is destroyed once this is over. If you decide to have him charged, let Sergeant Roberts there know.'

'What about that other girl. Is she going to be a witness?'

'I believe she will be if we can find the evidence.'

'How old is she?'

'The same age as you. Seventeen.'

'Isn't she scared?'

'Yes, I think she might be . . . but she thinks he should pay for his crime. She's of the mind that exposing him is the right thing to do, and it might stop him from ruining another girl's life.'

'What d'you think?' he said to Pamela Roberts as they clattered down the uncarpeted stairs.

There was a woman in a concealing scarf coming in as they went out. She turned towards the first door and fumbled in her shopping basket for her keys. Theo pulled the door to behind him.

'I think you handled her well. Not too much pressure, but enough to make her think.'

'Thank you. I wasn't fishing for compliments, but rather your impression of whether she was telling the truth.'

'I hope you don't mind, but I read up on the case you're handling. Charlie Parker is interesting. He was a serial groomer of sorts, and liked the high that came with it. Interesting that his legal wife had been his first lover. Marriage to her had lost its charm, but he had a responsibility with the child, and he took that seriously. Even so, he fooled himself into thinking he loved his mistress.'

Sharply, Theo said, 'Miss Bishop thought she was his wife.'

'He must have held her in great respect to have risked going through a sham marriage. He also trusted her with his mother, something he didn't confer on his legal wife. Miss Bishop would have represented an ideal woman to him, one to be set on a pedestal and worshipped.'

Hell! He could think of much better ways of enjoying Lauren. 'Explain grooming to me.'

'A man like Charlie usually has two or three women on the go, sometimes more. One he's married to, one who's his mistress and a third one that's being groomed. He puts himself out to get number three to like him. He buys her gifts and takes her out, like an old-fashioned courtship. When the time comes to take the relationship further, someone like Monica would trust him and be ripe for the plucking. I expect he sensed that one of his relationships was coming to an end. There are always subtle signals. Indifference, lack of sexual response. If his relationship with Miss Bishop had ended he would have slipped Monica into place and looked for another girl to start the grooming process all over again. I don't think Monica and her boss were sexually involved, but it was getting close. Either his legal wife or his bigamous wife, or both, were about to cash the marriage in.'

'Then Allingham came along and ruined his plans for Monica.' Charlie got upset, Theo thought. He was going to end the business partnership. But whether he knew it or not, Brian Allingham had put the drugs deal in motion. Charlie had then discovered he had no way of backing out of it. So he'd paid for the drugs, took possession of them and had then hidden them. Why? Why not sell them on? Because having them had tipped the balance of power back into Charlie's hands. Theo felt a buzz go through him. Things were beginning to come together. He gazed at the policewoman with a new respect. 'What about Brian Allingham?'

'The man's dangerous. He has a need for power over a woman. He drugs his victims so they're helpless, then becomes aroused by watching them being violated.'

'And Carla Allingham?'

'She'd be a willing partner, and would derive just as much enjoyment from what's going on as he does. I'd go so far as to say that I think the pair of them are capable of murder if they're thwarted, or feel threatened.'

Which left Theo with a very nasty taste in his mouth indeed. How sordid it all was.

'Perhaps Monica should move somewhere safer until this is all over,' he said.

'I'll go back in and see if she'd be prepared to go back to Bristol and stay with her mother for a while.'

'D'you think she will?'

'There was an eviction notice on her table. Now she's not working she can't pay the rent.'

'You have sharp eyes, Sergeant. Tell her I'll personally pay her train fare.'

Pam Roberts smiled at him. 'I didn't think you'd be such a soft touch, DI Ransom.'

He shrugged. 'I believe you've got daughters?'

'Two.'

'Then you'd hope somebody would help them if they were in trouble.'

Her smile faded. 'You're right. Wait there. I won't be long.'

Pam had only been gone for a few minutes when there came the rumble of an explosion, followed by a louder one. Bricks and debris flew through the air. The blast pushed against the car and it rolled over and over towards the other side of the road with him inside it. Bits and pieces of glass rained down on him. After a while everything went quiet.

His ribs hurt, his head throbbed from being banged back and forth and blood trickled from several wounds on his arms and head. He could smell petrol and he shuddered at the thought of being trapped in a burning car.

He was on his back, compressed into a small space, the car crushed to the top of the seats. Putting his feet against the crumpled door he managed to push it open, then flat on his back he clawed his way out and gazed at the house. The front had been blown into the street, and a gas pipe was gushing flame. There was no sign of Monica or Pamela Roberts. The roof had caved in to her small flat.

A man got out of a car at the end of the road. He started to walk towards him. He looked like Allingham, and Theo started towards him, his legs wobbling so much that they could hardly hold him.

'Allingham,' he called out. The man turned away, ran back towards a car, jumped in and drove off. It struck Theo as odd.

People were running towards him now. His legs collapsed from under him. He reached for his phone to thumb in emergency, then hauled himself to his feet. He had to keep this lot away from the scene, though he could already hear sirens.

He found his warrant card. Swaying back and forth like a drunk on Saturday night, he stood there, thinking that at least he could stand up, even if his sight was blurred and he felt sick. 'Keep away from the scene,' he croaked. 'It's dangerous.'

'Hey, are you all right, mate? Let me help you.' A muscular arm came round him in support.

Theo was grateful for it because the world was going dark. 'Keep them away from the scene until the emergency services get here. Make sure nobody smokes. Tell them . . . tell them . . . a policewoman and a teenage girl. Attic flat. Another woman downstairs. Tell them . . .' Theo heard the sound of sirens and began to shake with the relief of not having to be responsible for the carnage. But something urgent came to his mind and he clutched at the man's sleeve. 'Tell Lauren they're in danger, and to get out of the cottage.'

'I'll tell them. Now don't you worry about anything,' the man said, and gently lowered him to the ground.

That was the last thing Theo remembered before the world faded out to the sound of sirens.

Sixteen

The day had been quiet, and Lauren found herself with some free time to get on with her writing. Samantha didn't want a dry history, just something interesting and easy to read, especially if there was a hint of scandal attached to it. Lauren was enjoying what she was doing. She did her best to accommodate her employer, within the bounds of researchable fact and with dashes of conjecture, clearly written as such.

When Samantha had set eyes on Katie that morning she eyed her stomach and asked her outright when the baby was due.

Lauren noticed the effort Katie had made to bite her tongue, but all the same, her answer had been terse. 'It can't come soon enough.'

'You should have been more polite to Mrs Bamford, Katie,' Lauren had said after Samantha had left. 'She doesn't know the circumstances of your pregnancy.'

'Oh . . . I thought everybody did,' she said bitterly.

'No, but they can see that you're pregnant, and it's natural to ask when the baby's due.'

But Katie had forgotten her own troubles when Lauren had

taken her on the tour with the tourists. She'd been overawed by the size of the house.

'It's totally wicked, and to think Lauren grew up here,' she said to Samantha the next time they ran into her, and without one iota of envy in her voice. 'Your children are so lucky. Thanks for letting me come here with Lauren. I'm sorry if I seemed rude to you earlier. I feel so fat and ugly . . . like a toad.'

'I felt like that when I was pregnant.' Samantha looked from one to the other. 'I had the feeling I said the wrong thing to you this morning. Is there something I should know?'

Katie shrugged. 'I might as well tell you, since John Dunne knows and he'll probably tell everyone, anyway. I was attacked by three men. I don't know who the father is.'

'Oh, my God! And you had the courage to go through with the pregnancy.'

'I didn't know who to tell.' She sent Lauren a smile. 'When I did tell someone it was too late to try to do anything about it. Besides, it's not the baby's fault. People adopt babies all the time, even rich people like film stars. Someone will love it.'

'Of course they will.' Tears glistened in Samantha's eyes. 'How brave you are, Katie. If you need any help, let me know.'

'I have Lauren and my grandmother to help me.'

'Grandmother?'

'Betty Parker. Goodness, doesn't your husband tell you anything.'

'He tends to keep business things to himself, but he probably thought I knew.' Awareness suddenly filled her eyes and she looked from one to another. 'I know about Lauren. I'm not quite sure where you fit in Katie.'

Katie's eyes flickered her way. 'I'm Charlie Parker's daughter – from his first marriage, that is.'

Good old Katie, trying not to hurt her feelings, Lauren thought.

'Oh, I'm so sorry. You lost your parents in an accident, didn't you? And you're friends with Lauren. How . . .' She shook her head. 'I don't understand.'

Katie took up a defensive stance. 'Lauren didn't do anything wrong. She took me in when I had nobody to turn to. She's the only friend I've got, except for John Dunne and Theo Ransom.'

'Theo Ransom?'

'He's the detective who's handling the case, and he's Lauren's squeeze.'

A sigh gathered inside Lauren and she tried not to grin at the thought of squeezing Theo.

Samantha did grin. 'Theo Ransom? I've heard that name before somewhere. You must have mentioned him to me, Lauren.'

Lauren didn't think so. She'd been wary of telling Samantha anything personal since the publicity stunt, and she couldn't help saying, 'I hope you'll keep Katie's confidence.'

Samantha's face hardened. 'I know you think I deserved that, but I apologized for that newspaper article and I don't need reminding of it. Besides, the journalist put two and two together by himself. If you'd put me wise in the beginning it wouldn't have happened. God, no wonder you got on your high horse.'

'It wasn't really your business, and I thought Daniel had told you. I'm sorry.'

Samantha sniffed. 'He's not a gossip and neither am I. You can come and help me if you like, Katie. You can put the carnations in their vases and set the tables for lunch if you want something to do. We have two coaches booked in for lunch today, one after the other, and I'm a bit short-handed now my niece has gone back to school.'

Katie gazed at Lauren, as if asking for permission.

Lauren received a prickly look from Samantha. 'I promise I won't ask her anything personal, and I won't give her anything too heavy to do. I'll also pay her.'

'You needn't pay me,' Katie said. 'I don't mind helping out. After all, Mr Bamford put all that security in for us for nothing, and he said we could stay here if we needed a bolt hole. He's ever so nice.'

Samantha's eyes narrowed slightly, and her question, heavily laden with suspicion, was aimed at Lauren. 'Greg said that?'

'Don't worry. We won't bother you unless we absolutely have to.'

Katie offered Samantha Charlie's killer smile. 'That's what friends are for, isn't it? To help each other out. Everyone has been so good to us here.'

Samantha melted under Katie's onslaught. 'We've plenty of room here. And thanks, Katie. I'll accept your offer of help.'

Later, Samantha sought her out in the library. She had a newspaper in her hand. 'Lauren, I've just remembered why that cop's name was familiar. You might want to see this.' She placed a newspaper on to the desk in front of her.

There was a slightly blurred picture of Theo, obviously taken with a mobile phone. There was blood on his face and his eyes were closed.

POLICE OFFICER FIGHTS FOR LIFE AFTER TERRORIST BOMB BLAST the headline said.

'Oh, my God! Theo!' Lauren traced a finger gently over his battered face, and tears collected in her eyes. How could someone so vibrant be on the brink of death? Grief filled her and the world took on a grey mantle. She gazed up at Samantha, her eyes brimming. 'I don't think I can bear it if he dies.'

'Hey,' Samantha said and her arm came around Lauren's shoulder. 'He's not dead yet. Neither is the other police officer. They're both in the hospital, along with a teenage girl. You know how these papers dramatize everything.'

Her tears came even harder. Oddly, it was strangely comforting to be on the receiving end of Samantha Bamford's sympathy, because usually she didn't have much to spare for anybody.

'You know, Lauren. You're much too independent. Instead of trying to take everything on your own shoulders, if you'd told me earlier what was going on I could have been of help to you.'

'Why should you have been, when we were complete strangers? I gained an impression that you resented me, and it was because of my connection with Grantham.'

'I did resent you, but it wasn't because of that. Hell, I'll never have your class in a thousand years; it's in your genes. It was mainly because I thought Greg liked you too much.'

'Greg!' She was filled with astonishment and gave an involuntary laugh. 'I like your husband a lot, too, but he's been an absolute gentleman. He's talked mostly about you when we've been alone together.'

'John Dunne told me that Greg went down to your cottage the last time I went out with the kids.'

'He did, to fix the security system. Both Betty and Katie were home, and I went up to London that evening. You don't want to listen to what John Dunne says. He's a gossip, and he told Katie you were . . .' She shrugged. 'Well never mind. He can't help it. Not only is he lonely, it's also his age. His mind wanders and he gets terribly mixed up.'

'He told Katie what? Let's get that out in the open to start with.'

Lauren pulled away and wiped the tears from her eyes. 'He said that you and Daniel were an item.'

Samantha began to laugh. 'I was at school with Lucy, and she's my friend. She and Daniel still love each other and I'm acting as a go-between, trying to get them back together. I know exactly what went on to cause the split. I'll say no more.'

'I'm aware it was my mother. But it does take two.'

'Daniel knows it and regrets it. At the risk of offending you . . . hell, take a look at that portrait of your mother in the hall. No man in his right mind would say no to her. She's a man-eater. You're not unlike her in looks.'

'There is a difference. I don't poach other women's men, so you don't have to worry about your Greg, even though I do think he's a very nice man.'

'Is that the case?' Samantha grinned. 'So what were you doing married to a bigamist?'

'Damn you, Samantha!' Lauren's laughter choked in her throat when she looked again at Theo's battered face. Here was the man she would love for ever, and if he hadn't been in the right place at the right time today, he could have lost his life. Suddenly, the respect she felt for him and his kind, doubled.

Her eyes skimmed down the page. Monica Spencer's name jumped out at her. Intensive care. Not expected to live. The bigamy case had turned into something else now. It was no longer amusing. If the Allinghams were prepared to kill a young girl who might act as witness against them, then they wouldn't stop at killing all of them.

If Lauren knew where the drugs were she'd tell them, put a stop to it.

She desperately wanted to see Theo, but Betty would need to take it easy for the next few days.

'Katie and I are going to visit her grandmother tonight. She'll be released tomorrow if all is well, but she'll have to rest. We'll probably move into a hotel.'

'Move in here with us, like Greg offered.'

'No. They're not playing games now. They've just blown up

a house in London to try and kill a witness. I can't risk the danger it would represent to you. This is not about porn peddling now. It's about drugs.'

Samantha hugged her tight. 'It would be better if you stayed. Nobody can get near here at night. I'll hire some extra security guards. You can get on with the writing, and Katie can keep an eye on her grandmother.'

Lauren gave a wry smile.

'You could have those three upstairs rooms with the bathroom and kitchenette attached, then we won't get in each other's way. You can have food sent up from the cafe, so you won't have to do much cooking. It will only be for a short while.'

Lauren began to waiver. The rooms offered had been prepared for her bedridden great-grandmother, so she could live as independent a life as possible with a nurse and maid in attendance. Lauren had been a child then, and terrified of the ancient, shaking old woman with her fierce eyes.

'Just think. You'll be able to visit your boyfriend in a day or two without worrying about the two of them.'

That was the clincher for Lauren.

Katie was excited by the move to the Hall. Betty was dubious. An angioplasty had been performed on her, the ballooning and stents opening up the partially blocked arteries in her heart. She looked and felt much better, but had to take things easy for a few days. Betty had been brought up on meat and potatoes, and had loved her roast dinners with Yorkshire pudding and lashings of gravy. Now she was fussing about her healthy diet.

'I'll have salads for lunch. And I might as well try some of that foreign muck on rice,' she said. 'Though to give it its due, when I tried a bit in the past it was quite tasty.'

'You can walk up and down the corridor for exercise,' Katie told her. 'And don't you overdo it.'

'Go and suck eggs, you cheeky little pest,' Betty retorted.

Greg and a security guard went to the cottage with Lauren and Katie as they gathered together the clothes they'd all need.

'Betty said to bring the cats, the litter box and the cat food, otherwise they'll think they've been abandoned, then they'll go wild and kill all the wildlife.'

'Don't forget to water my geraniums,' Betty had told them. Lauren did, hiding her car on the Roman road and making her way via the track through the copse. There, she made sure that all was well before entering the cottage.

'And what about your driving lessons, girl?' Betty had said.

'I've cancelled them until further notice.'

Over the week Lauren had tried several times to contact Theo, but to no avail. She was worried sick about him. His answer phone was turned off and the phone simply rang out. His mobile was switched off. A call to his police station drew a polite response. They didn't give out information about their officers, but if it was about a case she should leave her name and number and DS Wright would get back to her.

She hung up. There was nothing in the paper or on the radio except for the same conjecture being repeated over and over again.

Frustrated, she told Greg Bamford what was happening. 'Do you think he's . . .' and she could hardly bring herself to breathe out the word, '*dead?*'

'I know a few people, I'll see what I can find out,' he said.

Within an hour he was back. 'Word is they've got the three of them under wraps. Your boyfriend is severely concussed, and he has cuts and bruises. They're keeping him under observation until the swelling in his brain subsides. He's not fully conscious.'

'And Monica Spencer?'

'Broken arms and ribs. The woman police officer has a spinal injury. She's been operated on, and after some rehab should be able to walk, even if it's with a limp. Both females have first degree burns which should heal up without leaving a scar. Luckily, a couch they were sitting on saved them from further injury. It was blown on to the bed with them on it, turned upside down and shielded them from the worst of the blast.'

'Oh my God! How awful it all is. How did you manage to find out?'

'As I said. Contacts. I used to be special forces and I know somebody high up. That former business partner of your late husband is a serious player. You don't have a picture of him by any chance, do you? I can scan it into the computer system and it will warn me if he comes into the house as a tourist.'

'You think he will?'

He shrugged. 'He'll have to get past the security first. Who knows. I'd rather be safe than sorry.'

'She found a photograph in Betty's album, of Brian with Charlie, and handed it to him that evening. Now she hadn't seen it for a while, looking at Charlie was like looking at a stranger. Odd to think that she'd shared the bed of this dapper looking man with his wide, ready smile. It seemed a long time ago. Correction. It *was* a long time ago!

'Which one was yours? No . . . don't tell me. It was the one with the smile. I can see Betty and Katie in him. I'll see if I can sharpen the snapshot up on the computer. Allingham has probably grown a beard by now.'

She managed a rueful laugh. 'Oh, hell, Greg. Have I got to keep an eye out for bearded men as well? I want to go and see Theo.'

'Like I said, he's being kept under wraps.'

Her chin came up and she said with all the desperation she could muster, for if Greg put his foot down she knew it would stay down, 'I don't care if he's wrapped up as tight as an Egyptian mummy. I want to see him. No, I'm *going* to see him. Which hospital is he in, please?'

His dark eyes contemplated her for a moment, then he smiled. 'I've arranged for you to visit him tomorrow. I'll take you up and bring you back myself. Now, is there anything you want from the cottage in the meantime.'

'Yes . . . Betty's sewing basket.'

'A sewing basket?'

'She keeps going on about it. She's making clothes for Katie's baby, even though Katie insists it's going to be adopted. It's best that she has something to occupy her, it keeps her out of mischief. And I've got to water the pot plants in the conservatory.'

'You've been watering pot plants?'

'Will you please stop asking me questions after I've told you the answer.'

'Ouch! Sorry. Considering the danger you're in, watering pot plants is a stupid thing to do.' He glanced at his watch. 'OK . . . we'll go now. Rain is forecast for the next few days. We'll put the pots in the garden and they can look after themselves. Where do you usually park. We don't want to give anything away.'

'On the Roman road on the other side of the copse. There's a track going through. It's a seven-minute walk, and I've marked the tree trunks with white paint.'

The countryside was filled with autumn leaves drenched in a sunset. It made her heart ache.

The copse was quiet except for the crunch of falling leaves under their feet. As they reached the edge of the garden Greg put a hand on her arm. The cottage looked secretive in its setting, like something out of a child's story book. The windows sent back winking gleams of light as the lowering sun was filtered through the moving leaf canopies.

Quite suddenly, Lauren remembered Harry Simpson, who hadn't been able to bring himself to quite leave the place. She wondered if he was waiting for his grandson to come back, to move in and keep him company.

'Is it always this quiet, here?' Greg whispered.

'Always.' Lauren liked the silence. Her father had told her the secret of it, that if she listened the silence would open its door and show her the noises it held inside it. When she'd grown up she'd realized that the secret hadn't been exclusive to them. But it had seemed special to her at the time.

She had been hurting, and had asked where her mother had gone.

She's left part of her with you. All you need do is close your eyes and you'll hear her voice, he'd said.

She closed them now, but there was still no mother, there never had been. She'd been too long gone and Lauren realized that she'd never allowed her mother back in when she'd tried. But she'd discovered other things held inside the silence. There were always other things to comfort her. There was the faint breeze that stirred the leaves, the whirr of birds' wings in the sky and the rustle of a mouse in the undergrowth. On the main road a lorry rumbling by and church bells in the distance on Sundays.

She reached out to the cottage and into its dark interior. She saw the old man sitting there, alone with his sadness, thinking of his grandson who'd gone to Australia and left him behind. Life was too short to abandon those who'd provided for you in the first place, and she thought of her mother again. She had nurtured her inside her body and given her life. She should be more grateful. It was about time she got over her anger and reached out to her, she thought.

'I can't see anyone around, shall we go in?' Greg said.

There was a faint creak . . . a sudden, raucous squabble

between a pair of birds above in the branches. They took flight in a thrash of wings and leaves.

She jumped and gave a little scream when a man stepped out from behind a tree and said authoritatively, 'Hey! You two. Step out of your hiding place and show yourselves.'

Seventeen

When her heart stopped thumping Lauren smiled at the man. 'We meet again, Sergeant Curtis.'

'Oh, it's you, Miss Bishop. Out ghost hunting again, are we?'

She laughed. 'Actually, this is where I live.'

'Ah . . . I thought the name was familiar. I was asked to keep an eye on the place for anything suspicious.' His glance went past her to Greg. 'And you are?'

'Greg Bamford, owner of Grantham Hall. In the strictest confidence, Miss Bishop is my guest at the moment. We were just about to collect a couple of items she needs. You're conversant with the situation, I imagine.'

The sergeant nodded.

'The cottage has a lights, camera and action security system in place. As soon as we've finished here I'll be arming it. If anyone enters the grounds the lights will come on, followed by the cameras. If they enter the cottage an alarm will alert my security staff up at the hall. They can see exactly what's going on here, and nobody will be able to get near the cottage without an electronic key to switch it off, which is personalized with a six number code. I can contact you if there's an alarm.'

'You will not take matters into your own hands, I trust—'

'Sergeant Curtis, I'm not a fool, and neither are my security staff. They're both ex-army and fully trained in the use of unarmed combat and non-lethal weapons.'

The sergeant nodded. 'While I'm here I'd like to see the inside of the cottage, if I may.'

It didn't take long. He nodded, satisfied, and helped them to carry Betty's geraniums outside. Lauren picked up Betty's sewing box and her knitting basket, and anything else that looked like something Betty might need in the near future.

Just as they were about to leave the policeman said, 'There aren't any animals in the cottage, are there?'

'No, why?'

He turned back and gazed into the kitchen. 'Funny, I thought I saw something move in here.'

Lauren managed to keep her face straight. 'I expect it was Harry Simpson.'

'Harry Simpson?'

'The resident ghost.'

'Very droll. It was more likely a shadow of the trees reflected on the window.' His hand strayed to the back of his neck and he headed for the door.

She exchanged a grin with Greg as she followed the sergeant into the garden.

Avoiding the rush hour, they made a swift journey to London, concealed behind the smoked windows of Greg's Range Rover. They arrived at eight thirty, going directly to the police station, where they were shown into an interview room.

A man came in and took a seat opposite. He didn't look friendly when he said, 'Miss Bishop. Mr Bamford. I'm Chief Inspector Kevin Crane. I understand you wish to see DI Ransom. May I ask what your business with him is?'

The man was looking her over, taking her in, judging her. She said, 'I imagine you know why I want to see him.'

'Tell me.' Sharp blue eyes came up to hers. Copper's eyes . . . cagey . . . and angry with her for what had happened to Theo, because he had to blame someone.

'I need to satisfy myself that he's all right.'

'He will be. Is that satisfying enough.'

She remembered that this was Theo's best friend, and his immediate boss. 'I need to see Theo for myself. I'm worried about him.'

'So am I, and your needs don't come into it. What if I say you can't see him?'

'Then you say I can't. There's no need to be so damned hostile, is there?' She glared at him, she couldn't help herself, and remembered a police superintendent that her father had known. She could prevail on that friendship if she had to. 'And what's more. You might as well know that I'll go above your head if need be.'

'You've already done that.'

Had she? So that's why he was angry, she thought. She slid a glance towards Greg, who remained impassive as he said, 'It was my doing. Miss Bishop knew nothing about it. Her style is less subtle in a kick arse sort of way. If she wants something she usually goes for it, head on. Her weakness is that she usually tells people in advance what she's going to do.'

'And you are?'

'Greg Bamford, of Bamford electronics. I'm a friend of Miss Bishop. I'm also her security adviser, and at the moment her personal bodyguard. She's worried sick about DI Ransom. It's no skin off your nose to give her the go ahead without subjecting her to the third degree, is it?'

Surprise filled her at Greg's words. 'I love Theo, why should he refuse, unless . . .?' Her glance darted back to the eyes of the chief inspector, and she didn't care if they reflected her fear as she whispered, 'He will be all right, won't he? He hasn't—'

'For God's sake, of course he'll be all right. Theo is tough, he's already begun to improve. I just think you happen to be bad for him, lady . . . a complication he doesn't need in his life at the moment.'

She went for the throat. 'Then you're judging me unfairly. What's more, you consider Theo to be less of a man than he is. He wouldn't thank you for telling him what he needs in his life. If I said he doesn't need you guarding his cave door like a fiery dragon, especially with me on the sharp end of your toasting fork, how would you feel?'

Greg laughed out loud.

'Theo happens to be my closest friend,' the man said gruffly, and had the grace to look ashamed. 'You're right.'

'I'm quite close to him, you know,' she said more gently. 'But I don't imagine he's mentioned me in a personal sense.'

'You'd be wrong about that. He has, and I am quite aware of the relationship between you. I tried to warn him off but he wouldn't listen.' He sighed as he lumbered to his feet. 'I'll ring the hospital and find out when's the best time to see him.'

* * *

Theo was in a room on the top floor with a view over London. Not that he could see it, Lauren thought. He was still unconscious. His face was covered in cuts and bruises, made to look worse by the criss-cross of suture strips, and the occasional stitch tying the worse cuts together. Both eyes were blackened and he needed a shave.

Tears sprang to her eyes and she took his hand in hers and said uselessly, '*Oh, Theo!*'

He didn't wake, though his eyelids flickered and he muttered restlessly from time to time as she told him what had been going on.

'Betty is home from hospital now. Both she and Katie said to tell you they hope you soon recover. The Bamford family has been very kind to us. We're living at Grantham Hall until everything is solved. There are security guards to look after us, so we're quite safe.'

The half an hour she'd been allotted slipped by all too soon. Loath to leave him Lauren took a ball point pen from her bag, uncurled his fingers and drew a flower on the inside of each. Then she wrote in his palm, *I love you, my darling Theo. Always, Lauren.*

Kevin came into the room just as she'd finished. 'What are you doing?'

She placed a kiss on the message, curled Theo's fingers back over it and smiled. 'Nothing for you to worry about.'

He looked at Theo's palm anyway, then at her. He wore a faint smile. 'I guess you do love him at that. I'll make sure he sees that. You're everything he said you were.'

'Then we're friends?'

'I might be able to get used to you in time.'

She guessed she'd have to prove herself first. 'How's Monica Spencer and the other police officer?'

'Monica is terrified. Who can blame her now she knows what she's up against. I don't think they intended to kill her, since the blast was downstairs. But it ruptured a gas pipe. which made it worse. She's lucky to be alive, but her mouth has effectively been closed. A pity, since we have the bastard on tape. As for the police officer, she'll have to learn to walk again. She has a family to support.'

'And Theo? I hate seeing him so helpless.'

'The swelling in his brain is rapidly subsiding. The neurologist expects him to be fully conscious tomorrow. And before you ask – no, you cannot visit him tomorrow, even if you're accompanied by the police commissioner himself. I'd be obliged if you'd stay away from him until this is over.'

'Is that an order?'

He gave a huge sigh. 'No, it's a request. You're a possible witness in this case, and could be up to your ears in it for all I know.'

'I assure you that I'm not.'

'I trust Theo's judgement in that, but be damned if the public will if it gets out. Fact. Theo is involved with you. That will damage his credibility, something that will ultimately be bad for him, career-wise.'

'I promise you, I won't knowingly do anything to hurt him. Thank you for letting me see him.'

His voice softened. 'Your muscle is waiting outside. Go home, Miss Bishop. Lie low. And if you have any notion where that drug shipment might be, for God's sake tell us.' He handed her a card. 'This number will put you straight through to me.'

'If I knew I would have told Theo long ago. Will you ring me and let me know how he is when he wakes up?'

He sighed. 'Don't you know when to give in?'

Knowing Theo would recover had made her dizzy with relief, and she couldn't stop herself from saying, 'Of course I do . . . ask Theo.'

He huffed with laughter, then he laughed again, his eyes filling with genuine amusement.

'Tut tut,' she said as she left. 'You have a dirty mind, Chief Inspector.'

He'd been dreaming that he'd been crawling across the desert, his face burned by the sun. He had a fine thirst on him now. His mouth and throat felt like the sand of his dream, clogged up with choking grit. His face itched. But the thumping in Theo's head was more bearable than the other times he'd woke. In fact, it had become a gentle ache. His eyes opened and he knew he was awake properly now.

This time he stayed awake. His eyes were less blurred and he saw a blue wall. Cautiously he moved his head to one side. Things swam a bit, but the blur soon righted itself. He could see a window covered with a splattering of raindrops. There was a view of the grey sky from his position. On the other side was a pale-blue curtain with knife-like horizontal creases where it had been steam-pressed. Beyond that was a door open to a corridor.

When a nurse walked past Theo croaked at her. She didn't turn back.

Another nurse looked around the curtain and smiled at him. 'Good, you're awake are you? How do you feel?'

She quickly interpreted his second croak and came to pour water into a glass. She stuck a bent straw into his mouth, said, 'Suck!'

The liquid disappeared inside him without touching the sides.

'You were supposed to drink that in sips in case you were sick,' she said with mock severity.

'You forgot to tell me.' He squinted at the badge pinned to her chest. 'I'll try and do it better next time, Sue.'

Sue was a cute blonde, short and well-rounded, like a little hen. She smiled at him and reached out for the bell. 'I'll tidy up your bed before the doctor comes.'

Tidying up his bed consisted of him lying to attention while the bed sheets bound him to the mattress.

'Comfy?' she said, and he didn't have the heart to tell her that he was dying for a pee.

Luckily, Kevin came in. He had a plastic container with grapes in it. 'These are from Rosie.' He ate a couple, placed the container on the tray and gazed hard at Theo, trying not to laugh. 'You gave me quite a shock when I came in,' he said cheerfully. 'You look as though you're laid out ready for the undertaker to collect.'

'I'm not ready for the oven yet. Give me a hand to go to the bathroom, would you, Kev?'

'Sure.' Kevin tossed the bedding into a tangled heap. 'Swing your legs round and sit on the edge of the bed. We'll take things slowly in case you get dizzy and fall on your butt. Did you know it's hanging out the back of your nightie?'

A couple of minutes later and Theo was staring at himself in the mirror. 'My butt's got to be better looking than my face at the moment.' He began to laugh. It felt good to be alive. It wasn't until he was about to wash his hands that he saw the flowers drawn on his fingers and the writing on his palm. He stared down at it, absorbing the message, enjoying the warm, crumbly feeling it gave him.

I love you my darling Theo. Always, Lauren.

Tears filled his eyes and spilled down his cheeks. Nobody had ever told him they loved him before. 'Lauren's been here?'

Gruffly, Kevin said, 'I guess you're not as tough as you thought you were, huh,' and he handed him a wad of tissue. 'Your lady visited yesterday. A shipload of marines with guns blazing wouldn't have kept her from seeing you.'

Theo dabbed gently at his bruised eyes, then blew his nose before smiling. 'Lauren's really something, isn't she?'

'I'll say. That's some woman you've got there. She took me apart and turned my words back at me when I got out of line. The man she was with was something else, too. He went over my head and pulled strings.'

'What man was that?'

'She has a bodyguard who goes by the name of Greg Bamford. Bamford heads an electronics firm. I looked him up. Former special forces. Served in Ireland with distinction. Runs a security firm on the side. I couldn't find out much there, I was told to leave it alone from higher up. Lauren Bishop and the two Parker females have moved into Grantham Hall until this is all over. They're being well looked after. I brought Bamford up to date, so he knows what he's going up against.'

'Thanks, Kev. I feel so bloody helpless. How long have I been here?'

'Three days.'

The nurse came back in with a cup of tea and two digestive biscuits for Theo. She gazed at the tumbled bedding in dismay. 'Detective Inspector Ransom! I've just tidied that.'

'He's a bachelor. He hasn't learned to appreciate the work a woman does,' Kevin said ingratiatingly. 'You couldn't find another cup of tea for your favourite policeman, could you Susie?'

Susie dimpled and went away again.

When the explosion came into his mind Theo said, 'Did anybody survive the blast?'

'Two did. Monica Spencer will be all right. She had superficial burns. She'll be going back to Bristol to live with her parents. She won't witness now.'

'Damn, just when we had Brian Allingham in the frame.' Heart heavy, he only just dared to ask, 'And Pam Roberts?'

'Pam will need some rehabilitation before she can walk again.'

Guilt hung heavily on him. 'I should have been more careful. I should have gone back up myself.'

'You did the right thing. Pam's trained in rape counselling.'

'What about the woman downstairs?'

'Dead. She was a bit of a mess, but was identified by her dental work. Bomb squad said she was carrying the explosive. It was a crude bomb, a stick of unstable dynamite and a fuse wired up to a clock. I think it was meant to scare rather than kill. It went off too soon, split a gas pipe and the gas ignited almost immediately. That caused most of the damage.'

'So it wasn't a terrorist act.'

Kevin looked like the cat who'd swallowed the cream. 'No, it wasn't. You'll never guess who it was, though.'

Theo smiled. 'Carla Allingham . . . hoist with her own petard. Who ever would ever have thought it.' He nearly laughed at the expression on Kevin's face.

'How the hell did you know that?'

'An educated guess. It's like this, guv. I remembered the odd behaviour of the man at the end of the road just after the explosion. I suddenly remembered I knew his face, and it was Brian Allingham.' His brow furrowed in thought. 'He stood there, watched his wife enter the house, then after the explosion he hadn't quite known what to do when she didn't come out. He got into a car and took off when he realized I recognized him. But I was too wrecked to get to him, anyway.'

'What sort of man would send his wife in to do his dirty work?'

'That boarding house only takes women as lodgers. They probably thought she'd look less suspicious to neighbours than a man. Plus, the woman was associated with a man who was involved with an IRA cell before her marriage to Allingham, so she might be familiar with the making of a crude bomb. I never gave her a second glance in the hall, and she was within arm's length. Does Allingham know she's dead?'

'The papers described Carla as critically wounded but it wouldn't take him long to put two and two together. They were more interested in Sergeant Roberts. A mangled cop always makes for a good story, and a woman gets us the sympathy vote, especially if she's got youngsters to support. They went to town on Pam Roberts.'

'Well, they can leave me alone.'

The nurse came back with the doctor in tow, looking self-conscious as she placed the cup of tea on the tray and rushed to tidy the bed clothes again.

'Those can wait, nurse. No, come back with that tea.' He picked up the cup and drained the contents. 'That's better . . . nobody stops to think that doctors need nourishment. Now, how are you feeling, young man?'

Theo was beginning to feel tired, and his head had a dull, but manageable ache to it. He wanted to get home, and he needed to get back to work. Brian Allingham now had a three-day start on him. He could be anywhere. Theo could almost smell the end of this case now. 'Fine . . . I feel fine.'

'Except for the headache.'

Theo shrugged. 'I can take aspirin for it.'

'You can, indeed, but I'd prefer you didn't. I'll give you a prescription.'

Theo was prodded and poked and tapped, his blood pressure and temperature were calculated. A light was shone into his eyes and he screwed them up against the glare.

'Your pupils are nearly back to normal. Any blood in your urine?'

Theo hadn't examined it that closely and said truthfully, 'I didn't see any.'

The doctor smiled to himself. 'Did you look?'

Here was a man who read between the lines. 'No, I admit I didn't.'

'I see.' Theo's facial wounds were examined. 'They should heal without leaving too much scarring. You'll have a small scar on your cheekbone and a bigger one on your shoulder where that cut is. It took fourteen stitches. You were lucky to survive, especially with your teeth intact, and it was sheer luck that the glass wasn't ground into your eyes. Your eyelids and eyes were full of it.'

The doctor was a ghoul, Theo thought.

'We'll keep you in overnight, Inspector Ransom, and I'll send you down for a scan in the morning. Depending on the outcome I might let you go home tomorrow. But you'll have to be monitored for twenty-four hours. Do you have someone who can do that?'

'Yes, Kevin said. One of the constables has offered to do it on her day off. She has nursing experience.'

'Right then. Take it easy for a while. Concussion can be dangerous and should be taken seriously. You can get up and move around today, but don't overdo it, and if you start to feel dizzy or nauseated tell the nurse.'

The doctor helped himself to a handful of grapes on his way out.

Kevin stood too. 'I'll leave you to it, then. I promised Rosie I'd pick up the dry cleaning. I'll bring your clothes in tomorrow, just in case.' He took a phone from his back pocket and threw it on the bed. 'Here's your phone. You'd better call your lady friend and put her mind at rest.' He scooped up half a dozen grapes.

Theo was suspicious. 'Hang on, Kevin. I recognize a quick escape when I see one. Who's been appointed to keep an eye on me?'

Kevin smiled broadly. 'The fair Davinia Graham. She practically drooled at the thought of looking after you.'

Theo's face fell. 'You should have asked Lauren.'

'She's all right where she is. We can't afford the resources to protect her, and you're next to useless at the moment. Besides, she'd put your blood pressure up.'

'But Davinia Graham? You said yourself . . .'

'She'll be perfect. She used to be a veterinary nurse.' Kevin stopped when he reached the door, and laughed. 'Actually, you'll have the services of an agency nurse for a few days, courtesy of the department.'

'Very funny.' Theo threw his pillow at him.

Sue advanced on him as soon as Kevin disappeared. 'I'm going to tidy this bed,' she said with intent. Her glance wandered to the grapes. 'Have you finished with those?'

Theo ate the last five while he still had the chance. 'Now, I have.'

Lauren was cautious when she answered the telephone. 'Yes.'

'It's me.'

'Hello you.' Her heart swelled with the relief she felt. 'I'm so pleased you've rung; how are you feeling?'

'I've felt better.'

'Poor Theo. I've been so worried about you.'

'I received your message, Lauren. Thank you for the flowers. What were they?'

She laughed when she remembered her efforts at drawing. 'Oh, *those* flowers. They were supposed to be forget-me-nots.'

'They looked more like sunflowers.'

'You kept bending your fingers while I was drawing them. Besides, it's the thought that counts.'

'Never will I forget you, Lauren,' and his voice was so soft and tender that it flustered her, so she didn't quite know what to say.

She realized that she'd stopped breathing, and drew in a breath. 'I do hope not.'

'I understand that you're all living at Grantham Hall at the moment.'

'Yes. The Bamfords are being so kind to us all.'

'Greg Bamford is a good man to have on your side, by all accounts. We're keeping him up to speed on the case. How's Betty?'

'A lot better after her procedure. It's becoming increasingly difficult to get her to rest.'

'And Katie?'

'She loves being at the Hall. Samantha Bamford has taken a shine to her. Katie is turning into a proper little busybody.'

'And you?'

'I find it difficult to be here at times. I keep recalling my childhood, and I expect to walk round a corner and see my father standing there.'

'Promise me that you'll be careful? This case is far from over though Carla Allingham is now out of the picture. And it appears that Allingham will stop at nothing to get what he's after.'

A tremor ran through her. 'Greg told me.'

'And the local police will keep an eye out for anything unusual.'

'Like ghosts in the cottage.'

Theo chuckled. 'In all seriousness there is something I need to ask you. Monica mentioned that she heard water in the background when Allingham phoned her, as if he was in the bath, and there was a boat engine. Can you think of anything that could tie that in with Allingham?'

'Only the Thames, and the fact that he's a Londoner.'

'I know he was in London four days ago. I saw him just after the explosion.' She heard him heave a sigh. 'Let me know if you think of anything, however silly you might think it is.'

'Theo . . . are you supposed to still be working while you're in hospital?'

'My mind's not going to switch off now. It's just woken up after three days of floating in and out of consciousness. Against all odds, my mind is as fresh as a daisy. I'm making the most of it. I love you, too, by the way.'

'You didn't mind the message. Hell . . . I don't know why I wrote that. I wasn't trying to push you into anything.'

'You mean you don't love me, after all?'

'No, I didn't mean that . . . of course . . . it's just. When we slept together—'

'I can't recall much sleeping going on.'

'Theodore, darling . . . do be quiet. I'm trying to explain.'

'There's no need to explain. It's quite clear. You tampered with my affection, then dragged me into bed and took advantage of me.'

She began to laugh. 'Can we just say it was a good shag, and we can do it again sometime, no strings attached.'

There was no laughter from him now. 'You don't want to marry me then?'

'I didn't actually say that. You've got to agree that marriage is old-fashioned these days. People just live together, or they go to bed and . . .'

'Fuck?'

She winced. 'I was going to say, make love.'

'Whatever label you hang on it, it simply means satisfying one's physical urges.'

'Theo, I don't want you to think that you *have* to marry me and provide me with children because we went to bed together.'

'Oh, good. I'm glad we sorted that out, since my own sentiments are not that archaic, either. But what about commitment, Lauren, does that mean nothing to you?'

'Of course it does. Why are we arguing?'

'I don't know. Yes, I do . . . I have a headache still. What's your excuse?'

'I don't know. It just blew up and now I feel totally miserable.'

'At least you're being honest about that. And you're right, Lauren. It was a fantastic shag, and we must do it again sometime.'

It was surprising how much those words hurt her, yet he'd only served up what she'd given him. 'I said the wrong thing, in the first place, didn't I?'

'I'm tired. Goodnight, Lauren.'

She couldn't allow them to part on a wrong note. 'Theo . . . I do love you.'

'I know you do. We haven't known each other long, though, and I agree, it would be a mistake to commit to anything long term. Perhaps once the case is over things will be different. Let's keep it superficial.' His voice was dispirited, drained. 'Kevin was right. He told me not to get involved, but I wouldn't listen.'

She thought her heart might break. 'Theo, don't say such things. You're hurting me.'

'Sorry, I wouldn't hurt you for the world. I'll be able to think straight once I get home tomorrow, I expect. Goodnight.'

He hung up before she had time to say anything else.

Hating herself, because she'd caused the hurt in him, Lauren turned to find Betty there. 'Boyfriend trouble?' she said.

She felt like crying. 'I read him wrong.'

'Don't judge Theo by my Charlie's standards.'

'Betty, don't. Charlie was your son. He was shallow, but he never deliberately hurt me in any way. And I'm not judging Theo. Charlie is in the past and it does no good to rake it all up.'

Betty shrugged. 'I had time to think about things while I was in hospital. Funny, but when you think you're going to die and you're given a new lease on life, you look at things a different way. I was thinking of Charlie, and of Katie. Charlie was selfish to keep us apart. And he did wrong by you. Everything around him was built on a lie and everybody suffered because of it.'

'It won't last for ever. I have great faith in Theo.'

'Do you? As far as I can see you've turned down a perfectly good man because of what happened between you and Charlie.'

'It's nothing to do with Charlie. Your son was a substitute for my father, though I never realized it until I moved back into this house. I loved my father, but although he was honest he was a charming and charismatic wastrel. No wonder my mother left him. But Theo isn't like that. Besides, I haven't turned him down. He didn't ask me.'

'But you said marriage was old-fashioned, so he must have mentioned it.'

Lauren sighed. 'The way he put it was – "You don't want to marry me, then?"'

'Do you want to marry him?'

'Yes . . . I adore him. I just didn't think he was being serious and I didn't want to push him into anything he'd regret.'

'So you fobbed him off. You're a ninny, Lauren Bishop. I never thought I'd ever say this about a copper, but that man's a lovely bit of crumpet. You don't deserve to have him.'

'I most certainly do. And I'm going to get him eventually.'

'How?'

Her voice began to wobble and she drew in a deep breath. 'I don't know yet. But when Theo finds those drugs it will be all over bar the shouting and I'll find an opportunity. Somebody must know about that storage place. Theo mentioned that Monica heard water and a boat engine when Brian phoned her.'

'Water and boat engine.' A smile inched across Betty's face.

Lauren stared at her. 'What is it?'

'This might be a bit far-fetched, but Carla Allingham's father used to be a bargee. Her half-brother inherited the firm and sidelined into narrow boats for hire. He has half a dozen for hire sprinkled around various canals.'

'So he might be putting them up. Well, Brian anyway, since Carla blew herself up.'

'Yes, well . . . I hope the bitch suffered after what she did to Theo and that police woman. Two kids she had. Poor little buggers having their mum blown up. Then there was that silly little tart from the office. It ain't right.'

'Carla's brother?' Lauren prompted.

'Nah! Bill Owens wouldn't give his sister or Brian the time of day. But there'd be nothing to stop them from hiring a narrow boat under another identity. He wouldn't even know. They had a few for hire to tourists in various canals, available through local travel agencies.'

So that's what Brian had meant about chickens coming home to roost. 'Do you know the name of the barge company?'

'Can't say I do? It shouldn't take the fuzz long to find out though.'

Theo felt miserable. He'd handled it all wrong. He gazed at the message in his hand and placed a kiss on it. Lauren wasn't superficial. She wouldn't have written it if she hadn't meant it.

He would put things right . . . apologize. He would propose marriage properly . . . on one knee with a diamond ring for her finger. He'd handcuff her to the bed until she said yes.

The pleasant possibilities that presented were set aside when the phone buzzed – and just as he was about to thumb in her number.

'It's Lauren,' she said, her voice like spiced honey, and his heart flopped about as though it was a paper bag filled with frogs.

'Lauren. I've missed you.'

'It's only been two minutes. I demand an apology.'

'It's been five minutes and twenty-six seconds. Will you forgive me?'

She began to laugh. 'Certainly not. The next time I see you, you're in huge trouble, Theo Ransom.'

'That sounds promising.'

'Betty has got some information for you.'

He heard Betty yell in the background, 'You can tell him, Duchess. It will put you back in his good book.'

Lauren was written on every line in his book, and had never left it.

'Barges,' Lauren said. 'Carla Allingham has a half-brother called Bill Owens. Betty said he doesn't have anything to do with the Allinghams. Bill Owens has half a dozen narrow boats that are hired out at various canals. She thinks he could have hired one of those without Bill Owens knowing. Is that helpful, or what?'

'Tell Betty I love her.'

She lowered her voice to a throaty purr. 'I'm jealous.'

'I love you more, Lauren. I'll never wash that message from my hand. Take care. I have a feeling that things are about to take off.'

'Love you,' she whispered just before he rang off, leaving him smiling.

Eighteen

The fact that there had been an explosion meant the news had picked it up. As usual, there was speculation . . . newscasters with serious faces, deep voices and correct enunciation pulled theories out of the air and they were accepted as the gospel truth.

There were photographs taken by mobile phones. Snaps of himself, of the remains of the car he'd been in, of the house. Witnesses had been interviewed. Pamela Roberts's teenage children had been photographed coming out of school. The older one had spotted the cameraman and had stuck her tongue out, the other had her finger raised.

Way to go, he thought.

I was just calling the dog in and there was a big bang, like an explosion. I says to Fred. Did you hear that? And Fred says to me that it sounded like a bomb had gone off. We went outside and heard all the sirens. Didn't we, Fred?

'One did go off,' Theo muttered.

Mr Butler was washing his car when he heard an explosion and saw the front of the house opposite fall down and the car roll over. He assisted the injured policeman and took charge of the situation until the authorities arrived. It appears that Mr Butler accidentally managed to get a shot of the surviving terrorist, which is now in the hands of the police. The other terrorist was a woman, who is now dead. Her identity is unknown.

He must call in and personally thank the man. There was a picture of the wrecked car, and beyond that in a little spotlight an extremely grainy snap of Brian Allingham standing at the end of the road. It could have been anyone.

Theo grinned. That would add a bit of fuel to Allingham's fire.

A debate went on about terrorism. Accusations were unfairly made and factions formed. Experts aired their expertise to other experts, who agreed or argued. There would be a lot of back-pedalling to do when the truth came out.

The bomb squad identified the dynamite as belonging to a demolition company that had gone out of business several years before. There was a tip-off, and some half a dozen sticks from the same batch were found in a derelict building by a canal. The dynamite was part of a legitimate purchase that had been reported by the company as stolen a few years previously. It was disposed of by the bomb squad without mishap.

There were signs of occupancy in the cellar, as if Allingham had been holed up there. As if any number of homeless people had been holed up there, in fact.

The police commissioner made a placating statement, and two weeks later the bombing was replaced by the news that a young couple backpacking in Australia had been murdered.

Theo suffered no ill affects from his accident. His father came to see him and talked about his mother. Andrea had left him.

His mother phoned to say she'd be home for Christmas. When he asked her how Trudy was she gave a snort and said, 'Don't mention that woman to me again.'

But Theo was frustrated. The case had gone cold on him. Despite Allingham's picture being distributed there had been no sightings along the canals, or anywhere. He had the feeling that it was a red herring, along with the dynamite. Allingham was sharper than he'd thought. He'd wondered if he'd found what he'd been looking for. He could be sitting on it because nothing much was shifting on the street, and the shortage of smack had escalated the price sharply. There was a spate of robberies, of mugging and bag snatching.

Carl Winchester and Colin Smith, alias Guns and Smithy scored eighteen months apiece in the manslaughter case. They sneered with bravado in the dock, but Theo noted that Colin Smith looked scared as they took him down, as well he might. He'd give him a few weeks then go and interview him about the assault on Katie.

The good thing was that Lauren, Betty and Katie had not been bothered since the explosion. Could it be that Allingham had gone to ground after he'd been named as a bomber. But where was he? Someone must be sheltering him because the nights were getting cold.

Theo had a couple of days off at the beginning of October. He rang Lauren. 'I'm coming down.'

'Take the train and I'll meet you at the station,' she said.

He threw a change of clothes into a holdall and headed for Waterloo station.

Theo saw Lauren from his window. Not far from her a man leaned against the wall. There was a deceptive casualness about him, but there was nothing deceptive about the muscles under his clothes. It must be Greg Bamford.

Lauren's smile was wide when he stepped off the train. She was wearing a cream coloured cable knit over jeans tucked into calf-length brown boots. Over the top a blue duffel coat, worn open. She slid into his arms and hugged him tight, holding on to him like there was no tomorrow.

'It seems like years since I've seen you. Let me have a good look at you. How are you? Have you recovered?' Her clear blue eyes went anxiously to his face, no longer bruised and swollen or crawling with spidery stitches, but still yellowed and sore in places. It had drawn a few looks from other passengers. She gently kissed the fading scars, then hugged him again. 'You've got no idea how much I've missed you, Theo Ransom. Is abducting a policeman a crime? I might keep you here if it's not.'

'I feel good. Yes I'm recovered. Yes it's a crime, and I might stay here for ever, anyway.' Warmth and contentment flooded through him. Theo had no need to think about his future. It was all tied up in this woman. He took her face between his hands and brought her mouth up to his. Her lips were soft and yielding and he thought it a good time to ask her, after he'd taken his fill. 'I'm afraid I'm old-fashioned after all. Would you marry me?'

Her eyes grew wide and she gave a husky giggle. 'Now, d'you mean?'

He grinned at her. 'If you've got a parson in your handbag, yes.'

'I'm afraid I haven't.'

'Will you? I'm falling apart without you.'

'At the risk of raising your ire again, of course I'll marry you. Betty said you're a nice bit of crumpet, and although our taste in everything is usually miles apart, this time I agree with her. Come on. I'll introduce you to Greg Bamford. He's awfully conscientious. He followed me in, in his car.'

The man was watching every passenger who came off the

train, and his seemingly casual glance didn't miss much. He
held out a hand when they were introduced. It was firm, with
no added pressure to prove dominance. Greg Bamford knew
his own worth and had no need to prove anything. 'We've met
before, Theo, except you were asleep at the time.'

'I believe I have you to thank for Lauren coming up to
London.'

'Lauren didn't recognize any danger in it, and would have
gone to see you with, or without my help.'

She said, 'Theo's a dangerous man in his own right. He blew
himself up without any assistance from me. I've just become
engaged to what's left of him.'

Greg smiled. 'Congratulations.'

'Thanks.' She slanted her eyes his way. 'We're going to shop
for frozen dinner and chocolate cake, then we'll be living in
the cottage for a couple of days. Is that all right with you,
Greg?'

The two men exchanged a grin and Greg said, 'He looks as
though he can handle anything that comes his way. Make sure
you use the security, Lauren. At least I can monitor the grounds.'
He took a two-way radio from his belt and handed it to Theo.
'I take it you're familiar with these.'

Theo nodded. 'Range?'

'About five miles. It will stretch to seven if you're in the
right place, but I doubt if you'll be going that far.'

'Tell Betty I'll bring Theo to the hall for dinner tomorrow
evening,' she said as he walked away.

'Will do,' Greg threw over his shoulder.

The autumn colours lingered, even though they were officially
in winter.

In the cropped fields a yellowhammer made the most of the
grain left in the stubble.

Underfoot in the copse the leaves were decomposing into a
soggy brown layer that oozed water. Everything had fruited
and the hedges were bursting with red berries. The trees shed
nuts and leaves to the ground and the squirrels scampered about
to fill their storehouses for winter. Ripe blackberries tumbled
down their canes. She must pick some she thought, and apples
from the tree, so she could make him an old-fashioned pie.

Lauren inhaled her childhood and felt the landscape hug her

tight, as though she belonged to it and it was claiming her back. How predictable the countryside was. Everything blossomed in spring, lived its life in summer, then spent an autumn of sweet decay before it died at its appointed time. That was how it should be. But this place only owned her childhood, and it couldn't have her back. She'd placed her heart and her future in Theo's hands.

He was behind her, carrying a box of groceries and she turned to him, certain that her smile gave off a golden glow. 'We'll be there in a minute. We have to wait and make sure no intruders are in the cottage.'

His radio gave a squawk and a crackle, and he answered it with, 'Thanks.'

'Was that Greg? What did he say, apart from crackle crackle?'

'We needn't wait. The cottage has been under surveillance since he got home.'

She chuckled, and when they emerged from the copse and they reached the porch, she held her hand up to the camera, showing off her engagement ring, a half circle of perfect diamonds set in white gold.

The phone rang as soon as they got inside. It was Samantha. 'Congratulations, Lauren. I like the look of the man. The ring's not bad either.'

The cottage had a musty smell to it, but was exactly how they had left it. She lit a scented candle then put a match to the fire while Theo unpacked the food.

'We'll have to pick some blackberries. I'm going to make you a pie.'

'Come here first, I need to tell you something,' he said. He took her head in his hands, his thumbs resting gently at each side on her mouth and his little fingers just curving into her ears. He gazed down at her, a smile edging across his mouth, and his hawkish eyes grew soft.

'What do you need to tell me that I don't already know?'

'When I first saw that message written in my hand I cried like a baby, because nobody had ever said that to me before. Not even my parents.'

The breath nearly left her body and she wanted to cry, herself. '*Oh, Theo!*'

'I love the way you say that.' He grinned self-consciously. There was a need in him to be all things to her. A child at her breast – her friend and playmate, hero, protector, conqueror and mate. What a paradox love was. It weakened and strengthened a man at the same time.

'That's what you said when you first came into the room, remember.'

'You were conscious?'

'No . . . but I knew you were there, and I've just remembered it.' He kissed her so tenderly that her body seemed to disintegrate and float off in different directions. When it came back together again she would probably be different, she thought. Her hands would be on the end of her legs, her eyes on her knees, and her feet would be sticking out the side of her head like ears.

When he withdrew from the kiss she kept her eyes closed. 'What do I look like now? Is everything in the right place.'

'Like you're part of me.'

She opened her eyes. 'You take my breath away, Theo Ransom. Kiss me again.'

'Later. You promised to make me a blackberry pie.'

'Come on then. Put your jacket on, and grab that bowl while I put the guard around the fire.'

Later, they ate an omelette followed by blackberry and apple pie swimming in custard. That evening they made love in front of the fire with Lauren hoping that Harry Simpson's ghost wasn't shocked by their abandoned behaviour.

No security lights woke them in the night. The ghost didn't rattle its chains and the phone kept its thoughts to itself.

Lauren woke at ten to find herself snuggled into Theo's body. Carefully easing out from under his arm she pulled on her nightgown, slid her feet into her slippers and went downstairs to run the bath. She switched off the alarm, then made them a mug of tea each and set it by the bath. There was a pleasant coolness to the morning that made her senses tingle.

Outside the sky was clear, the morning crisp and the grass powdered with frost.

Lauren kissed Theo's ear, 'Wake up sleepy. I've run us a bath.'

When he grunted and refused to open his eyes she slid her cold hands under the sheet.

His eyes shot open in shock and he uttered a succinct curse. It was better than she'd hoped for. Giving a giggle she ran down the stairs and out through the cottage door. He came after

her in all his naked glory, caught her halfway across the garden
and scooped her up into his arms.

Lauren began to howl with laughter. 'The security camera
is still on.'

He carried her back into the cottage holding her strategically
in front of him.

They sank into the bath, one at each end and still laughing,
then gazed at each other over their mugs of tea.

In the lounge, Lauren's phone began to ring.

'They can ring back,' she said, and they did, two minutes
later.

'I'll get it.' Theo rose from the bath and tied a towel round
his waist. 'Lauren's busy. Can you ring again in fifteen minutes?'

'Who are you?' a woman said.

'Lauren's fiancé.'

'Her fiancé? Don't be ridiculous! Put her on, will you. I'm
Portia, Countess Demasi.'

'It's Portia, Countess Demasi,' Theo said.

The shine seemed to drain from Lauren, as if it had been
sucked with the dust into a vacuum cleaner. Except her mother
probably wouldn't know one end of a vacuum cleaner from the
other. 'Mother . . . how lovely to hear from you?'

'What the hell is going on, Lauren? Who was that man . . .
what does he do?'

'He's a policeman.'

'A policeman!' Her mother's voice went up a few decibels,
so her words were clear to Theo. 'Are you completely devoid
of your senses, Lauren? First it was that low-life barrow boy.
Now it's a policeman. How common. What's more, you can
never find one when you need one.'

Lauren threw Theo a grin. 'I never have any trouble finding
one. Mother, will you stop it please? You've never met him and
you know nothing about him.'

'Then tell me about him. When did you meet?'

'I met him when he questioned me about . . . well, you know
who.'

'That was only a few weeks ago, and you allowed him to
take advantage of you? I know people in the service who matter,
Lauren. I shall make a complaint. He'll be dismissed. If you've
got to marry a policeman marry one with a future ahead of
him, like that one who was blown up in that explosion.'

'There's not much of a future in being blown up.'

'There is if you take out insurance,' she snapped. 'Your father would be appalled.'

'Oh, I don't know. He didn't have that much taste in women himself.'

'Lauren, whether you like it or not I'm your mother. I do deserve some respect.'

Theo was seated on the edge of the bath, trying not to laugh, and she grabbed his hand. The giggle she gave had a maniacal sound to it. She held Theo's hand against her face to gather strength from the contact. *Damn her mother! Damn trying to make peace with her! This was war.* If she could have stamped her foot in the bath without making waves, she would have.

Theo was kissing her ear. 'I also know people who know people in the police force, mother,' she managed to get out, because her kissed ear was turning into something more seductive. 'Do drop this. Why did you really call?'

'We're coming to the UK for Christmas. You haven't met my Count yet, and I thought this would be a good opportunity.'

'And you can meet my policeman, and be nice to him. He is Detective Inspector Theodore Ransom, in case you want to report him.'

There was a moment of silence, then her mother said, 'But isn't he . . .?'

'Yes he is. And no, I do not have an insurance policy on him.' Although she had to drag it out of herself, she took the first step towards reconciliation. 'We could all meet in London for dinner, perhaps. In the meantime you might remember that I'm an adult, and respect is reciprocal. Perhaps we could go forward on that basis and become friends rather than remain enemies. I do want my children to know and love their grandparents.'

'You tell her,' Theo whispered against her ear.

'Oh, my poor darling, you're carrying a baby!' her mother said faintly. 'It wasn't fathered by that dreadful man . . . what was his name . . . Parker?'

'No, I'm not having a baby. At least, not at the moment.' Lauren stopped her policeman's hand from advancing any further up her thigh. 'I must go, mother, something's burning.'

Theo took the phone from Lauren's hand. 'Goodbye for now, Countess. I'm looking forward to meeting you.'

'At least you have some manners,' she said, and quite un-expectedly.

'Yes. And you may look up my parents' pedigree in *Who's Who* if you wish. Elgar James Ransom and Sarah Fanshaw.'

'The feminist?'

'That's the one.'

'Good lord! Sarah and I went to the same primary school. She was such a brain.'

'The school on the council estate she grew up on.'

There was a moment of silence before, 'Are you suggesting I'm a snob, Detective Inspector?'

'Yes, indeed. I do think I might be suggesting that.'

Surprisingly, she chuckled before she rang off.

He set the phone on the side of the bath and gazed at Lauren, his mouth curving into a grin. 'How many children did you say we were having?'

Nineteen

The two days spent with Theo had been a joy. There had been an informal surprise engagement party at Grantham instead of the dinner planned with Betty and Katie.

Daniel had brought Lucy, and there was an air of happiness about them. There was no sign of resentment in Lucy when they greeted each other.

'Congratulations, Lauren. The last time I saw you was—'

'Four years ago, when I left the village to go to London,' she said quickly, not wanting Charlie to be shoved down Theo's throat all the time.

Lucy kissed her and whispered, 'I was sorry to hear of what happened. It must be dreadful for you. I do hope it's soon over.'

'Theo seems to think it will be.'

Theo had been cornered by John Dunne.

'They tells me you're a policeman from Lundun.'

'That's right.'

'I wants to ask you something. I don't suppose they ever

found my wallet – the one that was nicked from my back pocket during the war. It had five quid in it, a week's wages. They wouldn't even have bothered to investigate it, I reckon. Not with a war going on.'

Theo stifled a grin. 'As a matter of fact they found your wallet in the Thames river mud. The money was ruined, but the commissioner asked me to give you a fiver from the victims' fund.' He took one from his wallet and handed it over.

'I'll be blowed,' John said, and stared at it, almost speechless. But before Theo could move away he placed a hand on his arm. 'I want to tell you something. I saw that man in the paper . . . the terrorist. Talked to him. He bought me a shandy.'

Theo couldn't let anything go past, however remote. 'Where?'

'In Poole, I reckon, when that volunteer woman took me to get my pension and I managed to escape for half an hour. He got on one of them sailing boats that clutter up the harbour. When I were a lad it were a real port with proper ships coming and going and coal being loaded and stuff, not all these fancy boats the pleasure trippers use, dashing back and forth across the channel and getting up to no good. How can they afford them, that's what I want to know? Life's one long holiday for some.'

'Can you remember which boat it was?'

'Now let me see. Raunchy Rooster the boat was called. I wondered if she was named after a theatrical girl I once knew by that name. She used to wear a tail of rooster feathers and shake them around a bit. She had an arse on her like a steam roller, Raunchy Rooster did! I always liked women who were a bit on the buxom side, and who rolled about a bit. Like that Betty over there. She's a bit on the saucy side too, I reckon.'

'You should go and chat her up,' Theo suggested, trying not to laugh, and looking around for Greg. He caught his eyes and the two edged off towards the door.

When they were in the corridor Theo said quietly, 'The old boy said he saw Brian Allingham on a boat in Poole.'

'You believe him? He's a bit of a gossip.'

'Regardless, it has to be checked out and I'd like to do that for myself. Can I borrow a car? I could use Lauren's, but it hasn't got much go in it.'

'I'll take you. I'll just have a word with Samantha. She can keep Lauren busy. I'll meet you out the front. You might need some backup.'

'I'll phone the local police if I do.'

'I was thinking I would do.'

'It would be more than my job's worth to involve a member of the public.'

'I'm already involved.'

'So you are. OK. Lauren thinks a lot of you, so don't do anything that would require me to arrest you.'

He found his jacket on the hall stand. When they met at the car Greg was wearing a black leather jacket and a cap. Theo asked, 'Are you carrying a weapon of any sort, licensed or un-licensed?'

Greg grinned. 'You want to pat me down?'

Theo did, then nodded. 'Take the taser out from under your cap.'

'How the devil—'

'The cap sits too high. And you have a pistol to the right of your body, where it's natural for a left-handed man to keep one.'

Greg's eyes were steady on his. 'But you didn't touch me there.'

'The jacket is padded, and has been designed with a pocket to accommodate a gun. It hangs slightly lower on the right side.'

'You're a sharp-eyed bugger.'

'Something you set out to discover for yourself. Now you have. This isn't a pissing contest, Greg. If you're carrying other weapons say so now. If I find anything later, you're in trouble, and I don't care who you know or how long you've known them.'

'For someone who's after a man who was prepared to blow up three other people, you're mighty forgiving.'

'I imagine his wife was at the back of that. I'm not looking to kill anyone, especially myself. I want Allingham to go down for a long, long time – and I want to find him before he finds those drugs.'

'I get you completely.' Greg opened a solid compartment welded into the floor of the four by four. He locked the weapons inside and slid the carpet over it. He smiled. 'Satisfied?'

'Yes.'

'So am I. Let's get going then.'

Greg phoned someone he knew on the way. 'Find out who owns a yacht called Raunchy Rooster. It's moored at Poole.'

He got the answer five minutes later, and it wasn't what Theo wanted to hear. The yacht was registered to an Elizabeth Parker.

The quay was almost devoid of pedestrians. Down near the water the air was cold, with a breeze coming off the harbour. The water was alive, moving in constant shining ripples that were fired by lights coming from the various buildings lining the quay. There was a drunk sitting against the steps of the Customs House, his chin sunk on to his chest.

Greg lifted the man's head up, then gently lowered it back into the same position. Bamford didn't leave much to chance, Theo thought.

The Raunchy Rooster was exactly where John Dunne had said it was. She was tied up to boats either side. 'She's not going anywhere in a hurry,' Greg whispered, clicking off his torch.

They stepped on to the see-sawing deck from a small mooring jetty. Everything was padlocked, shut tight. Theo rattled the padlocks.

A man came down the jetty. 'What's going on here?'

Theo flashed his warrant card. 'We're looking for a man who was living on this yacht last weekend.'

'Terry Ogden? He left this morning. A bit sad he was, on account of his wife having died. He said he was going to pick up his niece, whose staying at some fancy country house around here, and he was going to return to London.'

'In the yacht?'

'He said he'd hire a car.'

Which meant he was going to steal one. 'Can you describe Terry Ogden?'

Terry Ogden, alias Brian Allingham, was described in great detail.

'If he returns before you leave, don't approach him because he might be armed. Call me instead.' Theo handed over his card.

'What's Terry done?'

'I'm afraid I can't discuss that with you, sir.'

'I was going to leave tomorrow, but I might leave tonight, instead, just in case,' he said worriedly.

'You do that, sir. Goodnight. Thank you for your help.'

'Allingham wouldn't have told anyone what his plans were,'

Theo mused. 'I've got a hunch that he fed that info to the yachtsman in case we cottoned on to him.'

'I'm inclined to agree. With Allingham on the loose you'd better stay at Grantham tonight. Let's get back to the girls. I've got a jittery feeling.'

Something that was borne out by a phone call from Lauren. 'I think we've got trouble, Theo. We can't find Katie.'

'Shit!' he said, then, 'What happened?'

'Katie said she was tired and was going to bed. She went outside to call Ginger and Tiger in, and she never came back.'

'OK, Lauren. Try not to worry. Perhaps she had a fall or something. We'll be there in five minutes.'

Greg put his foot to the floor and they headed back to the village at speed. The party was finished and the guests had gone home, but lights were blazing. Theo was relieved to see Lauren waiting for him. But so was Betty and Samantha, and they all had frantic looks on their faces.

Lauren told him, 'We've searched the whole house.'

'Ginger and Tiger came back without her.' Betty's face was screwed up with fear.

'Rennie and Rob have searched the grounds, as far as they can.'

'No sign of her,' the security man said.

They looked at the videos. There was a crowd of people milling about, all saying goodbye to one another. Then cars began to leave.

'There she is,' Theo said.

The video stopped, then Greg zoomed in on the rounded shape of Katie. It happened quickly. They took it through, frame by frame starting from the moment when Allingham stepped out of the car. He reached out for Katie from behind and slapped something over her mouth. She struggled a bit before his hand cut across her face, but soon lost her fire. She was bundled into the back of the car. The man leaned inside for a short while.

'That slimy maggot, what's he doing to my granddaughter,' Betty said, so obviously distressed that Lauren feared for her health and took her hand to comfort her.

'Taping her up I imagine, he wouldn't have time for anything else,' Greg murmured, more for the women's benefit than anyone else's, because Theo knew as well as Greg that Allingham could quite easily be strangling her.

The man straightened, and for a moment they saw his face in the flash of a headlight, which only confirmed what they all knew. He called out something and waved. The vicar waved back. So did Daniel.

'Cool move,' Greg muttered.

Allingham closed the door, got into the driver's seat and drove out through the gate sandwiched between the car of the vicar and Daniel Mather.

He backtracked the tape, wrote down the car details and handed it to Theo.

'Nicely timed too.' He noted the time. 'If he's on his way to Poole we must have passed them coming back in,' Theo said savagely.

Theo moved to the other end of the room and took out his mobile. A conversation took place.

'The car is a stolen one,' Theo said a few moments later. 'The local police know the score. Curtis will keep his eyes on the yacht.'

Betty said, 'What yacht? I thought Brian was on a barge.'

'No, that lead fizzled out.' He watched her intently when he said, 'It's a yacht named Raunchy Rooster. It's registered in the name of Elizabeth Parker.'

''Ere, what's going on? That's my name,' Betty said. 'I haven't got no bleeding yacht. I wouldn't know one end of one from the other and I get seasick walking across a bridge over the river. You don't think . . .?'

Her reaction satisfied him. 'No, Betty, I don't think you're involved. I trust you completely. With your granddaughter in danger, I know you would have told me everything that might be of help.'

Betty burst into tears.

Lauren said. 'You've had a bad shock, Betty, so you go to bed and rest. Theo will find Katie and bring her home. You'll see. I'll wake you if anything happens. I'll come with you.'

Lauren's phone rang.

'Lauren, it's me,' Katie said. 'I'm scared.'

'Katie, love, where are you?'

'She's with me,' Brian Allingham cut in.

Lauren was comforted by the fact that somebody was listening in to the phone call. 'Let Katie go . . . you've done her enough damage.'

'You know what I want, Lauren. Charlie only loved three people in his life. His mum, you, and his precious daughter. He was furious about the drugs and was going to ditch them into the sea. So I sent him the tape of what had happened to Katie, and threatened to distribute it if he did. He and Jean were on their way round to confront me. I told him I was going to tell her about you, and he said to go ahead because he was sick of living a double life. He said he was going to divorce Jean and pay more attention to you.'

Poor Charlie. It wouldn't have made any difference. Their relationship had been already over, and it had been too late to resurrect it, she thought.

'Ironic that they copped it on the way. Listen now. If I don't get what I want I'll kill Katie, then I'll come after you and Betty. That is, unless you remember where the goods are?'

'Yes I do remember. They're locked safely away in a storage facility.'

'Then I want the key, and I want to know where the storage facility is.'

'I'll tell you that when I give you the key. I want Katie first, and if I don't get her I'll throw the key into the sea.'

There was a short silence, then he laughed. 'Fair enough. Go to Lyme Regis and walk to the end of the Cobb. I'll give you further instructions from there. Be there in one hour.'

Theo came in, placed a finger over his mouth and nodded.

'Will do. You'd better bring Katie with you, Brian.'

'It's me who's setting the terms. Once I get what I want you'll have the kid back.' He rang off.

'Do you have the key?' Theo said, thrusting a tiny dagger of hurt into her heart, so she was curt in her reply.

'I would have already given it to you if I had.'

'Hey, I love you. I can't help switching to police mode now and again, though. Feel free to kick me.'

She kissed his cheek instead. 'A key is a key. I'm sure I can give him a key of some sort. He won't know the difference until he tries to use it.'

'You heard him. He won't hand over Katie until he gets what he wants.'

'I've got the key,' Betty said tearfully. 'Charlie gave it to me to look after.'

They both turned, gazing at Betty with disbelief. Theo said

calmly, 'You'd better fetch the key, then you can tell me where the storage facility is situated. I'll interview you later, then talk to my superior. I'll be guided by him as to whether charges should be laid against you.'

Lauren didn't bother to defend Betty. Although the woman looked crushed, Lauren knew she deserved it.

The Cobb was uneven underfoot, and Lauren was thankful she was wearing flat shoes. She reached the building at the end and stood there waiting.

If Theo had got his own way she wouldn't be here. He'd wanted to wait for a female police officer to go instead, but admitted there was no time to spare.

'Brian knows what I look like. I'm not going to risk Katie's life,' she'd told him. 'With or without your permission, I'm going.'

Greg had fitted her up with a radio, and an earpiece, which she'd removed on the way here. Nothing must get in the way of Katie's freedom.

The tide was nearly in, the moored boats floated above the dark sandy bottom of the cove. She could hear the slap of water against them.

She'd been waiting ten minutes. This was ridiculous, she thought. Brian must have seen her walk the length of the Cobb alone, and if she'd alerted the police they would be too far away to be of assistance. He would know she was here. So where was he?

A noise caught her attention. 'Psst.' Lauren could just make out a rubber boat beneath her. He must have floated in on the tide. 'Have you told the police?'

'You've got to be joking.'

'Where's the key?'

'First, I want to see Katie.'

He indicated the shape in the bottom of the dingy. 'There she is.'

'Katie?' she called out.

The shape wriggled and strained, gave a high-pitched and panicky, 'Mmmmm.'

Brian pulled Katie upright. 'The key and the address, Lauren.'

'Tell him and get away with Katie. Your safety and hers comes first,' Theo had said.

'The address is on the label.' She told him it anyway, and held out the key.

He snatched it from her hand, without even questioning it.

'Give me Katie.'

'Here she is.' He pushed Katie out of the boat and she sank beneath the dark water. The next minute the rubber boat had gone off into the darkness.

Without thinking Lauren jumped into the water and groped around the bottom. Nothing. She went up, took a deep breath and dived down again into the pitch black water. Her hand closed round some cloth and she managed to get Katie to the top. Treading water, she tore a strip of tape from Katie's mouth and opened it.

'Breathe,' she shouted in her ear.

Katie swooped in a breath, then gave a terrified scream and began to struggle against her bonds.

'Stop panicking,' Lauren shouted when they surfaced. 'I can't swim if you struggle, and we'll both drown. They'd floated out from the Cobb and her hand touched against a mooring rope. She caught hold of it and held Katie with the other hand, keeping the girl's head out of water and talking to her all the while to calm her down.

'Everything will be all right, Katie. I won't let you go, I promise. Theo and Greg will find us soon, and they'll untie you. I haven't got enough hands. Let's shout for help. One, two, three, *Help!*'

They could see the light from the men's torches bobbing as they ran along the Cobb.

'Over here by the boat,' Lauren shouted when they were level with them. The light played over the water until it found them. Theo jumped in and took the trussed up Katie from her. She followed him to the Cobb and Greg pulled Katie out. Theo pushed her up to Greg. He gave her a hug when he clambered out, but he said nothing just held her in his arms as they stood there, shivering and squelching with water.

Greg took a knife from a sheath on his belt and cut through Katie's bonds. She couldn't stand up by herself so Greg carried her.

Beyond the Cobb an engine fired into life. A white light shot into the air and began to slowly drift downwards. There was a faint whoop whoop.

'It didn't take the coastguard long to find him,' Theo said.

Katie spoke out. 'I hope he gets a thousand years in jail.'

'With all the charges against him he probably will. I'm going to change clothes and catch the first train back up to London. I want to be there when the drugs bust goes down.'

'I'll drive you, it'll be quicker. We could go now. It will give me a chance to talk to you,' Greg said.

They reached the place where she'd left the radio equipment and Lauren casually scooped it up.

'Lauren—' Theo said, clearly exasperated.

'Theo. I love you and I'll always love you, even when you're being bossy. I'm alive, you're alive, and more importantly . . . Katie's alive, thanks to you, my darling.'

He was being manipulated, and he liked it. He grinned, picked a length of slimy green weed from her hair, then kissed her.

Twenty

Lauren showered, changed her clothing then went back to the hall. She'd decided to stay there that night, so Katie would be reassured. And tomorrow was Katie's birthday. They were going to have a quiet party between them. Now they'd move back to the cottage and have it there.

And just as well she'd decided to sleep there, for just before dawn Katie woke her by turning on the light. Her expression was alarmed. 'I've got pains in the bottom of my stomach. They woke me up, and I think the baby's coming,' she said.

'But the baby is nowhere due yet.' Pulling on her clothes Lauren got out of bed. 'I'll wake Betty. See what she thinks.'

Just then Katie's water broke.

Betty came out of her bedroom, rubbing her eyes. 'What's going on?'

'The baby is coming.'

'Oh Gawd! I'd better ring for an ambulance. I only had one kid and that was too many years ago to remember.'

Katie groaned. 'I don't think I can wait that long. I can feel its head stretching me.'

Taking the sheets and a blanket from the bed Lauren folded them into a pad. 'You'd better lie down, Katie. Get Samantha, Betty. She's had children.'

'I'm not going along those cold corridors with all those statues and things. It will give me the willies. Besides, I don't know where she sleeps.'

'Then phone her,' Lauren almost yelled, when Katie began to strain.

Samantha arrived just as the baby's bald little head came out; still buttoning up her blouse. 'Leave her to me. Betty, ring the bell at the bottom of the stairs. When one of the security guards appears, tell him to keep a look out for the ambulance.'

She turned to Katie. 'The baby's head is turning. Let me just feel for the cord. Lauren go and find something warm to wrap it in. A couple of flannel pillow cases from the cupboard at the end of the hall should do.'

When she came back, Samantha was saying, 'With your next contraction try and give a bit of a shove. The baby's only small, so it shouldn't be too hard.'

She'd hardly got the words out of her mouth when the infant slithered from Katie. She and Samantha smiled at each other when it gave a warbling cry.

'It's a girl,' Samantha told them all.

The baby was placed on Katie's stomach and the pillow case laid over her.

'She's too early, so we need to keep her warm, Katie. The afterbirth hasn't come away yet, but the ambulance officers can see to that. I can hear the siren, so they're not far away. Look at her. She's so petite, like a little doll.'

Despite Katie's constant declarations in the past that she didn't want to see her baby, mother's instinct combined with curiosity got the better of her. Tears came to her eyes at the first sight of the child her body had produced. Tentatively, she touched the translucent skin on the child's face, then peeled back a corner of the pillow case to see her better. The infant brought her fist up and stuck her thumb in her mouth. Katie smiled. 'Look at her hands, they're like little seashells. She's so beautiful.'

Betty's face broadened into a smile when she came back. 'There's a pretty one for you. What are you going to call her?'

'I don't know.'

'Well, she's got to have a name, hasn't she? I mean, you'll never forget a child you gave birth to, it ain't natural, and especially since she'll share a birthday with you. So you might as well give her a name to remember her by, instead of thinking of her as "she".'

Once again Katie's hand reached out to touch her child. Tears filled her eyes and she expelled a defeated breath, almost like a sigh. 'It feels as though I've been given a special birthday present. I can't give her away. What happened isn't her fault, is it? We've been through a lot together today, and if it wasn't for Lauren we both would have drowned. At least she'll have a mother to love her.'

'And a great-grandmother,' Betty reminded Katie.

'And a godmother,' Lauren said. 'Happy birthday, Katie darling.'

To which Samantha added, '*Two* godmothers.'

The child gave a little whimper, her hand left her mouth and she grabbed at a handful of air.

Katie giggled. 'She's waving at you. She must approve then. Gaining confidence the new mother looked round at them all. I'm going to call her Elizabeth, Lauren, Samantha, after all of you. You don't mind, do you?'

None of them did.

After the ambulance had taken mother and child away, Samantha smiled. 'It's dawn. Going back to bed will be a waste of time. How about we meet in my kitchen for a champagne breakfast in one hour.'

Later in the day, when Lauren had captured the cats and was putting the cage into the car along with Katie's possessions, Samantha handed her a printout from the Internet.

Detective Uncovers a huge cache of illegal Drugs.

'I'll read it when I get home.' She hugged Samantha. 'It's going to be wonderful not to have to look over my shoulder all the time, but I can't say I'm going to miss the excitement. Thank you for being so kind to us all.'

'I enjoyed having you here, despite our skirmishes. I was thinking that I might let some rooms out next summer. That little suite you're in to start with. Americans pay big money to stay at stately homes.'

'A good idea.' Lauren started the engine. 'I'll see you tomorrow, Samantha. I'll come in and finish editing those ancestral histories.'

'Before you go, I was thinking that if your name goes on the booklets as the author, then perhaps you wouldn't mind if your family crest did too.' She shrugged. 'All right, I'm being shameless. But think about it.'

Lauren nodded. It wouldn't hurt to think about it.

Samantha held out a tape. 'By the way, here's something for you. That man of yours has got a good body on him.'

Lauren blushed. It was the security tape from the cottage.

Three weeks later Theo knocked at the door of Blackbird cottage. It was opened by Katie, who gave him a sunny smile.

'Lauren and my gran are at the fête,' she said. 'If you hurry you'll be able to catch Lauren's speech. It starts in fifteen minutes.'

'It's you I want to see at this moment.' He went inside and handed her an envelope. 'The results of the DNA tests.'

He crossed to the crib where a tiny child was sleeping, and smiled down at her. Such a beautiful, innocent and dainty being to have emerged from such a terrible crime, he thought.

'I think you made the right decision in keeping her, Katie. Are you sure you want to go ahead with the assault charge? Smith has confessed, but the other two will deny it. Not that it will make much difference. We have film evidence that Allingham and Winchester were involved in another assault. And a couple of other young women came forward when they knew that Allingham was facing a long sentence.'

'Yes, I'm sure. They shouldn't be allowed to get away with it. Besides, it will satisfy my need for revenge after what they put us all through. My counsellor will be with me every step of the way. And anyway, I want you to win.'

'How can I lose with you on my side?'

She turned the envelope over. 'Do you know what's in it?'

'No. I figured it was your business, so I asked them to seal it without telling me the result,' he said gently. He hesitated, then said, 'I haven't found your tape. I think your father may have destroyed it. If you were my daughter I would have. There was a tape he made of himself stored with the drugs. I think he made it in case anything happened to him. He dropped Allingham in it. The drug deal wasn't of your father's doing, but once he was involved he had to go along with it. He named names, and we've been able to charge several dealers. Your father was in over his head and didn't know which way to jump. I just thought you'd like to know.'

Of course it could all be bullshit, Theo thought, but while watching the tape he'd been able to judge for himself the attraction of Charlie Parker. He'd been very plausible.

'But my father was still in that porn stuff,' she said.

'Yes, he was. But selling porn to adults is not illegal. Don't think too badly of him.' Katie hadn't mentioned the child porn, so neither would he. Charlie might or might not have been involved in that, but Theo thought it was more likely that he was.

'Thank you, Theo. You've been really kind. I want to ask you something. Will you be one of Lizzie's godfathers?'

He gave Katie a hug. 'I'd be honoured.'

'Then here's your first duty.' She shook her head. 'I'm going to tell Lizzie the truth when she asks. If she wants to know who fathered her she can open the envelope herself when she's old enough to handle it. You might think that's cowardly, but I don't want to keep dwelling on what happened. Who knows, when I'm older I might meet a nice man who will understand how I feel, and who will accept Lizzie as part of the family. In the meantime I've got my gran. We're going to look after each other.'

She held the envelope out to him. 'Will you keep it safely until then?'

There was a lump in Theo's throat. He hoped Katie would find happiness in the future. 'I'll do my best. And if you want to change your mind at any time, you only need to ask.'

Lauren had just opened the winter fête at Grantham Hall when she saw Theo at the back of the crowd. A smile lit up his face at the sight of her.

She excused herself from the people who wanted to talk to her, and moved to where he stood.

'Can you get away?' he asked her.

'There are end to end coach parties starting in an hour. At the moment I'm supposed to be on the arts and crafts stall. Come and buy something. I can recommend a framed water colour by local artist Katie Parker, or a crocheted knee blanket by Betty Parker. No, forget the knee blanket. John Dunne has just bought it by the looks of things.'

'Is there anything by Lauren Bishop?'

'I'm afraid not. She's neither arty nor crafty.'

Theo bought Katie's water colour, a portrait of Tiger and Ginger, then said, 'I'd like to see Betty while I'm here. My boss has decided not to lay charges. But Betty is to be formally cautioned.'

'What's that?'

'I'll take her to the local police station, where a senior officer will reprimand her. No further action will be taken, but the caution will be on her record. If she breaks the law again the caution will be brought to the attention of the court.'

'Betty will find that horribly embarrassing.'

'She's lucky she isn't going to prison. The punishment is less than she deserved. She put everyone in danger by withholding that key.'

'She knows that. But Charlie was her son, and she loved him. She didn't believe he'd be mixed up in a drug deal. And quite frankly, neither do I.'

'You both could be right. I have some news on that because, although he was involved, I don't think the intention was there. I'm inclined to give him the benefit of the doubt on that, at least.'

'I'm so glad, Theo. Betty will be pleased, too. She's taking a turn in the cream tea room. Have you seen Lizzy yet? She's so sweet.'

'I have seen her. Katie has asked me to be her godfather.'

'And will you? Greg will be the other one.'

'I think I can manage it.'

'Betty and Katie have decided to stay on here. The owner has decided to renew the lease on Blackbird's Nest, rather than sell it. And Betty has found the papers for the yacht she didn't know she had in an envelope with her personal certificates. She's putting the boat up for sale and will be able to buy a decent car with the proceeds. Katie has just got her driving licence, so they'll be able to get out and about without me. In fact, I'm beginning to feel rather superfluous to them now.'

'Good, because I want you all to myself, and soon. I'm pleased they decided to like each other in the end.'

'Staying enemies became too hard to cope with when everything was going on and they had to rely on each other. They wanted to like each other right from the beginning, but Betty had taken a stand and found it hard to back down from it. Now they have the baby to dote on. It makes up for them both losing Charlie, I suppose.'

'He was a rogue, but if he hadn't been I wouldn't have met you. Do you . . . *miss him.*'

'I was with Charlie for four years, so I can't promise that I'll never think of him.' She leaned into him and kissed the corner of his mouth. 'I will say that the very first moment we met I knew you were special and we were meant to be, Theo. Not meeting you would have been a tragedy.'

He grinned. 'I know when I'm being buttered up, but I love it. Carry on.'

'Enough is enough. Oh, yes, I remember, I do have something to tell you. I heard from my solicitor, Mr Gregson. No doubt you remember him. My former home has sold for a good price. He feels that when this is over and it's gone through probate, I might get back some of the money I put into it. Though Betty and Katie will be taken into consideration, too.'

Theo took her hand and kissed her knuckles. 'What about you, Lauren? You fit into this place so well. Do you have any desire to stay here? Greg has offered me a job.'

'What do you want to do, Theo?'

'It depends on you entirely. I do know that I want to leave the police force. If you want to stay here I'll take Greg up on it.'

She sensed the reluctance in him. 'I thought you'd rather be your own boss. Didn't you tell me you'd always wanted to start a detective agency?'

'I still do. But Kevin has a wife and children, and a mortgage to service. He prefers the security of the police force. I do have someone else in mind. Pam Roberts, who was injured in that explosion. She could work from the office while I do the leg work. And if I decide to go it on my own, I've already got clients, because Greg said he'll throw some work my way, and recommend me to one or two people.'

'Excuse me a minute, Theo.' She smiled at the vicar and his wife, and sold a cross-stitched dressing table set and six padded coat hangers to them, then turned back to him.

'I'd be happy to live wherever you want to. I've enjoyed working at Grantham, though I'm glad I don't have the responsibility of it. Samantha will give me a reference and I thought

I might learn to use a computer properly or something. I also have some money of my own we can fall back on.'

She remembered the twenty-five thousand pounds she'd taken from the safe and a blush crept under her skin when Theo grinned. She said in her defence, 'Betty and I pooled our available cash and we divided it between the three of us. I still have my legacy though.'

Daniel Mather came over, greeted Theo then kissed her cheeks. 'You look lovely, Lauren. Being in love obviously suits you.' His eyes skimmed over the stall. 'I suppose I'd better buy something.'

'There's a blue tie-dyed bandanna you might like, or some yellow bedsocks knitted by the Misses Anstruthers. They made one each, and one's a bit longer than the other.'

'Perfect if you have odd feet, then,' Theo remarked.

'You'd be surprised how many people do. I might buy them myself. The Anstruther twins always put in such an effort for their age.'

'I suppose we could each wear one to bed in winter.'

Daniel laughed at Theo's remark and picked up the bandanna. 'Hmmm . . . this is quite nice, isn't it. It looks familiar. Who made it?'

Lucy came over. 'It looked as though Theo was trying to have a serious conversation with you before my husband stuck his nose in. Can I help out on the stall early? I know you have a coach party due soon.'

'Thanks, Lucy, your husband wants to buy the bandanna you made, I think.'

Throwing on her jacket, Lauren took Theo's hand and towed him out through the front door. There was a view over the bare, brown fields and hedgerows. The trees were stark, sketches of pencilled beauty. Rooks' nests were exposed to a marbled grey sky and the hedgerows pearled with November mist. Wood smoke scribbled from chimneys.

'You will miss this place if I take you away,' he said.

'This will always be there if I need it.' Lauren snuggled into his warm body and lifted her face to his to be kissed. 'Follow your heart, and I'll follow it with you, Theo darling,' she said afterwards.

'Do you have a current passport?'

She nodded.

'Let's go to Las Vegas. We could marry and spend our honeymoon there.'

'When?'

'Tomorrow or the day after.'

She touched his face gently. 'We could, but we've all been through a lot together, and Katie and Betty will be disappointed if they aren't invited. And I'd like to invite my mother, and your parents and your friends and everyone at the manor, though it might get a bit fraught when Lucy sets eyes on my mother. I've been hoping they'll be civil towards one another.'

Theo sighed. His father and mother would definitely be fraught, and he doubted if they'd be civil, wedding or not. But then, he'd formed a positive feeling that they'd been unhappy living apart, and the crisis was over. Who knew what the future would bring?

'Oh, yes . . . and Samantha has offered us a reception at Grantham Hall if we get married here. And the reverend is looking forward to doing the ceremony—'

Theo began to laugh. 'All right, all right . . . I give in.'

'I haven't finished.'

'Yes, you have.' He drew her close and kissed her long and hard.

'*Oh, Theo, I do love you,*' she said, her voice sort of husky, so, as always happened when she said it like that, his knees melted like butter in the sun. 'I'd so love to run away to Las Vegas tomorrow with you.'

And that was how it was.

NEWPORT COMMUNITY
LEARNING & LIBRARIES